Game Plan

KARLA DOYLE

COPYRIGHT

DEDICATION

For Amanda, for always, always believing in me.
(Also for being nitpicky and pushing me when necessary!)
I am so lucky to have a cheerleader like you in my corner.

For Todd, my personal hero, for your love & support.
Thank you for giving me the freedom to make my dreams
come true.

And for Grace, my fabulous editor and an amazing person.
I wouldn't be here without you.

Chapter One

"Scott's really working the team spirit today with that kelly-green golf shirt buttoned up to the eyeballs." Lasha sniggered as she pointed to the opposite set of bleachers.

Andie swatted her friend's hand down. "Stop pointing, he'll think you're motioning him over here."

"It's been what, two years now? Your ex needs to get laid so he can get over you."

The trouble with that theory was Scott's indifference to sex. A concept so foreign to Lasha, she'd obviously blocked it out of her mind. Andie cocked an eyebrow at her best friend.

"Right. The only briefs Scott likes to dive into are legal ones." The focus switched as Lasha checked Andie out, head to toe. "You're the one who needs to up their nudetastic action quotient—from zero. That'd throw Scott off the reconciliation trail."

"I'll get there," Andie said, at which Lasha rolled her eyes. "I will, eventually." With any luck, before her lady parts shriveled up. So far, though, she hadn't met anybody she wanted to go out with. Or plain old hit the sheets with. Really, where did forty-year-old, barely divorced moms go to meet available men?

The idea of cruising clubs and bars at her age gave her the heebie-jeebies. And there weren't a lot of prime candidates at parent council meetings. The two males present last month had passed their best-before date a decade ago. She probably shouldn't be so picky, but since she had no plans to get serious at this point in her life, if ever again, settling for a soft-bellied man with a decreasing libido who excelled at intellectual conversation wasn't happening. She'd had one of those.

Lasha wandered off, searching for her next sexual plaything, most likely. Dylan left the on-deck circle for his turn at bat.

Andie rose from her spot at the end of the front row bench and laid on the hooting and clapping. Her son looked over his shoulder and rolled his eyes. At twelve, Dylan rode the line of being glad for his mom's attention and wishing she'd blend into the crowd like normal mothers. As long as he still smiled at her antics, she wasn't about to give them up. This season, he remained her little boy.

And damn, the boy could hit. His worm-burning line drive zipped past the first baseman and found a home halfway into the outfield. Dylan rounded second, had a look, thought better of getting greedy and dove back to the bag. He'd be proud of those bruises tomorrow. Cheers and whistles filled the air as she watched her son brush dust off his knees. The noisy fans all but drowned out the warning she heard a second too late.

"Ow—what the?" She grabbed her ankle, hissing at the heat spreading above the bone. Everyone around her remained focused on the game. Nobody had noticed her crumple in pain. Not even Scott from across the diamond, even though he'd barely taken his eyes off her for five innings.

She eased onto the bench and rolled her leg sideways. A baseball-sized welt had already formed above her right ankle. The foot she used for sewing. Terrific.

"Hey, are you okay? I yelled over at you."

"Apparently you need to get a better set of lungs, because I didn't hear you." The snarky response left a bitter taste in her mouth. "Sorry, that's the pain talking, not me. I'm not always a bitch."

"No worries, I get it. Taking a hit stings. It's my fault anyway. I shouldn't have drilled the ball that hard on the sidelines. Here, lemme take a look at that ankle... Damn, it's rising faster than a twenty-year-old virgin getting a lap dance."

Andie's first thought was that the guy needed to shut up, there were kids nearby. Her head snapped up to tell him so and the thought fell away. Kneeling in front of her was what could only be defined as a prime candidate. Full head of light-brown hair with exactly the right amount of messy, incredible blue eyes and lips designed for making out. And since the buttons on his baseball shirt had been neglected, Andie was treated to a view of one spectacular naked chest.

"I take it back, your lungs look fine," she said, and clapped a hand over her mouth. Major slip of the internal thought process.

The hunk looked up at her, totally amused. "They do, do they?" He scooped her foot into his hands and placed it on his thigh as he examined her ankle.

Strong fingers gently but thoroughly traced over her flesh. Yes, he was merely checking for damage he might've caused. It was still the best contact she'd had in forever. Her own hands got the job done, but they didn't send a thrill through her system. Thank god she'd shaved her legs this morning. Not that he'd notice or care.

Andie's mind headed for the scenario he'd mentioned. Except she became the dancer, gyrating over the bulge in his lap. And he was no virgin. Uh-uh. In her version of the strip-club seduction, the athletic stud beneath her was a sexual MVP.

"It's not serious, but it needs to be iced." The deep richness of his voice yanked her out of the premium-grade fantasy. "You bring any ice packs?"

She swallowed and shook her head. No way could she speak to him again. Not after telling him his chest looked good, and especially not after picturing herself grinding onto his cock. God, her face must be beet red. The way he grinned—he had to know. Oh, but he was pretty. And much younger than her. Too young for her to be picturing naked and sweaty.

"I'll grab you some ice from my cooler." He sprinted away. Baseball pants had always been one of her favorite things about the game. On this guy, they were downright erotic.

Lasha slid in beside her. "Who in the name of tasty treats was that?"

"Just some guy who hit me with a ball. A case of being in the wrong place at the wrong time."

"Just some guy, huh?" Lasha raised an eyebrow. "So switch places with me. Maybe I'll get lucky and be in the wrong place too."

"You don't want one of these." Andie turned her leg so Lasha could see the now-monstrous bump.

"No, but I'll take one of those." Lasha nodded toward the pure testosterone jogging their way. "I wouldn't mind if he groped my leg like he did yours, or looked my way with those come-play-with-me eyes, either."

"Shut up, he'll hear you. There was no groping. No bedroom eyes. And he's too young."

"Not for what I had in mind." Lasha looked at Andie's face and laughed. "Not for what you had in mind, either."

"Shut. Up."

"Why don't I go watch your offspring kick some tween butt until you're strong enough to stand on that horribly injured foot." Lasha moved off as the baseball hottie dropped to his knees. "Make sure you get his number, Andie, in case you need him to reimburse you for crutches or something."

Later, she would kill Lasha for embarrassing her this way. Right this minute she had better things to do. Like soak in every detail of the specimen kneeling in front of her.

Nice, round muscles filled out his shirt. Great shoulders and pecs did it for her in a big way. This man had both going on. He lifted the injured leg to his lap again, seating her foot on the fly of his uniform pants. She stared at her toes, willing them still, when all they wanted to do was jump free of their strappy sandals and wiggle against his crotch. Good god, she needed to end this before she did something stupid.

"That's cold." Reflexively, she tried to draw her foot away. He held it and the ice pack in place while looking up at her. With his level of hotness, the ice would be water in minutes. Boiling, even.

"Your friend is right, we should exchange numbers."

"I'm not going to sue you for the price of ibuprofen tablets, don't worry." The motion from his chuckle shifted his shirt. A hint of ink on his finely shaped chest peeked out at her. Tattooed men ranked highly in her personal fantasy time. Bad, meet worse. She was so toast.

"I like these shoes. Sexy."

And things just got toastier. "Not your size, sorry."

"I prefer them on you." He winked and swiped one finger across the high-gloss, hooker-red polish on her big toe. "You have very pretty feet. Nice toes."

"Thank you, I grew them myself." She hadn't flexed her flirt muscle in years, but it sprang into action. Pheromones and adrenaline rushed her system, sending heat to her unmentionables and a chill to her nipples. Strange how the body worked. And utterly fantastic.

After inspecting her toes and the injury a couple minutes more, he met her eyes again. "Keep the ice on for ten minutes. I've gotta go, I'm playing on the other diamond and my game is about to start. But you should call me later. For ibuprofen, cold packs, a foot rub, whatever you need. I deliver, 24/7."

"A foot rub—are you a registered massage therapist or something?"

"Strictly amateur. But I do more than feet, and I guarantee satisfaction."

Well that about sealed it. The toys were coming out tonight. The big ones. "Thanks, but I think I'll survive."

"I'm going to worry about this beautiful foot unless I see for myself that it's improving."

Andie couldn't take her eyes off his mouth as it stretched into a glorious, open grin. He had nice, straight teeth. Really white too. Probably a non-smoker, one of the criteria on her wish list. She had no business sizing this guy up. He couldn't be more than thirty-two. Thirty-three at most. Way too young for her.

He pressed a scrap of paper into her hand, letting his fingers linger a little longer than necessary. "My number." Another sizzling smile later, he was walking away, backward.

She set the ice pack aside and stood, taking a tentative step toward the chain link fence beside the diamond. Pain shot up her leg and she winced. He stopped and she waved him to keep going. "I'm okay." She was so not okay.

He shook his head. "Call me, I'll come over and ice it for you."

"What if it's the middle of the night?" Wow, she did not say that in front of all these respectable family types.

"I'll be lying awake thinking about those pretty painted toes anyway."

Andie glanced around. No one had heard the exchange, everyone was intent on the game. Her son's game. Where her attention should be, instead of flirting with a strange man, regardless of how hot he was. Much as she wanted one more gawk, one more sexually laced comment, she kept her eyes on the juvenile baseball players wearing Jell-O green. But she wouldn't soon forget the major player in gray and black.

Getting bumped to this shitty, small ballpark wasn't pissing Mason off anymore. And for the first time in his life, he wished he played catcher. Playing deep centerfield meant he couldn't see the neighboring diamond. If this inning dragged on much longer, he might not get another look at the woman he'd sort of purposely hit with a ball. Andie. The name suited her—uncommon in a totally good way.

He'd noticed her as soon as she got up and started cheering. Sure, lots of people yelled, whistled and clapped. Especially at kids' games. But Andie's actions seemed different. More enthusiastic, for one, and genuine.

Of course it helped that she was hot. Not in any overdone or obvious ways. A long, brown ponytail poked out the back of her ball cap. Very cute. She wore a formfitting white t-shirt and rolled-to-the calf, skin-tight jeans that accented a trim waist and very fine ass. Even in those basic things she oozed sex appeal.

So he'd ditched his regular warm-up routine and chucked the ball her way. He intended it to land at her feet, not ricochet off her body. In a way, it worked out better than his original plan.

Up close she didn't disappoint. Pretty face to match the nice body. Big, round blue eyes, clear and sparkling as an untouched lake. Plump lips that begged to be kissed. Then there were the shoes. Not your average mom shoes, that's for damn sure.

He could barely look her in the eye once he touched her leg. No way could he hide it. One look at his face and she had to know he was thinking of fucking her wearing nothing but those shoes and a smile.

A lazy fly ball fell into his glove making the third out. About time.

He reached his team's bench as the other game wound up. One of the boys hopped the fence and practically bowled Andie over with a hug. Must be her son. That a kid his age showed affection that easily said a lot about the parent.

Or parents. Shit, where'd the guy with the fluorescent-green golf shirt come from? She'd definitely been alone during the game, aside from the female friend who'd eyed him up as though he were dinner. If there'd been any sign of a man at Andie's side, Mason wouldn't have made a move. And her hands had confirmed it—no wedding ring. No tan line where one usually sat. Fair game in his mind.

Their attraction was mutual. He was positive about that, because when he touched her leg, the sparks between them were almost visible. One simple touch and his cock had started rising. Her expression told him she had some control issues of her own brewing too. No way he'd misread the chemistry.

But from the dynamic in his line of sight right now, golf-shirt guy had to be Dad. What Mason couldn't tell from this distance was whether he was something more.

"You got a thing for the MILF on diamond two?"

Mason forced his eyes from Andie and tried not to glare at his idiot teammate. Only a classless jerk referred to a woman as a Mother I'd Like to Fuck, no matter how sexy she was.

"I appreciate good-looking ladies, sure."

"Ever been with an older woman? I hear they'll do anything and everything to get some hard, young dick." The loudmouth stared toward Andie and adjusted his junk. "She looks all right. I'd do her."

"Don't be so fucking disrespectful, Ev."

Evan snorted. "What's up your ass—what, was she your babysitter or something?"

"No, your older sister babysat me, and not only did she help me with my math homework, she taught me about oral sex too." A huge bullshit lie, but Evan's head looked ready to pop off, which was awesome. He'd apologize later. To Evan's sister, not to the dickwad.

"Fuck you, Lang."

Mission accomplished on getting rid of Evan. Too late, though. The crowd at the other diamond had turned over and new teams were on the field. No sign of Andie anywhere. Shit.

Mason's mind stayed on Andie for the remaining innings. One, because she'd gotten under his skin in a big way. Two, because he couldn't stop thinking about dumbass Evan's comments. Yeah, she was older than him. Maybe a few years, maybe a few more than that. So what? He didn't care about an age gap and neither should anyone else.

But what if they did?

He was getting way ahead of himself—the odds of her using that piece of paper he'd slipped into her palm were slim. If she did call and they hit it off... his friends and family were good people. Nobody he cared about would give a rat's ass about an age difference. What losers like Evan thought counted for jack. Now that that was settled, he'd just have to wait and hope for the phone to ring.

Andie hated feeling pissy about Dylan spending every weekend with his dad. She didn't blame Dylan for wanting to go. No boring hanging around the house when he spent time with his dad. Scott used his wealth to great effect. This weekend, they were off to Toronto. Tickets to both Blue Jays' games, premium dugout seats—nothing but the best—and a field-view room in The Dome's Marriott Hotel so Dylan could watch the teams warming up. They'd done things like this as a family until she asked for the divorce.

A little pang of regret popped up. Squashing it was as easy as recalling Scott looking on while she packed for an excursion, then taking out whatever clothing he deemed inappropriate for Mrs. Scott Finch to wear publicly. Bye-bye tops that even hinted at cleavage and jeans that accented her curves. His replacements—pressed pants and bland blouses. Knee-length skirts. Monochromatic outfits in tan, navy or pastels. And decently sexy high heels? Never. Not for a woman of her social position. Gag.

No, she was never going back to living that way. Not with anybody. Sometimes, though, being alone sucked. Like tonight, and all of the weekend nights that she ate alone, watched a DVD alone, drank a glass—or several—of Cabernet alone. Still, she'd take the trade-off. Being alone meant wearing what she wanted, painting her nails hooker-red and shaking her ass to a rocking beat. She liked belonging to herself.

Though, belonging to a sexy man for a smoldering night of fun once in a while would be nice.

She moved mindlessly through the nightly routine. Teeth brushed and flossed, face washed and age-defying night moisturizer applied. She hobbled through the empty house to her bedroom. Turned down one side of the covers and slid into the king-sized bed.

The crisp, cool sheets tickled her skin. She shimmied out of her sleep shorts and camisole. Why not sleep naked—it's not as if anyone would walk in on her. A breeze drifted through the screen, raising goose bumps and sending her nipples to attention. She trailed her fingers across the peaks. A shiver rippled through her, sending a jolt of sensation between her legs. Nice, but she needed something stronger. She licked her fingers, drew them into her mouth like a cock. God, she needed to do that for real, and soon. Somebody virile and totally hot. Like the guy from the baseball game.

Mason, according to the scrap of paper on her bedside table. A fitting name for a guy with a solid physique. No doubt his cock would be hard as stone too. She sent the moistened fingers back to her nipples, toying with them by rolling and squeezing. She closed her eyes and imagined him.

A man like Mason would take charge of the pleasure. She squeezed the buds until heat bloomed in her breasts and made a beeline lower. She snaked one hand between her legs, slid two fingers inside her cock-deprived channel, then dragged them up to her clit. A few light strokes to tease like his tongue would do. She pressed harder, rubbed faster, imagining his face there. Orgasm hit and finished too quickly. Not nearly satisfying enough.

Masturbation usually helped her sleep. Not this time. Tonight it made her more aware of being alone in bed. Because that's what she needed to dwell on... not. She stared at the clock for three insanely long minutes. Half past ten. Too late to bug friends. They all had kids or significant others, or some combination thereof, except for Lasha. By this point in the evening, her best friend would be incommunicado due to much more thrilling sexploits. And that left Andie a little green.

Not that she wanted Lasha's brand of freewheeling promiscuity. Just some adult companionship once in a while. A couple hours of fun. The no-strings-attached kind—and if it came with some nudetastic action, as Lasha had called it, the vibrator collection in her bedside drawer would probably appreciate having a night off.

She flipped on the bedside lamp and picked up the slip of paper. She'd had plenty of chances to throw it away—at the ball park, when she stopped for takeout, at home—but she'd kept his number. Using it would be crazy. And yet the phone was in her hand, her fingers pushing the buttons.

One ring, two. Her heart beating its way out of her chest almost drowned out the third ring. Good, he wasn't home, saving her from one giant, embarrassing mistake.

Then he answered, "Hello."

Most people used the simple, standard greeting in question form. Not Mason. His hello was a statement that slid into her ear like a caress. An invitation. As if he knew she was naked and had recently come while fantasizing about him.

"Sorry, I think I've called the wrong number."

"I don't think you did, Andie."

Dammit. Foiled by Lasha's big mouth and caller ID. Now what?

"I'm glad you called, I was thinking about you." Rustling followed a beat of silence on his end. "How's the foot?"

Ah ha. That kind of thinking about her, the guilt-ridden kind. "I iced it when I got home, like you said, and the swelling has gone down a lot. But your sloppy throw cost me a night of dancing, so you know." The around-the-house-by-herself kind, but he didn't need to know that little detail.

A low laugh that curled her toes filtered through the line. "That's too bad. But I'm sure your date found other ways to entertain you. Better ways."

"My date?"

"The guy from the ball park. Glasses, green shirt."

"Oh, him." So, Mason had seen her talking to Scott after the game. Interesting. But she and Scott giving off a couple vibe? Not possible. They'd barely touched each other while married and Andie always kept at least a foot between them now. Still, if people—such as Mason—got the wrong impression, she obviously needed to make some changes.

"He's my ex. Definitely not a date."

"In that case, I'd like to make it up to you."

Andie listened to more shuffling on Mason's end. She rolled to her back and it struck her—the rustling sound could be bed sheets. Mason lying in bed, stretched out in his naked glory...

The mental image made her mouth water. And reach for her southern parts. "You don't owe me anything. I'm fine. That's really what I called to say."

"At ten-thirty on a Friday night?"

The amusement in his tone initiated a blush she was glad he couldn't see. "Busted. That was lame, I admit."

"Lame but cute, and I like that you're owning it. So, how about it, are we on?"

God, he had a sexy voice. Like broken-in leather, rough and soft at the same time. She could listen to him talk for hours. About anything. So why not do it—accept his offer, grab the opportunity before it disappeared. Before she chickened out. "Okay. Make it up to me sometime."

"Now works for me."

No backing out. She looked down at her naked body. Freshening up in a bath would be nice, but take too long. "I need a few minutes to get dressed. Where should we meet?"

"By the fountain at Museum Square. We'll go from there."

"Okay, it's a...a meeting." She slapped her forehead. Lame, lame, lame.

"It's a date, Andie. I'll see you soon." Mason waited for her to hang up before reaching over to disconnect. As soon as he'd seen her name on the call display, he'd switched to speakerphone mode. He wanted her voice in the air around him. And yeah, he wanted his hands free for other things.

The guys from his team had razzed him plenty when he bailed on pub time. Not because he skipped partying for sitting by the phone—none of them put those pieces together. Instead they ribbed him about work, since morning appointments were the excuse he gave. He could live with that. Only he needed to know the truth.

By the time the phone rang, he'd already fallen into bed, horny from thinking about her all evening. He'd been halfway to finishing when her voice echoed through the speaker. Talking to her made it worse. He palmed his cock once, and again. He needed release, but not now. He grabbed clothes and hustled from the bedroom. He'd come later, after some close-up time with Andie. Then he'd have every detail of her face and scent committed to memory. It'd be worth the wait.

Downtown was busy. Not surprising, the temperature and clear sky made it an ideal night for bar-hopping. His buddies would still be at it, meaning he and Andie had a few less options. If the team saw him out with a woman after ditching them, he'd never hear the end of it. And he'd rather they didn't have something to ride him about next time out. If anyone was going to ride him, it was Andie.

He stuck his hands in his pockets and shifted his hard-on as inconspicuously as possible. Stupid move, thinking about sex again. His balls would be blue by the time he got home. He cut around a group of Goth wannabes and spotted Andie, sitting on the edge of the fountain. She hadn't seen him yet. He slowed up and enjoyed his last minute of anonymity.

She'd called this a meeting, and even though he'd corrected her to date, he wasn't sure she'd agreed. Her outfit definitely said date. The skirt showed lots of shapely leg and the sleeveless shirt hinted at some fine cleavage. Very sexy, top to bottom. The last time a woman had appealed to him this much was... never. Not Stacey, his ex-fiancée, and nobody since, either. He stopped short. Took a breath and let the hit to his system settle. Damn.

She noticed him then. Her face lit up, putting the dozens of strings of white lights decorating the Square to shame. If he previously owned an ounce of cool, it vaporized into the early summer night. He didn't need a mirror to know his smile went ear to ear.

"You look—" What words could he use without scaring her off? "You look beautiful. And incredibly sexy, if you don't mind me saying so." He offered his hand and she took it, letting him pull her to a stand in front of him. The heat of their connection zinged through him. Some long-lost reserve of control sprang up to save him from yanking her body to his and kissing her breathless. He'd have to do it before the night ended. That much he knew.

"Where can I take you?" He kept her hand, adjusting their fingers to link together. "What would you like to do, other than dance?"

Andie's mouth parted and closed. She shook her head but, to his relief, with a smile on her lips.

"It wasn't a yes or no question, and if I ask you one of those, I really hope you'll be nodding, not shaking your head."

"That's a safe bet, unless you're asking if I'm ready to go home." Her face went pink, an indication of what it cost her to make the statement.

The blush only made him want to kiss her more, but he pushed the greedy thought aside. "No chance of that question happening." He motioned with their joined hands and they began walking. "Unless I'm asking to go with you."

Well, now. Fantasizing about sexing it up with Mason was one thing. Knowing that it might become reality before they said goodnight was a whole other ball game. One Andie hadn't played in years. Even before the separation and divorce, sex had been infrequent—to the extreme—and lackluster. And yes, she blamed that on Scott.

But what if it wasn't all Scott's fault? She might be horrible in bed and not know it. Because, let's face it, being a pro at getting yourself off didn't guarantee pornographic results with a partner. Especially with a younger man. The whole prospect made her suddenly weak in the knees. She stumbled slightly and turned on her swollen ankle, prompting Mason to wrap his arm around her waist. Totally worth the stab of pain in her leg.

"Sorry about the ankle."

"The smile on your face makes that hard to believe."

"I wish I hadn't hurt you, but I'd be lying if I said I'm sorry that it got you here."

Even with the wedge-heeled sandals that were killing her ankle, she only reached his chin. She'd been eye-to-eye with Scott. Looking up at a man was kind of sexy. Oh, who was she kidding—it was ten kinds of sexy. So was his firm grip on her waistline.

"You're putting too much weight on that foot. If you put your arm around me, I could support you better."

"What are you, a doctor?" Sarcasm or not, she took him up on the suggestion. Her hand slid across his lower back and hooked into a belt loop. The ass that had looked so fine in baseball pants lay a mere hand's width lower. Itching to grab it as she was, she restrained herself. She was forty, after all, not fourteen.

Mason steered her toward a small restaurant. "How about here?"

"It looks busy." And by busy, she meant bright. Outside, with moonlight and intermittent streetlights, she was relatively comfortable. But once they were across from each other, under the unforgiving glare of hanging pendant lamps, there'd be no escaping the obvious—their age difference. "Plus, it's nice out. Maybe some place with a patio instead."

They'd stopped on the sidewalk. The set of his body indicated they weren't going any farther. Neither would her fantasy date after a few minutes at a table. At least she didn't have to worry about her bedroom skills anymore.

"Patio next time. Let's go in and get one of those tables at the back." He squeezed her waist. "I don't want to share you with everyone on Dundas Street. I want you to myself tonight."

The promise in his voice made her tingle. Mistake or not, she let him lead her to the door. Well, there were worse places to be humiliated than a quiet bistro with semi-private seating.

A cute little thing of about twenty-five led them to the booth Mason requested. Sashayed in front of them better described her action.

Mason's hand stayed on the small of Andie's back, and when she peeked over her shoulder, his eyes were on her, not the perky butt in front of them. Go figure.

Andie eased onto the maroon upholstery, giving the hostess a smug smile when she caught her openly gawking. Mason's preference had the younger woman stumped too.

Theirs was one of those curved booths able to seat an entire family, yet perfect for cuddling. He slid in close beside her and put one arm over the back of the bench. Voila, instant twosome moment. The twirpette grudgingly took their drink orders and huffed away. Once she was alone with Mason, his eyes surveying her face, Andie's nervous dread returned.

"I'm older than you," she blurted.

"I'm taller than you."

"I have a twelve-year-old son."

"I have a one-eyed cat."

"You're just making fun of me now. Your cat has nothing to do with this," she said, motioning between them.

His fingers dropped to the back of her neck and trailed along her shoulder. "Neither do the other things. None of them affect how well we'll match up."

Chapter Two

Mason's comment, his fingers on her skin and the lure of his incredible eyes, left her speechless. A waitress arrived with their drinks. Not the hostess, but equally young and cute. Great. In acknowledging the new girl, Mason broke their connection. Briefly, but long enough for Andie to regroup.

She clinked her glass against his beer. "To matching up."

He laughed and took a long pull from the bottle. Over the edge of her drink, Andie watched his lips on the rim and the slide of his Adam's apple as he swallowed. Her eyes followed the line of his throat lower, into the unbuttoned zone of his white shirt. Geez, the man was hot. She tipped her glass, all but draining it. The vodka in the screwdriver worked its magic immediately, and that warm, easy feeling washed over her. Maybe it relaxed her a bit too much, since orange juice was dribbling from her chin. Not quite as smooth as his drinking method.

He caught the drops with his index finger. "Got it."

She giggled. Like a schoolgirl, for crying out loud. Blame it on the alcohol. His featherlight touch rounded the cap of her shoulder, teased the lower edge of her collarbone, then returned to her neck. Thank god she'd chosen the cowl-neck top. At least her bullet-hard nipples wouldn't show. She needed to make conversation, and fast. Before she did something stupid like climb onto his lap.

"Do you really have a cat with one eye?" Ugh, that was the best she could come up with?

"I do. Somebody found him in their backyard, pretty banged up, more than the eye, and brought into an animal shelter. I…" He paused, obviously deciding on what to say next. "I adopted him after he'd recuperated and nobody claimed him. He's a cool cat, thinks he rules the roost."

A ballplayer with a soft spot for animals and eyes that a woman could drown in—she was in so much trouble here.

"What about you, any pets?" he asked, and she cringed. "Not a good question, I guess."

"Touchy subject, that's all. My ex took our dog when I asked for a divorce." An unladylike snort escaped. "She was my dog, but her registration papers were in his name. She's still my dog, even though she's no longer mine." She shrugged. "I can't bring myself to get another pet…I know that probably sounds stupid."

His face was intent but undecipherable. "How long has it been?"

"Two years."

"Do you have visitation rights?"

Was he mocking her, or serious—Andie couldn't tell. He was getting an honest answer, regardless. Let him think whatever he wanted. "I tried that in the beginning. It tore me up, giving her back after a few hours together, or a weekend. And then I got a call from the vet, accidentally, because they still had my number on file. Apparently, Scott had dropped her off for tests because she'd quit eating and become very lethargic. Everything came back normal, thank god. Turns out it was stress. Doggie depression, because of me. So I gave up the visits altogether for her sake." Oh great. Her voice had gone all shaky and tears threatened at the corners of her eyes. "You probably think I'm totally ridiculous. Most people do. I got all this stuff in the agreement, yet I get blubbery about a dog he won't let me have."

Mason covered her nervous hand with his big, warm one. "I think you're great. Not even a little bit ridiculous."

Being married to a lawyer had taught Andie a thing or two about phoniness. Mason's smile seemed understanding and sincere. Here she sat, telling a stranger—who happened to be her smoking-hot date—about her divorce, without instantly regretting having opened her mouth. There was just something about this guy.

"He's keeping her to spite you."

"Pretty much."

"That's a dick move."

"I've always thought so. Let's talk about something else. Anything, you pick."

He raised an eyebrow and smiled. "Dangerous thing to do, leaving the field wide open. What if I choose... sports?"

Was that really what he wanted to say? Hmm. "Baseball, I'll participate. Everything else, I'll nod in all the right places while thinking about how attractive you are."

He laughed, the sexy sound drawing the attention of every female within earshot. "So if I talk about baseball, you won't be thinking about how I look?"

"I happen to be a great multitasker. I promise to be mentally undressing you while we discuss the ins and outs of the game."

"Andie, I'm kissing you now. I know I should wait 'til later, but I can't."

"Me either." She put her hand to her lips—they were a bit too loose around Mason.

He angled his body toward her. Gently removed her hand, pulling it into his lap. He abandoned it there and reached for her face. His fingers brushed her cheek, down the side of her neck. Her heart raced as though this was her first kiss. In a way, it was. She hadn't kissed any man other than Scott in seventeen years, and the last ten of those had been sporadic at best. God, what if he could tell how rusty she was? What if she...

"Stop thinking," he said, close enough that his lips nearly touched hers.

"Okay." Before she could internally club herself for the dumb answer, he kissed her. His mouth was soft and warm with the perfect amount of pressure. Her lips parted, allowing his tongue to slip inside. She tasted beer, a hint of cinnamon and a boatload of endorphins.

Next thing she knew, her arms were wrapped around his neck. Oh god, his hand was on her bare leg, just shy of her hemline. If her thighs didn't burst into flame, it'd be a miracle.

She parted, granting him access. Sweet heaven, he took the invitation, advancing until his wrist bumped the fabric of her skirt. Then he stopped. Sort of. Forward motion might have ended, but his fingers continued moving in a random, swirling pattern in very close proximity to her panties. Her very damp panties.

She moaned into his mouth, a sound that was unmistakably erotic in origin. To her ears, anyway.

He broke the kiss, but didn't move away. "Are you hungry? They have great bruschetta here."

He was asking her about bread while caressing her inner thigh. After making out with her in a public place. Maybe the kissing hadn't affected him the way it did her. She wanted to straddle him right then and there—not order appetizers and talk baseball. Instead, she let her arms fall away from the softness of his hair. She eased back a bit and waited for her head to clear.

"Um no. My stomach is still full from the takeout I grabbed earlier." And the butterflies he'd unleashed while making love to her mouth.

"If you'd called me sooner, we could have had dinner together. I had the Chinese-for-one special, also known as the dateless-loser meal."

"I can't believe someone like you ever needs to go solo." Let him read whatever he liked into that one. Her nipples tightened at his chuckle, straining against the lacy bra. He followed up the laugh by reaching for his beer. As in, removed his hand from her leg. She hid her disappointment by dusting off the remains of her screwdriver.

"Want another?" he asked after emptying his bottle. He raised a hand and made the number two at the waitress while pointing to their table.

"That move would never work for me. I'd be waiting fifteen minutes for somebody to notice I wanted something."

His gaze swept over her, covering every visible inch, right down to the pushed-up skirt on the bench seat. "Not if the servers were guys."

Andie surveyed the restaurant. "I can't disprove your theory because there's not one male employee on the floor." No wonder he'd chosen this place. All the pretty young things made for nice scenery. Age-appropriate scenery. Unlike her. She tugged at her too-short skirt. Adjusted the neckline of her top that showed a bit too much boob for a woman her age.

"You're wrong." Mason didn't look at the waitress when she dropped off their drinks. His eyes stayed on Andie.

"Kind of hard to be wrong when I didn't say anything."

Mason saw through her forced smile. Totally self-protective. Ditto her body language. He could guess the reason. But she couldn't be further off base.

"I'm not looking at anybody but you, Andie. Why would I, when you're the most gorgeous woman here?" He reached for her hand and dove in. It had to be said. Directly, so they could be done with it. "At the ballpark earlier, I threw the ball your way intentionally. You're hot and I wanted to meet you. Yeah, you're older than me. Who cares? I'm attracted to you in a very big way. And that kiss... I'm still trying to recover." He'd had to force his hand from her leg, because he was this close to stroking her right here in the restaurant. He got the feeling she would've let him. And that had him ready to burst.

The sparkle returned to her eyes, making the speech worthwhile. Good, they were back on track.

"How big is very big?" Her cheeks turned pink with the question.

For a second he considered placing her hand on his bulging cock. A move like that and she'd think he asked her out strictly for sex. That wasn't the case, even if he did want to fuck her until they both dropped from exhaustion and satisfaction. His fingers twitched over hers. To be safe, he grabbed his beer and downed a mouthful. But he still needed to answer the question.

"Right now, uncomfortably big."

Her lips curled into a slow, sultry smile. One he wanted to slide his cock into and fuck 'til he came. He closed his eyes briefly, needing to get control. Yet again. Enough to make it through their date in a semi-gentlemanly state. He spread his legs a bit in an effort to make the boys more comfortable. Suddenly, they had company.

Andie's hand cupped his cock. She caressed it through the denim, firmly stroking his length, with a squeeze thrown in here and there for added torture. Her eyes were pure fuck-me. Any reservations she'd had were gone. Along with his resolve.

"Let's get out of here," he said, and she nodded. He dug into his pocket for some cash, tossed a couple of bills on the table and pulled her out of the booth with him. He guided her forward with his hands on her waist. "Money's on the table," he barked at the waitress as they passed. He pressed his cock against Andie's ass while pushing the heavy door open. Stupid move, it put him one step closer to exploding. The night air was warmer than average for June, but it had nothing on the heat they were generating. And they were still fully clothed.

Most of the businesses along Dundas Street lived in joined brick buildings. Not many alleys existed, but lucky for him, one was nearby. His arm around Andie's waist made it that much easier to snag her into the narrow laneway with him. The passage might've been four feet wide, max. No security lights came on and minimal moonlight filtered between the buildings.

The darkness made it private enough to steal a couple minutes of making out, because he couldn't wait until they got to his truck. He didn't ask permission or give her warning. Just pressed her up against the brick wall and shoved his leg between hers to hold her in place. Her startled yip quickly melted into a low, throaty sound that made his cock ache. Shit, they'd never make it home at this rate.

"Do you want this?" He hiked her skirt up past her hips, fingered the edge of some very tiny panties. If she said no, he was fucked. Not in a good way. "I can't see your face. Tell me."

"I want you." Her voice was soft yet hungry, and Mason didn't miss the twist she'd put on his question. She wanted him, not this. She couldn't have said anything sexier.

"Lift your hips, I want to feel your ass." Her skin was warm and firm in his hands, the tiny string disappearing between her legs a total tease. "I wish I could see you." He tugged the scrap of material down. Pushed her naked ass against the bricks, making her jump. "Too rough?"

"No, I-I like it."

"Good." Face to her neck, he inhaled. She smelled sweet, but not artificial like perfume. Fresh and natural. Fucking delicious.

She shivered when he got to the spot below her ear. Thrust her tits into his chest and moaned a little.

Fuck. He found her mouth and swallowed the sexy little noise. Her tongue invited his in. Demanded it. Putting the brakes on this pit stop wasn't going to be easy.

He snaked his hands between them and under her shirt. Found two perfect handfuls encased in lace. He toyed there until her breath caught, the sound making his cock strain against the fly of his jeans. What noises would she make when he had her naked and coming? He put his hands on her hips, pushed her away from him, back to the wall. The pouty sigh she made was cute, but he wanted her moaning. Maybe even begging.

"Mason…"

That'd do. The whisper of his name killed the last of his control. His hands skated across the flat, smooth skin of her stomach. Lower. Fuck, she was on fire. Wet too, and smooth as everywhere else. His married buddies often complained about their wives letting themselves go, and for some reason he'd half-expected that to be the case because Andie had an ex and a kid. Shame on him.

He sank two fingers inside her and she said his name again, her voice soft and needy.

"Fuck, babe, you're making me crazy." He began working her clit with his thumb. "I can't wait to make you come."

Andie couldn't hold back from moaning. At this rate, he wouldn't be waiting long. Hearing that her orgasm was his goal… deal maker.

His skilled hands guaranteed she'd come. He touched her as if he'd done it a thousand times, as if he knew everything that turned her on, as if he loved doing it to her. Her head rolled side to side as the sensation built. His fingers were relentless. Rubbing hard and fast, taking her to the peak, then easing into long, slow strokes before she had the chance to tumble over.

"I'm gonna make you come now." He breathed the words into her ear. "On my face."

He was going to do that here? How?

"Hold on to me, babe," he said as he dropped to his haunches.

She grabbed his shoulders, relaxing as his mouth took possession. His tongue moved against her clit with the perfection of her favorite vibrator, but better, because he was a hot human male, and totally in control. Nothing solo ever felt this good.

"Oh god…" His fingers filled her again, first one, then two. He found a magic spot inside, touching it with each mind-blowing stroke. Apparently he'd acquired the schematics for her anatomy, because he knew exactly where her buttons were—including some new ones—and how to push them for maximum effect.

His hair was soft and thick, and he took her grip on his skull as a sign to finish the job, it seemed, because that's exactly what he did. She flew over the edge, bucking and grinding, totally and shamelessly riding his face. The alley echoed her half-spoken words and moans. Anyone walking by could hear. Not only did she not care, she liked it.

"My legs, I'm going to fall."

He nuzzled her clit with his nose. "I'd never let you fall."

"I can't take any more. Too sensitive." Reluctantly, she let go of his head. He straightened, taking the strain off her wobbly legs by way of pinning her to the wall. That pin of his needed some attention.

"You are so sexy. Your shape, your taste, those sounds you made when you came for me. I don't want to stop. I could lick you all night."

Just, wow. In her entire life, nobody'd said anything like that. Nor had anyone dragged her into an alley because they had to have her right then. Mason was a freaking sex god. And oh, was she ready to do some worshipping.

"It's my turn." She grabbed two handfuls of hard biceps and shoved. Sure, she only budged him because he let her. Her skirt dropped into place as she backed him to the opposite wall. The black lace panties chosen for his eyes, not for a dark laneway, slid to her ankles. She stepped out of them. A small price to pay for the hottest experience of her life. Worth it, even if they were the nicest pair she owned.

A low laugh bumped out of him when he hit the bricks. Again when she yanked the shirt from his jeans and fumbled with his belt, button and zipper. He didn't lift a finger to help. Just leaned his sexy self against the wall and let her have at it. She couldn't see him fully in the darkness, only lines and shadows. Still, his eyes were on her, she'd bet her entire lingerie drawer.

She hit bottom on his fly and shivered. In a matter of seconds his cock would be exposed. Hers to fondle, suck or plain old have her way with. She pushed the denim aside and ran her hand over his bulging briefs. Thank god for a decent-sized bulge. Not that she wanted a man who was freakishly large or anything. Significantly endowed and thoroughly stiff, that's all. Stiff before she put in an hour's work, for a change. She peeled back the jersey and wrapped her hand around him. Any woman who likes sex and has a shred of honesty knows that size does matter. Mason's cock didn't disappoint.

"Now I wish I could see you better." She sank to her knees, working at the layers of clothing until he sprang free. She palmed him a few times and heard his breath catch. Good, the torture went both ways. She let her hand slide to the base. Steadied his cock as she consumed it in a long, slow glide. This was exactly what she'd been aching for—a mouthful of rock-solid, delicious man at her mercy. Mason fit the bill perfectly.

"Oh, fuck. Holy motherfucking Christ." He groaned, then half-laughed. "I hope you're not a devout churchgoer."

She released him with a noisy pop. "Hell no."

"Halle-fucking-lujah." His fingers twined in her hair and he guided her back to his cock.

She smiled as she sucked him in. This was already the most fun she'd ever had on her knees. She took him deep, working him with her tongue, then eased off, maximizing the suction when she got to the tip. Judging by the free-flowing expletives above her, he was a fan of the technique.

As she started her descent again, Mason tightened his hold on her hair and thrust. His cock touched the back of her throat. A quick breath through her nose and the initial gag reflex passed. Using his hands and hips, he now controlled the rhythm and depth.

Her nose hit the hard flatness of his stomach, again and again. Asphalt and rubble stung her knees as she jerked forward, back, forward, back. He'd taken complete control. Moaning filled her ears. Hers. She'd never been more turned-on in her life.

"I'm gonna come." He released her hair and tried pulling out.

No way, not yet. She wrapped her arms around his hips and grabbed his ass, keeping him deep. "Mmm hmmm." Kind of hard to talk with a mouth full of cock. She urged him by sucking and licking. He got the message.

"Your mouth feels so damn good." His fingers slid through her hair, cupped the back of her head. He thrust into her mouth again. "Oh fuck yeah…" His body tensed. His cock pulsed and a stream of warmth splashed the back of her throat.

She was no expert at swallowing but did her best. The rest she wiped away with her hand, as subtly as possible, onto her skirt. The salesgirl at H&M had given her a big spiel about patterned fabric being great for hiding spilled coffee and such. Hopefully it did the same for blowjob overflow.

Mason reached for her hands and helped her to her feet. Pulled her into his arms. Kissed her face. Stroked her hair. His erotic dominance melted into sexy, masculine tenderness that tugged at something inside her. God, she was already gonzo for him, and it had been what—an hour? There had to be a goofy, infatuated grin plastered all over her face. Good thing it was dark.

"I'm not in the habit of making comparisons, but that was the best head I've ever had."

"It was pretty good, wasn't it?"

Mason's laugh bounced off the brick walls. "Try fucking amazing." He laid a long, deep kiss on her lips, one that made her shivery all over again. "Let's get out of here."

"You keep saying that."

He released her briefly while he got everything properly tucked away, then took hold of her hand. "The next stop will be a lot more comfortable."

After checking the street for onlookers, Mason led Andie out of the alley. Half a dozen or so people sat out on the patio of a nearby café. None of them so much as glanced in their direction. Hard to believe nobody'd heard them, because they'd sure made plenty of noise. In hindsight, it'd been a pretty selfish move, though she'd clearly been on board from the get go. Still.

"Hey, hold up a sec." He stopped under the first streetlight. He needed to look at her, take in every little detail. He'd messed her silky, smooth hair with his greedy hands. Her lips were red and swollen from kissing and sucking him off. Her knees were either bruised or dirty. Maybe both. All proof of his intensity and her eagerness. Damn, he had to get her to a bed, fast.

She shifted foot to foot. Tried to rearrange her hair one-handed. "I bet I'm a mess."

"A little sexed-up looking, but beautiful."

Her body relaxed and she smiled. Even blushed a little. She obviously had doubts about her appearance, and that was total bullshit. She was a fucking goddess. If anyone had told her otherwise, they were blind and stupid, and lucky for him, they were history. He had no intention of joining them.

"Where would you like to go?" He pulled her close and kissed her nose. She put her arms around his neck and it felt—right. Right enough to take her to his place, maybe for the night. "My house, yours, the back of my truck under the open sky…"

"Your place, but in my car."

Planning ahead for her getaway, he could respect that. "Lead the way."

They walked, arms wrapped around each other, until they returned to the Museum Square. Andie slowed and hit the crosswalk button. Ah, shit. Downtown parking was scarce, especially on weekends. Friday nights were the worst. She must've parked behind one of the north side businesses rather than in one of the public lots to the south. If they crossed here, they'd walk past The Lazy Fly, the pub sponsoring his ball team. At this hour all the guys would be hanging around the front patio. Worse, they'd be half in the bag—at least—and lacking filters. They'd have a heyday with the fact that he bailed on guy time, but got caught out on a date. Then there was Evan, who'd been an utter jackhole when completely sober. He wasn't getting a crack at Andie close up and while intoxicated.

Traffic stopped for the flashing lights. "Why don't we cross at the next light," Mason said, guiding her from the curb. "This side has some nice stores, we can window shop along the way."

"But I'm parked right over there, behind the jewelry store." She cocked her eyebrow at him. "I'm not really in the mood to shop, window or otherwise. And I love shopping, for the record."

The jewelry store was adjacent to the pub. He looked past Andie's sexy-cute face, scanning the patio. Yup, there they were, five of them, at least. So he'd tell her the truth. No big deal. She'd understand. Women knew better than anyone that men could be idiots.

"I'd rather not take you past The Lazy Fly right now. That's where my ball team hangs out after our Friday games. A bunch of them are out front right now. You know how guys are."

She didn't waste a glance on his teammates, just started walking. "I suppose I do."

Assholes avoided, excellent. He pulled Andie tight to his side. "You ever go in there?" He motioned at an independent deli that boasted a nice little restaurant in back.

"Sometimes."

He waited, but nothing followed. Maybe she hated the place and didn't want to say so. "A buddy of mine owns this store," he said as they passed The Sports Net. "If you ever need runners, this is the place to go. Though I'm a big fan of your footwear choices so far, I gotta say."

"Thanks."

Another single-word answer. This one came with a phony smile. Something was up, but her arm was still around his waist. Could be nerves about going back to his place. Understandable, their first date had jumped to the fast track within the first ten minutes. Maybe she was having second thoughts.

Much as he wanted to bury himself inside her, he was fine with waiting. 'Til the second, third, fourth date—whatever. He'd tell her so before they got in her car. Get rid of any pressure or doubts she had.

"This is mine." She fished keys from a tiny purse and unlocked a shiny compact sedan. She didn't get in, didn't step aside for him to drive. "I think it's best if I head home. Alone. Sorry if that makes me a tease."

"That you are not. Not even close." The most willing, uninhibited woman he'd ever been out with worried that she was a tease. Craziness.

"Okay, well. Thanks for a fun evening." She'd opened the door and slid inside before the last word left her mouth.

He stopped the door and leaned in. "Hey, you're not even going to let me kiss you goodnight?"

She tilted her head toward him and puckered up, guppy style, without letting go of the steering wheel.

What the hell just happened? He might not know much about her, but he knew she'd done a one-eighty, and he knew expressions in general. Andie's face was irritation and impatience. Too bad, because he wasn't done with her yet.

"I'd like to see you again, for dinner, a movie. Dancing if you want, once your ankle feels better."

For the longest minute she simply stared up at him. "Would we go out of town?"

"We could, sure." Whatever she wanted to do, they'd have a great time. He could feel it.

"I don't think so, Mason." She tugged on the door, forcing him to step aside or be whacked on the hip by a hunk of steel. It slammed and she lowered the window. "We both got what we wanted tonight. As much as I'd like to enjoy you again, I'm not interested in being anybody's dirty little secret." She nodded at his feet. "Watch your toes. I don't want to be responsible for putting you on the DL. I'm sure your teammates wouldn't be impressed by that, either."

He stepped back and she took off, leaving him scratching his head in a cloud of parking lot dust. There'd been times in his life when he was too smart for his own good. This was not one of those times.

Chapter Three

Andie hated waking up in an empty house. Too quiet. A few years ago she'd have traded anything for this kind of silence. Now it made the thoughts in her head seem extra loud. Mostly, her mind was on last night with Mason. She didn't regret the sex part. No woman in her right mind would wish that away. The humiliation part, on the other hand, really sucked.

Finding out he was embarrassed that his friends might see them together had nearly toppled her. Her guard had been safely in place until he pulled her into that alley. Mostly. Okay, only a little. Dammit.

Enough with the self-pity. She threw off the sheet and tried out the ankle. A bit stiff, but otherwise fine. Good thing, she had five aqua bridesmaid dresses to make for the Palmer wedding three weeks from now. They'd come begging a few days ago, after the groom's mother realized the job wasn't as easy as it looked. Ha. Andie loved last-minute gigs like this. More money per dress and less whining from the clients because they didn't hold the power. Being in control was nice.

In the bathroom, she peeled off her pajamas and leaned over to start the shower. Her gaze snagged on the mirror.

She'd seen the reflection of her ass thousands of times. Lord knows she checked it frequently enough, ever on the lookout for cottage cheese dimples and orange peel ripples. No sign of the above, but it was pink instead of the usual never-sees-the-light-of-day white. Had to be from rubbing the brick wall.

She hopped onto the toilet seat for a better view in the vanity mirror. Oh, yes. Her knees were worse. Stained and scratched from when she'd lost control with Mason. Control she'd given to him or allowed him to take, the line kind of blurred between the two.

She'd been fifteen the first time she truly made out, and that was… good god, twenty-five years ago. In all that time, she'd never had so much as a hickey. Look at her now. The woman in the mirror smiled back, full of smug satisfaction. She was officially ready for adult-grade dating.

Scott's cell number lit the phone display around five-thirty. The Blue Jays had wrapped up their afternoon game with a victory fifteen minutes earlier. She hit the talk button, ready for Dylan's recount. She already knew the details—she'd listened to every at-bat while working. But her baby boy always called to tell her about his day, and that's what mattered.

"Hey, how was the game?" she asked by way of answering. "I miss you."

"I miss you too, And."

Not Dylan, but his dad, his voice dripping with a sarcasm-desperation mix. As usual, he'd shortened her name to a single syllable—one of his habits that irked the crap out of her. One of many.

"Hello, Scott. I hope you're not talking while driving. It's dangerous, illegal, and the fine is over one hundred dollars."

"Nice to know you still care, hon. Not driving. Dyl and I are waiting for a table at The Grindhouse."

She cringed. She was absolutely not his hon. "Put Dylan on, I'd like to hear his voice and say goodnight."

"He's in the restroom."

She took a breath, exhaled quietly. Must be cool, not let Scott win by showing irritation. "And you're calling me because…?"

"I thought you might like to join us for the rest of the weekend. If you left now, you'd be here in time to catch a late movie with us. I'm sure I could arrange another seat for the game tomorrow. I know how much you enjoy baseball."

More than she was supposed to, by Scott's standards. The time she'd jumped up with the stadium crowd in doing the wave, he'd turned a shade of purple she couldn't name. "Thank you, but no."

"Dylan would love it if you drove out."

Typical Scott tactics. If bribery doesn't get the desired result, play the guilt card. And it'd worked at the beginning. More times than she could count. Not anymore, though. Scott had filled her head with so much worry, she'd taken Dylan to a family counselor. Behind Scott's back. That hadn't pleased her ex. God, if Scott knew that Dylan had been encouraging her to start dating lately… She shuddered to think what brainwashing he might try on their son. Scott wanted his family photo back in the frame. Period.

"Well, And—what do you say? Come watch the Blue Jays beat the Yankees with us, like old times?"

Like old times. While she missed the family parts of their life together, she didn't miss Scott's constant attempts to make her over into his vision of a proper wife. The wardrobe adjustments. Suggestions that she dance with less hip movement. Clap more daintily. Invite the right people over for cocktails, instead of her over-the-top best friend.

Nor did she miss the permanent frost that'd settled in their bedroom. Physical contact had become almost non-existent after Dylan's birth. A consequence she hadn't foreseen, and one she couldn't regret, because it had given her—given them—a beautiful baby. But she didn't want to spend the rest of her life that way, either.

"Is Dylan back from the men's room yet?" she asked, ignoring the taunting request.

"No." Scott's voice switched to its cool, lawyerly tone. "Would you like him to call you later?"

Andie dropped onto the couch with a sigh. "Just tell him I love him."

"Lucky kid."

No degree needed to read between those lines. They weren't having this conversation again, not a chance. She ran a finger over the pink scrapes on her knees. "Goodbye, Scott."

Everything was done. Appointments, paperwork, tending to boarders and overnight patients. Mason's mind had been on Andie through it all. Okay, maybe not while his finger was up Trixie's butt, expressing her anal glands. Other than that, pretty much constantly. He still didn't know what went wrong.

One of her last comments stuck in his head, though, crystal clear. She'd gotten what she wanted from their date. He'd shielded her from his loudmouth teammates only to have that jerk, Evan, be right about her all along. A cougar on the prowl, simple as that. He hated the term, hated himself for thinking it. Especially about Andie, who really didn't strike him as the casual hook-up type. Maybe that was wishful thinking on his part. Wouldn't be the first time he'd been wrong about a woman. This time he wouldn't get burned.

Hugo met him at the door of his small, wartime bungalow. The cat had his rumble cranked to maximum, out of loneliness more than hunger, since his bowl hadn't been touched. Looked like Mason had two choices—bring home a friend for his friend, or let Hugo live at the clinic. Yeah, well, no mystery how that one would play out. Some guys enjoyed solitude, to the point of avoiding all commitments like the plague. He wasn't built that way.

Tonight he'd be surrounded by commitments. Katie and Logan's engagement dinner—attendance mandatory. His sister had a celebration planned, meaning food, drinks and hugs aplenty. There might even be speeches. God help him if anybody started crying. Yeah, he had a rep for being a sensitive male, but tears... He was still a guy, for fuck's sake. Seeing women's faces go blotchy and their noses turn bright red made his cock shrink up like a scared turtle. It was worse than a cold swim.

He strolled in for the six o'clock reservation at ten past seven.

"Big brother, over here," Katie called from a large table near the window. Her fiancé, Logan, sat next to her, one arm draped over her shoulders. Lucky bastard glowed almost as much as his baby sister. Both sets of folks were at the table, plus the groom-to-be's sisters and a few close friends. All couples, no singles. Another burn for him.

He scanned the table as he walked over. Some glasses, that's it. Ah, hell. "You didn't have to wait for me." So much for dragging his feet getting here. They should have been into their main courses by now. He planted a kiss on Katie's forehead, then one on his mother's cheek. Shook hands with Logan. To everybody else, he nodded. Somebody'd saved a chair for him, directly across from the future Mr. and Mrs. Brenner. Awesome, he got to stare love in the face for the next hour or so.

He dropped into the seat and grabbed a menu. Anything to avoid being part of the wedding conversation. Fuck, when did he turn into a bitter asshole? His little sister deserved better.

Mason survived appetizers, dinner, dessert and engagement presents. Barely, and by the grace of a couple pints. Sports highlights on the TV over the bar didn't hurt, either. The party ended by nine. As the last friends filtered out, Logan excused himself to hit the john, leaving Mason and Katie remaining at the table. And she had the let's talk look.

"You seemed off tonight. Bad day at the office?"

"Everything's fine. Just keeping it toned down, that's all. Tonight is about you guys."

Katie laughed. "I'm going to assume that what you really mean is that you're thrilled for me, and how lucky my fiancé is, etcetera." She shook her head. "For such an incredibly smart guy, you can be really dumb with words."

"Cut him some slack, Katie-Kat." Logan returned, giving her an affectionate yet scolding look. "You know how guys are."

"I sure do, baby." Katie snuggled into Logan's side, despite the fact that he was on a separate chair.

Didn't matter that his little sister was twenty-six and soon to be married. When she and Logan looked at each other that way, Mason had to find somewhere else to focus his attention. Logan's comment about the way guys are bounced around in Mason's brain while he pretended to watch commercials on the overhead. He said the exact words to Andie last night, when he explained why they should avoid walking past the pub. She'd agreed. Or had she?

"Hey man, you have an admirer. End of the bar. Sat down a couple of minutes ago and hasn't stopped looking at you."

With Logan's sense of humor, the admirer could be anybody. Like a huge, hairy biker dude. Mason shrugged, but grabbed a quick look over his left shoulder. Andie, alone. That'd never do. Goodbye resolution to forget about her.

"Have a good night, you two." He stood, shook Logan's hand and kissed his sister's. "And congratulations, kiddo. Logan's a lucky man."

Katie's face lit up. "Much better. Now, who's the woman that has you jumping out of your seat?"

"Somebody I met at a ball game. And I'm not jumping."

Katie issued him the raised eyebrow of doubt. "Invite her to join us."

So his well-meaning sister could cross-examine Andie? Yeah right. "You've got better things to do than sit here and make small talk with a stranger. Go home. Plan a wedding. Celebrate—but don't tell me how." Mason had known Logan since they were kids, and was well aware of Logan's adult preference for kink. Hell, he used to envy the guy for some of the stuff he got up to. Thinking of his baby sister in those scenarios made puke rise in his throat. Hypocritical, but true.

He issued a final wave and turned toward the bar. If Andie had been watching him before, she certainly wasn't now. More like the opposite. He'd bet his last dollar she was deliberately not looking at him. No acknowledgement whatsoever when he slid onto the neighboring stool. Her phone must be pretty damn interesting, because she was glued to the screen.

He caught the bartender's eye and motioned at Andie's drink. "And a Sleeman, in a bottle." Mason pushed the full glass of red wine her way, finally winning her attention. "Thanks."

"For what?"

Damn, that voice. Soft and feminine without being weak. She could read the back of a cereal box and he'd get hard. He should've called her today.

"I have a list. Very detailed." He took a long draw from his beer, enjoying the pink sweeping her face. "But right now I meant it as thanks for improving my evening."

Her eyes flitted around the bar area before returning to his face. "Where are your buddies tonight? Not here, obviously."

"Hard to say. Home with their girlfriends, wives and kids, most likely. Except for one jerk who's probably busy fucking a Fleshlight because no living human would want him."

"Ouch, harsh."

"Harsh but true." He shrugged. "My baby sister had her engagement dinner here earlier, otherwise I'd be home too."

"With your girlfriend or wife and kids?"

"With my cat." Mason crossed his arms on the bar, keeping his eyes locked with hers as he leaned into her space. "That's the only pussy waiting for me at home. Or anywhere."

"That's unfortunate." She picked up her wine, obviously trying to hide her smile behind the glass.

"I agree."

"It's early. You may get lucky yet."

He angled on his stool and slid closer. "Tell me this is inside information, not a random pep talk." No answer from Andie, who kept sipping her drink. But she'd definitely relaxed. She didn't seem pissed at him anymore, either. He'd take it. Take it and run with it. "You look beautiful tonight. Again."

"It's nice to know some men have low standards."

"Some do. I don't."

"I'm not dressed to impress." She fidgeted on her stool, smoothing invisible wrinkles from her clothes before moving on to tuck a wisp of loose hair behind her ear. "And this stupid clip thingy is barely holding my hair up." Her long, delicate fingers touched her mouth. "I don't even have lipstick on."

Some women said things like that to encourage compliments. He didn't get that vibe from Andie—the way she downplayed her attributes seemed legit. Not like she lacked self-confidence, that wasn't it. She simply didn't realize how fucking gorgeous and sexy she was without all the prep and plasticity of other women. An effortless beauty.

"Your naked lips remind me of last night, and that t-shirt is lethal sexy. As for your hair…" He fingered some of the escaped strands at the back of her neck. She shivered, and he smiled. "I like it this way, up, off your neck, with these wavy bits hanging down. I also like how easy it would be for me to grab that clip and let your hair loose, so I could feel it wrapped around my fingers."

The tip of her talented tongue slid across her bottom lip, making his cock twitch. She jumped when her phone vibrated on the bar, scooped it up, read the text and scowled while combing the crowd. So much for their promising moment.

"Problem?"

"I just got stood up."

Well, fuck him. He'd been warming her up for somebody else. No wonder she'd avoided making eye contact until forced.

"This is your fault," she said while clicking a message into her phone.

"Consider this my apology." He slapped cash on the bar, stood and walked out. No looking back.

Andie's head snapped up at Mason's abrupt departure. He weaved through the tables without a backward glance, disappearing through the front doors. That left her alone, confused, and more than a little worked up.

"You shut him down good," a male voice said from behind her. Its owner took over Mason's stool and gave her a thorough look-over. "His loss is my opportunity."

Gross. Not a lot of men successfully pulled off lines like that. Mason could—this guy, not so much. Around her age, nicely dressed and not altogether unattractive, he did zero for her. Clearly, he had no clue. He kept smiling, or rather leering, his eyes working a circuit between her mouth and her boobs. Mason's comment about her t-shirt echoed in her head. Too bad she hadn't brought a sweater.

"What's your name, baby?"

"Ida." She gave one of her coldest faces. "Ida rather have a root canal than tell you my name. Baby." Juvenile, yes, but it had the desired effect.

"Bitch." He slid off the seat and slunk away.

The bartender laughed as he wiped the bar in front of her. "Nice. That jerk's here every weekend, harassing the pretty ladies. Nobody ever gets rid of him that easily."

"I'd say thanks, but that makes me sound like a bigger bitch. Which I'm really not." Why did she feel the need to explain herself to a total stranger? Because she was a wound-up, messed-up wreck, that's why. "Him, I meant to get rid of. The first guy I scared off was unintentional."

"You mean your boyfriend? Ah, he's just jealous. I'm sure you'll work it out."

Andie stopped toying with her drink and stared at the dark-haired server. He thought Mason was her boyfriend. Huh. "What makes you think he's jealous?"

The bartender averted his eyes, toweling an already-dry glass for all he was worth. Definitely spot free by now.

"Come on, tell me. Please."

He hung the glass in an overhead rack. "Giving advice is murder on my tip jar, but how can I say no to such a pretty face?" He placed his palms on the bar in front of her. "Whatever you said when you looked at your phone pissed him off. Possessive-like. Not a generally annoyed look, like a guy gets after waiting an hour for a woman to choose an outfit, or listening to her complain about not getting enough cuddling."

"God, women are the worst." She loaded on the sarcasm, and it didn't go unnoticed.

"Women are the best thing on earth," he said with a big smile. "But you drive us nuts, especially if we're really into you, which your man clearly is."

Andie freed him with a thank you. Despite her feelings at the end of last night, she hoped the bartender had it right. She swallowed the last mouthful of wine and hit mental rewind. Then smacked herself upside the head.

The bartender removed her empty glass. "Guess you figured it out."

"Too late, but yes."

"I'd say you've got time to save this one." He nodded toward the front of the restaurant.

She swiveled, scanned the room and came up blank.

"Outside," he said from behind her.

Through the oversize front windows, she located Mason. He sat in a corner patio chair, long legs stretched and hooked at the ankles, nicely muscled arms crossed over his chest.

Eyes fixed on the door. No beer on his table. Totally unapproachable looking.

She fished a five from her purse and placed it on the bar. A decent tip, considering she'd already given twenty percent when she paid. The bartender gave her a wink and a nod. Here's hoping his advice was on the money.

The closer she got to the door, the tighter her stomach clenched. She stepped out into the summer night and connected with Mason's eyes immediately. His expression stayed cool, borderline angry. She made a straight line toward him, cell tucked in her palm, ready to go. The breeze chose this less-than-convenient moment to blow an errant lock of hair in her face. Stupid, good-for-nothing hair clip. She puffed at the strand—repeatedly—rather than use her hand, since she wanted to hide the phone from Mason's view. A very anti-dramatic effect. But good for breaking the tension a bit, if she read his face correctly.

"This is the person who ditched me tonight," she said when she'd reached his feet. She thrust the phone in his face before he could protest. Grudgingly, he looked at Lasha's picture on the screen. Recognition registered in his features. Still didn't look convinced, though. She switched applications and pulled up the text conversation. For extra sass, she pried one of his hands from his chest and slapped the phone in his palm. Let him look all righteous and smug after reading those snippets.

She shifted foot to foot while he read. For only a couple of texts, there was significant R-rated content. Lasha had made explicit comments about Mason's body—all true, Andie could vouch for those—along with referencing Andie and Mason's sexy evening. Because yes, she'd spilled some of the details. How could she not? Lasha's final text contained a suggestion for what Andie could get up to tonight, both to, and courtesy of, the gorgeous man reading her iPhone. The smile on his face must mean he liked the idea.

Mason offered the phone, catching Andie's hand when she reached for it. "This is where I apologize for being a Neanderthal." He opened his legs and pulled her between them. "Which explains why I'm alone, but why are you?"

"Um, because my friend took off when she saw us getting ready to make out at the bar."

"Not just tonight." He drew her close enough that her knees brushed his fly. His hands cupped the back of her legs, climbing the hamstrings and stopping at the bottom curve of her ass. He squeezed, his fingers curling between her legs. Her skin practically caught fire as his gaze slowly moved up her body. Cool blue eyes never looked so hot.

"Do you need to get home for your son?"

She shook her head. "He spends weekends with his dad. I'm free until tomorrow night." Too much information... it probably seemed as if she were begging for an invitation to spend more time together.

"Meaning I have a chance to fix my mistakes, starting with the one from last night." He grinned, one part sexy mixed with two parts sheepish. The effect was one hundred percent charming. "Only I haven't figured out exactly what it was."

"I guess it's a good thing you've got all night."

Chapter Four

These had to be the same hard-ass plastic benches from his kid days of bumper bowling. In fact, he'd bet nothing had changed at B&D Lanes in decades. Except his opponent. Andie lit up this dreary place. She even made the clown-like rental shoes sexy. But bowling, for chrissake. He still couldn't believe he'd brought Andie here instead of taking her straight home to his bed. After an hour of watching her cute ass sway as she lined up her shot in the lane directly in front of him, his reasoning didn't feel so reasonable.

She'd given no hint why their date died on the pavement last night. He'd said or done something, that much was obvious. He could've straight out asked, but no, he'd chosen this method. Hopefully a nice, light evening would wipe the slate clean. Show her that he wanted to spend time with her, get to know her, not just take her home and fuck her long and hard.

They'd spent the past hour swapping random details. Education, career choices, favorite foods and movies—basic date conversation. She'd been offered an assistant designer's position at some fancy fashion place in Toronto after college, but had come back to her hometown and set up a dressmaking shop instead. Big-city living didn't appeal to her—another thing they had in common. Once she'd learned he was a veterinarian, she'd bombarded him with questions. Not the usual kind. Really detailed stuff only a true animal lover would want to know.

He liked that. He liked everything about her so far. Her interests and core values. Her quick and dirty sense of humor. Hanging out with her was fun and interesting. But holy hell, let them get to the getting-naked stuff soon.

"Strike!" She did a little jump and wiggle thing, then cruised back to him. "That turkey makes it game. You want another rematch?"

"Hell no." He yanked her onto his lap. Thrust up against her ass while brushing his lips along her jaw. "It's hard to bowl in this condition."

"Oh?" She gave a little grind. "Oh. I guess that might be a problem if you use a standard approach. You could assume the straddle position and roll the ball through your legs."

"Rearrange that last sentence a bit and I'm all over it." A simple tug on her waist had her pressed up tight to his chest. Close enough to kiss, something he'd wanted to do all night. Her lips opened the tiniest bit. Soft, pink and moist from her tongue. His cock jerked in its denim prison, desperate to get inside her—anywhere, everywhere—and find release. One kiss suitable for a public audience wasn't going to cut it.

"Andrea Finch, I knew it was you." The voice came from a woman beating a path toward them, a reluctant male in tow. "Didn't I tell you, John? I said, 'that woman over there looks like Scott Finch's wife'."

Mason cocked an eyebrow at the beauty he wasn't going to get to kiss. "Andrea?"

"Don't you ever call me that," she whispered, and extricated herself from his lap.

He'd be a gentleman and stand beside her—in a couple of minutes. Whoever these people were, they probably wouldn't appreciate looking at bulging proof of his affection toward Andie. Plus, she'd put herself in front of him, her ass in his direct sightline. A winning view for him.

Andie shook the man's hand, then stuffed hers in her jeans' pockets. No handshake for the woman, whose face said she got that message, loud and clear.

"It's ex-wife, Judy. And I go by Andie, I always have." She turned her attention to Judy's husband. "How're you, John? Busy with lots of cases?"

Another burn for Judy. Mason faked a cough to hide his smile. He and Andie wouldn't be doubling with John and Judy anytime soon. Fine by him. They looked about as much fun as a trip to the accountant. From the conversation, John practiced law. So did Andie's ex, though not at the same firm. More good-to-know details.

"You haven't introduced us to your friend, Andie." Judy didn't seem to care that she'd cut her husband off midsentence. "Apparently Scott got all the manners in your divorce settlement."

What a nasty bitch. Mason rose from the chair to stand close behind Andie. Nobody got to shit on her while he was around.

"That's right. Scott got the book of etiquette. I got the sex toys. And your poor husband probably got arthritis inputting that list in the divorce papers."

"I'm not sure it was the typing, but my wrist did get plenty tired," John said with a grin. Judy turned fire-engine red and practically spit flames. It was fucking priceless. Andie didn't need a protector—she did just fine on her own. Soft and feisty. Fuck, that was hot.

Mason reached around Andie and shook John's hand. "Mason Lang. If I ever need a lawyer, I'll look you up." To be polite, he offered his hand to John's wife. She looked at it as if he were offering a dead fish. No shake. No problem. He'd rather put it on Andie's body, anyway. "Andie's been handing me my ass for the last hour, so we're calling it a night here. See you around, John. Judy."

But Judy wasn't finished with her bitchfest. "Don't keep your boyfriend out past his curfew. You wouldn't want him to get grounded."

Angry heat rolled off Andie. In the next seconds, Mason readied for a fight. Not participating, only watching. He'd put every cent he had on Andie.

John nixed the cat scrap by hauling Judy away in a less-than-graceful way. Lots of flailing and verbal protests. An uptight bitch like that wouldn't recognize John's actions as the service they were.

"Babe, I have to ask," Mason said, going for the most serious tone he could manage. She tensed as he turned her to face him. He had to bite the inside of cheek to keep his mouth straight.

Resignation flashed across her face and she sighed. "Go ahead."

"Were you serious about the sex toys?" Confusion filled those beautiful blues until he couldn't hold back a grin any longer. "'Cause if you were, I think we should go to your place instead of mine."

"That's your question?" She thumped his chest, prompting him to yank her closer. "Come on, you have to be wondering about my age. Especially after that crapshow."

"Nope. Just the toys."

"I'm forty, Mason." She eased backward. Fiddled with a renegade piece of hair. "Four-zero. It matters."

"Not to me." He tucked the strands behind her ear, stroked her cheek and the line of her neck. So pretty. "To hell with idiots like her. I couldn't care less about anybody's opinion on the subject, other than yours."

"What about your baseball buddies? The ones you were too embarrassed to walk by while I was on your arm."

And there it was. Of course that's what she'd thought last night. Like his sister pointed out, even with eight years of university education, Mason could be as dumb as the next idiot. Somebody ought to teach a course on effective verbal communication with women. The thing would sell out.

"Hey." He snared her by the belt loops and waited for her to really look at him. "I bailed on the guys last night, blamed it on having to get up early for work, when really I was hoping you'd call. That's why I didn't want them to see me. I know how teenager-stupid that sounds, but it's the truth." His eyes stayed on hers. She believed him, right? All her best frontal parts melted into his body. He let himself relax and enjoy, even though the key areas didn't quite line up while standing.

"This isn't working for me," she said, pulling away.

Shit. Shit. "Because of the age thing?"

First she smiled. Next she grabbed his collar, yanked his head down and laid a kiss on him that would've made poor Judy faint dead away. Hell, he practically lost consciousness.

"Because of the height thing. I'm in flat shoes and you're a tower. Now, to answer your earlier question, yes, I have some toys at home."

He had his bowling shoes off in about five seconds and began tugging at her laces.

She burst out laughing. "What I don't have are condoms."

He held her calves while expediting her shoe removal, scooped both sets up and grabbed her hand. "There's an open-to-midnight drugstore on the way."

"You don't know where I live."

"Trust me…" He gave her fine ass a playful smack. "There's a drugstore on the way."

Andie grinned like an idiot after Mason entered the pharmacy. Holding it in while they'd made the five-minute drive from the bowling alley had been murder on the jaw muscles. The night had certainly taken a series of turns, and it was heading in a good direction. Not good, great. Here she was, sitting in Mason's truck, waiting for him to return with condoms so they could go to her house and have sex. Possibly involving toys she'd only used while alone.

Sex. She'd be having it in about twenty minutes. The real deal, fully naked, maybe even with the lights on. Her mouth went dry. That couldn't be good for her breath. There had to be a mint in her purse. Dammit, not a one. Maybe she should go into the store and buy some Tic Tacs. But what if she ran into another Judy-type acquaintance and they saw her with Mason and a box of condoms? Tonight's drama would be public knowledge by tomorrow as it was. Every social circle intersected at least six others in this itty-bitty city.

Oh god, was she sweating now too? She fiddled pointlessly with the controls, but he'd shut off the truck and taken the keys. Where were the good old days of windows that simply rolled down?

The driver's door opened and she jumped. A small shopping bag slid across the seat, followed by the soon-to-be wearer of said purchase. Gone was the button-down shirt, tossed into the backseat of the crew cab in one fluid motion. That left a white t-shirt that hugged some fine biceps. So round and hard, they begged to be touched. Same with his hair. After last night's encounter in the alley, she knew it was soft and thick. And his smile, that perfect mouth and what it could do... Now she had damp panties to go with her sweaty body and tangled nerves.

"You okay?" he asked before turning the ignition over. "We can change the plans, no pressure."

God, he did sweet almost as well as he did sexy. "No change. I just want to wash the grimy bowling alley feeling away first."

"I can help with that." Leather creaked as he released her seatbelt buckle and pulled her toward him, draping his right arm around her shoulder. "I'm pretty handy with the shower sprayer."

"I bet you are." Hair tumbled down her back. The clip bounced on the seat behind her. Mason's fingers spread through the length, easing away the tangles and her doubts. "That feels so good." How long had it been since anybody had touched her this way? Forever, literally.

"Keep moaning like that and we won't get out of this parking lot with a full box of condoms."

She'd been moaning? "Okay."

His left hand slid up her thigh and cupped her hot zone. He leaned in, close enough that his lips brushed her ear while he spoke. "Okay you'll stop moaning, or okay, bust open that box and fuck you right here?"

"Yes."

His words flipped a switch inside her. How many times had she fantasized about something like this? Scott had never done public displays of affection—not kissing and certainly nothing better. It wouldn't be appropriate for a man in his position, blah, blah, blah. Mason, by comparison, seemed more than willing to fulfill her secret exhibitionist desires. Last night, oral sex in an alley. Tonight, screwing in a parking lot. To hell with clean and horizontal, she wanted to mount him right here in the front seat and ride him until the windows steamed solid.

His finger flicked the seam of her jeans back and forth against her clit. She rocked her hips for more friction. So rough and torturously good.

"Right there, harder…" She clapped her hand over his, pressing both tight to her body her as she writhed through a fast, raw orgasm. "Oh my god, sorry."

"Are you fucking kidding me? I haven't even gotten you naked in a bed yet, and you're already the sexiest woman I've ever met."

"I really want to get to the bed part, but first this." She clawed at his zipper, dug through layers of denim and cotton until his cock stood free and ready. Zero finesse, all business. "This is even prettier, now that I can admire it properly."

He laughed. "My cock is pretty?"

"Very." She stroked it base to head, licked her lips. "And mouthwatering."

"I'd hate to see you go hungry," he said, and nudged the back of her head.

"Wow, you're offering yourself up for a blowjob, just for me?"

"I'm a considerate kind of guy, what can I say?"

The automatic door on the drugstore slid open for a departing customer. A dark-haired man carrying a bag of diapers walked in front of Mason's truck en route to his vehicle. He didn't give them a second glance. No reason to, yet. At this point they were nothing more than a couple sitting in a parked truck at a late-night pharmacy. A few minutes later and the guy would've seen her head bobbing up and down. Now that might've gotten his attention. Another car pulled in a few spots away and its driver hurried into the store.

Mason wore a smile so mischievous and sexy it should be illegal. His head cocked in question.

Could she do it—suck him off in the front row of a parking lot, where anyone coming or going from the store had access to the show? A small risk, considering the late hour, but a possibility nonetheless. Somebody could catch them. They might slow their walk to stare a bit, might even stop and watch. Heat pooled between her legs. Part of her wanted that.

"Let's go to your place." He shifted, made a move to put things away.

She stopped his hand, shook her head. "I'm not done here."

"Andie—" Whatever sweet thing he was about to say died when her lips closed over the head of his cock, slowly slid to the base, then sucked him hard all the way to the top. "Do that again."

She repositioned herself on the bench seat, on her knees, ass in the air. And sucked. Slow and hard at first, like he wanted. The more he vocalized his enjoyment, the hotter she got and the faster she went. His cock thickened. Got steel hard. His hand fisted in her hair and she nearly came from wanting to.

"Babe, stop." He used his hold on her hair to angle her head to the side. She looked up with his cock still filling her mouth. "Do you have any idea how sexy you are with those perfect lips wrapped around my cock, staring up at me with those beautiful eyes? I need to be inside you."

She took her time releasing him. He watched each inch as it eased from her mouth. Nobody had ever looked at her that way, consumed by hunger for what she gave.

As soon as he was free, he grabbed the bag that had fallen to the floor. Plastic and cardboard went flying. He ripped the packet with his teeth, then smoothed the condom down his length while she watched, riveted. Sex with a condom was a thing from her distant past. And sweet heaven, it had never been a sexy show like this.

"My turn to watch. Jeans off. Now." His eyes followed her hands as she worked the zipper and shimmied out of the denim. "Leave the panties on."

"They're not as nice as the ones I left in the alley last night." She rose to her knees beside him, the sound of his laugh working like a magnet on her hips.

"I don't mind owing you a pair, but these look pretty great in my opinion." He trailed one finger across the front of the skimpy blue thong, let it slide lower, back and forth over the strip of fabric covering her clit. He pushed the material aside. Dipped his finger inside her and gently urged her closer. "C'mere. Ride me."

She swung her leg up and over. The goal—a sexy transition to straddling his lap. The reality—whacking her right foot against steering wheel.

"Ow, crap. Shit. My ankle." She crumbled onto the seat beside him, throbbing foot cupped in her hands, half crying from pain and half laughing at killing the mood, klutz-style. "Do I have the moves, or what?"

"You really do." A huge smile lit his face. He patted his lap, right next to his cock. "Foot. Let me take a look at it."

"It's just bruised. It'll be fine in a minute." She tried flexing it and winced.

"I'm the doctor here."

"You're an animal doctor." Mason had her right foot across his thigh before she could blink. "God, you move fast."

"I'm always quick with the feisty ones," he said while checking her ankle with a series of gentle pokes and stretches.

"I'll be sure to keep that in mind if we ever make it past the oral sex stage." She toed him in the ribs with her left foot. With her panties still askew and her legs slightly parted, Andie was well aware of the mostly naked view she'd be providing if he looked her way. And, bingo. She had his attention. A couple of adjustments to the seat and tilt steering, that's all it'd take, he could cover her with his body and slide inside.

"Can you sit up yet?"

So he still wanted her to ride him. Okay by her. "Yup. Good to go." This time, she'd lose the attempt at sexy flair. Eyes on the prize.

"Then buckle in. We need to be at your house five minutes ago."

Mason breathed a sigh of relief when Andie wiggled into her jeans. Driving across town with her nearly naked beside him would've been torture. He tucked himself away and shoved the condom in his pocket. Nine more where that came from and they weren't coming off empty. He stole a quick glance at the woman he intended to use them all with, then backed out of the spot. Yeah, he'd never look at this parking lot the same way.

Andie stiffened as he pulled away. "That Buick is gone."

"The guy left while you were... occupied."

Her eyes went wide. "Did he see anything?"

If he were with any other woman, he'd tell her no immediately. Reassure her that the dark tints and height of the cab ensured complete discretion. Not that he'd ever had another woman suck him in public like that. Only in his dreams. With Andie, though, he wasn't sure no was the answer she wanted to hear. The way her lips curled into a wicked smile, the glint in her eyes when they drove under a streetlight—the woman had a naughty streak. He bet even she didn't know how deep it ran.

"There's no way he could see your face. Probably not mine, either." Not a lie, but not the plain truth. A perfect answer, given the expression on her face. The idea of getting caught turned her on? He could cater to that, hell yes.

"Sorry we didn't get to finish things."

He reached over and grabbed her hand. "I'm not. I'd rather have you laid out on a big bed when I fuck you. The first time, anyway."

Andie lived in the swankiest part of town. No shock there, her ex was a lawyer and a member of the prominent Finch family, either of which meant big money. Having both to his credit—Mason could only imagine what the guy was worth. The woman beside him didn't come off snooty or privileged. Exactly the opposite. Maybe that figured into her divorce. He wanted to ask, wanted to know everything about her, really. There'd be time for long talks. Later.

She pointed to a monster executive home. "This one. Number 67."

He swung into the driveway. Colored, stamped concrete, top notch, to go with the house. Tasteful outdoor lighting showcased pristine landscaping and immaculate grass. "Nice place," he said while opening the passenger door.

"You want it? It'll be on the market soon."

"Big move or little move planned?"

"Downsizing, staying in town." She dealt with the security system and gestured for him to enter. "I don't need a place… like this," she said, waving her hand at the foyer.

If she meant massive, he could see why. The foyer was almost as big as his kitchen. Speaking of kitchens, holy shit. His main floor could fit inside this one. Dark cherry cupboards, black granite, black appliances. Not Andie's picks, he'd bet.

Maybe it wasn't the size of the house she wanted to change, but the style. She pulled a beer from the fridge and handed it to him. A Bud Light Lime. This, he pictured her choosing.

"It is a lot of house for two people." He leaned on the counter and cracked open the beer. "But you might remarry, extend the family with more kids." His move had been calculatingly casual. Her outburst of laughter was spontaneous and one hundred percent natural.

"Mason." She leaned into him, hands spread flat on his chest. "You have nothing to worry about. I'm not out to snag you for marriage version two-point-oh, nor will I trap you with a baby. You're safe." She tiptoed up for a long, soft kiss. "I'm going to grab a shower. Finish your beer and meet me upstairs."

The Bud crawled down his throat. He should be chugging it back and doing a happy dance. A funny, gorgeous, fucking sexy woman waited for him upstairs. She didn't want his future or his sperm, just tonight and his Glad-wrapped cock.

He poured out half the beer and rinsed the bottle. Climbed the plush, carpeted stairs that led to what would undoubtedly be the hottest sex of his life. Afterward, he could walk away, satisfied and commitment free. Too bad he didn't want that this time.

One upstairs room had lights on, its door half closed. He pushed it open slowly. Andie stood, bare from head to toe, fishing through a drawer, several items of lingerie hanging from her wrist.

"Put them all back. I want you just the way you are."

Chapter Five

His voice alone did things to her. Worked its way through her system like a stimulant, turning every nerve ending to high. She didn't look at him directly, just let the panties and bras slide back into the drawer. Facing the mirrored dresser, she arched her back and leaned forward while applying lip gloss.

In the reflection, his eyes traveled up and down her body, paying particular attention to her ass and the slight spread of her legs. Being naked didn't bother her. Good metabolism ran in her family and she'd never lost sight of keeping fit. While she might not be able to compete with a hard-bodied twenty-year-old, she more than held her own in the over-thirty class. She maintained her figure for her sake and no one else's. That Mason seemed to enjoy looking at it was icing on the double-fudge cake.

The t-shirt went up and off. His hands moved to the fly of his jeans, took the zipper down slower than she'd have thought possible. God, she wanted to turn around. He hooked his fingers under the waistband and pushed. Denim and jersey went down together, leaving his cock free and ready. Head to toe, Mason was the finest specimen she'd ever had the pleasure of almost looking at. Even with his socks on.

"Turn around," he said, so she did. "Come here."

She did that too. As slowly as possible. Patience afforded her a better look than she'd have had launching herself across the room, as she wanted to do, so it was worth it. He had all these glorious muscles, not crazy big, but definitely the product of serious hours inside a gym. His chest had a small dose of short, brown hair and the tattoo she'd only seen a hint of under his ball jersey. A cross, and a detailed one, at that. Huh. That came as a surprise, given his vocabulary in the alley. Regardless, the tattoo only added to his hotness factor.

She stopped in front of him, barely able to breathe or think with his naked body so temptingly close. She raised her hand and traced the ink work with the tips of her fingers, making him shudder.

"You shiver and my nipples get hard," she said.

He slid his hands up her sides and cupped her breasts, thumbing the hard peaks. "Babe, they were hard before you even turned around."

"I'm pretty sure you were looking at my ass, not my nipples."

"I am an ass man, and yours is amazing, but it didn't stop me from appreciating your beautiful tits in the mirror."

"I don't think anybody's ever called them that."

"Beautiful? That's a sin."

She gave him a playful nudge. "No. The other part."

"Tits?" he asked as he started walking her backward. "Does the word bother you?"

"No." She expected to feel the bed at the back of her legs, but they passed it.

"So it won't bother you when I say I want to suck your tits?"

"No, not at all."

He lowered himself into the reading chair by the bay window and pulled her between his legs. "What if I tell you I want to suck your beautiful tits in front of this open curtain? That while I'm sucking your tits, nibbling your perfect pink nipples, I'm going to rub my finger over your clit again and again, until you come, right here, where anyone on Paradise Ave can see. Does that bother you at all?"

She shook her head, not trusting her voice to come out steady.

"I'm gonna need to hear you say the words." One finger began a back-and-forth motion, as promised. "Just to be sure."

Every window in the house was tinted. Mason wasn't aware of that fact and she wasn't about to spill. Standing naked at the glass always gave her a little thrill, even knowing nobody could see a thing. Standing here in front of Mason while he promised to do oh so good bad things made her tingle all over. She'd never done anything like this with Scott. He didn't like to play.

"I want you to suck my...um...tits." A hot, naked man was in her bedroom, waiting to pleasure her, and that lame-o attempt at sexy was the best she could do? She rolled her eyes as her cheeks burned. "When you call them tits, it makes me feel sexy. When I use the word, I feel like an idiot."

"That's no good." Mason smiled and leaned back in the chair, cock in hand. "I definitely want you feeling sexy, not stupid." He used a slow, steady rhythm, never taking his eyes off her. Now that was sexy.

"This is way better than internet porn."

"Yeah?" A red-hot smile slid into place. "And is this what you do when you're watching porn—just watch?"

"Sometimes I fold laundry." The deep sound of his laugh made her best parts tighten with need. "But mostly I play with myself."

"I'd like to see that."

"Let me grab the hamper." She took a fake step away, enough to make him reach for her. His hand closed around her wrist. Not tight, he didn't need to use his strength to keep her there. The rush of sensation that came with each touch, the draw of his incredible eyes, she'd do anything he asked, with or without words. So self-assured and in control, Mason was a man who knew what he wanted and expected to get it. He affected every nerve ending, every cell in her body. He was exactly what she'd been missing.

He drew her back to the spot in front of the window. Directed the hand he'd grabbed to the needy place between her legs, then let go. His eyes stayed on her while he lazily fisted his cock with his right hand.

He wanted to watch her touch herself? Expert at masturbation she was, but never for an audience. Her heart rate kicked up its pace as she slid one finger between her folds and circled her clit without touching it. Self-inflicted tease torture, the kind she used when she wanted to draw out the process. A little more pressure wouldn't tip the scales. She rubbed across her clit, igniting the need to come. Mason's eyes were transfixed on her motion. Hand still working in his lap, he pumped faster, matching her rhythm. A bead of pre-come formed on the tip, begging to be licked.

"I need your cock in my mouth." He answered her by jerking forward and sealing his lips over her nipple. "Okay, I can wait a few more minutes." Vibrations from his muffled laugh tickled the sensitive skin of her breast. She wriggled against the sensation. He nipped the bud, hard enough to make her gasp—and press her eager body closer. If only he had two mouths, one for each breast. His hand moved up her body and pinched the lonely nipple. Oh, sweet heaven. It never felt this good when she squeezed them.

His teeth scraped the flesh as he released it. He skimmed his hands down her stomach, anchored them on her hips and urged her downward, to her knees. Wordless, intense and perfect. He angled his cock with one hand, using the other to cup her cheek. She looked into his eyes and opened for him. Let him guide her lips down his shaft until there was nothing left to take. How did he know everything she wanted?

"Your mouth is fucking paradise."

Sexy, perfect words. She gulped his cock base to tip, over and over. Fast, because she was way past being able to go slow. Her nipples rubbed the edge of the chair with each pass, the raw silk piping creating a burning pleasure that shot through her body. Mason's scent, his intoxicating man-ness, rushed her senses. She stroked the strip of soft, smooth skin below his balls. He cursed under his breath and tilted his hips, giving her better access. She ventured lower, massaging the ring of his ass with small, firm circles.

"Jesus, Andie..."

She jerked her hand away. Oh god, he hated it. He hated it and probably thought she was a freak for doing it. "Sorry. I'm sorry... Apparently not all the tips in those sex articles are good ones."

He shifted forward in the seat, putting them in very close proximity. "Fingering my ass was an experiment?"

"I wouldn't exactly call it fingering."

"Because..."

"No penetration." The words squeaked out as heat rushed her cheeks, making her blush like a virgin. First the flub with the dirty talk, now this. Oh yah, she was proving to be quite the dud at seduction scenes.

He rose from the chair, grabbed her hands and pulled her up, into his arms. The smile on his face matched the erection pressing against her stomach. Huge. "You can use me as your sexual guinea pig anytime. But right now," his fingers ran down the seam of her ass, cupping it at the bottom with a hard squeeze, "it's my turn to experiment. And babe, there's gonna be penetration."

Halfway to the bed, he hooked his arms under her knees and hoisted her up. The head of his cock rubbed her clit. A couple of small adjustments and she could have him inside her. And man, she needed that. Big time.

"Where are the condoms?" The last thing she wanted was an accidental pregnancy from her first time out of the gate.

"Front pocket of my jeans." Cool softness hugged her body as he deposited her onto the duvet. "We don't need them yet."

"You're going to make me wait even longer?" Not that she minded having him hovering over her, kissing his way down her neck and over the curve of her breast.

"Impatient much?" He caught her nipple between his teeth and tugged. "It's been what… twenty-eight hours since we met?" He gave her a devastatingly hot smile before his mouth disappeared beneath her breast to continue its southbound journey.

"Yes, but it's been years since—" Oh, *oh*. She glanced down. The sensual movement of his head combined with the fluttering of his tongue against her sensitive parts rendered her momentarily mute. His fingers slipped inside her. She relaxed her hips, opening wider. At the deepest point of each thrust, his knuckles brushed her ass, teasing her rear entry. No man had ever touched her there, though it certainly ranked highly in her fantasy time. Mason would be different. He'd touch her everywhere, fuck her everywhere. Do everything she dreamed about and maybe some extra stuff.

Her legs shook as she tipped over the edge. She shoved her hands through his hair, clutching his head, melting against his face. Shamelessly enjoying what he gave. When the last wave of ecstasy rippled through her, she dissolved into the bed. Satisfied with a capital S, large font, bold and in italics. Most of the women she knew would kill for one orgasm like that. Yet seeing Mason resurface, licking his lips and smiling, she greedily wanted to shove him back down for another round.

"Wow."

"Yeah?" He put his tongue on her clit and gave it a little swirl.

"Very wow." So much so, she could barely take the light teasing he was administering. "Are you a good vet?"

"The best."

Confidence suited him. He wore it as naturally as skin. "You're not going to ask me why I'm asking about your job right after you made me come like a rocket?"

"Nah, but I like that part about the rocket."

"That was my point. If the vet thing doesn't work out, you could become a gigolo. With your skills, you'd be rich."

"Would you pay for my services?"

"I might."

"I wouldn't take your money. Burying my face between your legs is my pleasure."

"God, you're smooth."

"You'd rather I was rough?"

One look at his hungry smile and the sinful glint in his eyes and she was done for. Whatever he did to her, however he did it, would end with a trip to the moon. She didn't doubt that for one second.

"How about now…" She rocked her hips side to side. "Have I been patient enough?"

"Hell yes." He disentangled himself from her legs, turned her on her side and smacked her on the butt. "Go get them."

No need to tell her twice. She rolled off the bed and practically dove for the pile of clothes he'd left on the floor. Digging through his pockets revealed four condoms. Ambitious. She raised an eyebrow at him while holding them up, fan-style.

"I know, I should've brought the whole box."

The bed shook as she plopped down beside him. "What, it's not enough that you wrecked my ankle with a baseball, now you want to cripple me by way of fucking?" Before she could blink, he'd snagged the condoms from her hand and flipped her onto her back. His cock tapped her inner thigh, edging closer, then retreating. Driving her wild.

"Definitely not cripple, but I like the idea of having you confined to a bed for a few days. Also, you're damn sexy when you talk about fucking." He tore into one packet and handed her the goods. "Put it on."

"Pretty sure I don't have a cock. Feel free to go back down there and conduct another search, though."

"What, I wasn't thorough enough the first time?"

"You missed a spot."

A groan slipped out, even though he tried to keep his cool. Was she saying what he thought she was saying? Because it sounded like an invitation to play with her ass. No man in his right mind would refuse that suggestion, not with Andie, who had a fucking phenomenal booty. Round and firm with skin he wanted to touch for hours. He closed his eyes, pictured spreading her cheeks, feasting his eyes. Touching her. The sound of her moan as he worked his finger inside her in preparation for bigger and better things. Shit, he couldn't, not this time. Thinking about it had him at the edge. Any attempt at the real deal and he'd lose it altogether.

"Don't think that you have to…" She turned away, burying her cheek in the cushy blanket. "I mean, I know that not everybody wants to do stuff—back there."

"Are you kidding me?"

She sucked her bottom lip between her teeth and shook her head. Her chin quivered when he touched her cheek. A little stroking across her smooth skin and he coaxed her to look at him. Those eyes, so honest. And damn if he didn't see insecurity lurking there. Unbelievable.

"Babe, every guy wants to do things back there, especially when their lady is beautiful and sexy like you."

"Not every guy," she whispered.

No way. That explained the stammering and the timid eyes. Fucking moron, her ex. "This guy does. I'm ready to explode just from thinking about your sweet ass. From thinking about every part of you. Your soft, sweet-smelling hair, those delicious pink lips, all the way down to your red toenails." He rolled to his back and eyed the condom in her hand. "Put it on me."

The simple act of her holding his cock at the base made him suck in a breath. Gentle and tentative as her touch was, it launched him into a worse state. He barely fought back the urge to thrust up into her hand. To pump until he came in her fist.

The hand with the condom wavered above his cock. "Do these things come with instructional diagrams, because I've never done this before."

Some women did adorable, some were sexy. Andie pulled off both at the same time.

"I'll help." Electricity flared between them when he put his hand over hers. "Pinch the air out of the tip, like this. Now put it over the head and roll it down the sides."

"Is this good?" she asked while smoothing the latex along his shaft.

Good—fuck, it was great. Sensations assaulted his system, even with the damn condom buffering her touch. His balls clenched. Mouth went dry. The best he could do was nod and pray she noticed. His plan to draw things out, give her a couple of orgasms before sinking himself into her? Yeah, that was history.

"Climb up here."

She swung one shapely leg over his chest. Centered herself over his throbbing cock and brushed her heat over the tip. She lowered slowly—holy fuck, was it slow—taking him inch by agonizing inch. Heaven swallowed him whole. Her muscles squeezed him, amplifying every pulse of his cock. Baseball. If he thought about his swing or the batting order, maybe he'd last until she hit bottom. Hell, he hadn't been wound this tight since he was a teenager.

She ground herself onto him in deep, deliberate circles. "You feel so good inside me."

The words were real, and that made them hotter than any forced dirty talk. For a few seconds he simply looked up at her. The sensual line of her neck, the fullness of her tits, the spot where her waistline dipped in and her hips began their sexy outward curve. Fuck, she was beautiful. Natural. Totally relaxed with her sexuality. A rare combo. One he could get used to, easily.

Her back was smooth and soft under his palms as he guided her forward enough to catch one nipple in his mouth. The soft little moan she made went straight to his cock. He tipped his hips, thrusting, driving his pubic bone against her clit.

"Oh god—that—I—" Her voice was a throaty whisper, the disjointed words proof of her pleasure.

He was ready to come. Too fucking soon, but knowing she was on the edge with him zapped the last of his control. He pulled her down, mashed her tits against his chest. Then it was warm lips, desperate tongues, clashing teeth. Anything to get closer. He cupped her butt. Swiped some lube from their fucking and eased the tip of one finger into her ass. And fuck, did she welcome him.

"More," she whispered between kisses.

Hell, yeah, he'd give her more. He pushed deeper, and was rewarded by the sexiest fucking moan he'd ever heard. It filled his head, rang through his body, made his balls clench with need. He thrust hard, burying his cock to the hilt. Andie writhed on top of him, eyes closed, sweet lips parted and gasping. No turning back now.

"Babe, I'm gonna come."

"Uh-huh. Please... yes."

His pulse pounded in his ears, he wouldn't have heard a parade go past, but he was completely tuned in to her soft voice, answering. Telling him what his senses already knew— she was already there. He let go, joining her in the best feeling alive.

She lay plastered to his chest, unmoving and silent, until he started to pull out. "I wish you could stay."

What the hell? Did she sense that he was the type to fuck and run, or was she politely telling him to split?

"I suppose it's nature's part in the whole male anti-cuddling thing."

Now he was really lost. "How's that?"

"Post-sex slippage. No matter how much I put my Kegel exercises to use, I can't keep you in there." She sighed, rolled off to his side and propped up on one arm. "There, you're free."

So she wasn't booting him out. Good. He made a quick trip to the bathroom to deal with the condom, then slid onto the bed, facing her.

"Here I am, ready to cuddle. What's your preference, face-to-face or spooning?" The sound of her giggle stirred his cock. When she turned her back to him and nestled that sweet ass against his hips, every drop of blood in his body changed course to southbound. He cruised one hand over her curves and down to her sweet spot, eliciting an approving moan. They weren't going to get much sleep tonight.

Chapter Six

Mason expected Andie's designer kitchen to have a high-tech, fancy coffeemaker. Gourmet beans from some obscure mountaintop plantation. Instead he found a plain, stainless-steel kettle—the old school, stovetop kind that whistles—and a jar of instant. Her house oozed pretentiousness. She didn't seem to have an ounce.

They'd stayed up past two, alternating between fucking and talking. He'd woken at seven with Andie's face on his chest, her leg draped over him and her hand curled around his cock. She looked beautiful, peaceful and unbelievably sexy. And, unfortunately, not nearly as alert as the part of his anatomy in her grip. So he'd snuck out rather than disturb her. She needed the rest. He had plans for her today. Big ones.

He whisked eggs, chopped red pepper and grated cheese. Found spices in one of the million cupboards and put a large skillet on to preheat. His cell vibrated on the counter as he poured the ingredients into the pan. A quick glance at the screen told him it was the after-hours service, meaning he had a possible emergency to deal with. Maybe he'd get lucky and it'd be as simple as calling a worried client. He stirred the eggs while he called for the details. Damn. A legit emergency, one he had to go in for—now. So much for surprising Andie with breakfast in bed.

He turned off the burner and charged up the stairs, laid a quick kiss on sleeping beauty to get her attention. Pulled on clothes as he explained about the Great Dane with possible gastric torsion, a life-threatening condition that even surgery couldn't always resolve.

"Oh, no. Can I do anything?"

"Cross your fingers it's something less severe and be ready for me when I get back." He leaned over the bed and gave her a deeper kiss than he had time for, given the circumstances. "I made breakfast. I wanted to feed you in bed, but I'll have to do that next time. Go grab it while it's hot."

Her whole face lit up. Damn, he'd love to slide back into bed with her. Push the covers off and settle his mouth between her legs while watching sunlight dance on her skin and pleasure play across her face. He gave his head a shake and pushed to a stand.

"I'll see you soon," he said from the doorway. She didn't answer. Just smiled and waved her fingertips. For the first time in years, he couldn't wait to get back to a woman, instead of putting distance between them.

Sunday morning dragged into afternoon. No Mason on her doorstep. No call or text. Disappointment set in, despite her best attempts to ward it off. Last night had been the most incredible night of her life. Fun and passion with a ridiculously hot man who'd even made her a gourmet-style breakfast. She had no business expecting anything more to come of it. And yet here she was, foolishly staring at the phone for hours on end.

She jumped when it finally rang, then dropped the handset on the floor. Twice. One more ring and it'd go to the machine. "Shit!" Damn klutz gene was going to make her miss the call. She quickly jabbed the talk button and attempted a sexy yet casual hello.

"I assume that extra-friendly tone was meant for one of your gentleman callers, not me." Scott seldom let emotion color his voice, but his agitation was obvious.

"Excuse me?"

"I received an email from Judy Fenwick, detailing your run-in last night at the bowling alley. She said you were draped all over some man, and when she came over to catch up with you, you were offensive and raunchy."

Nasty bitch. "Only by Judy's standards."

"And mine, from the account I received."

"Judy was her usual, obnoxious self. She was rude to me…and my date." There. Maybe Lasha was right, and he'd put the idea of reconciliation aside now that she'd publicly moved on.

"Irrelevant. I have a reputation to uphold. Your behavior and activities reflect on me, despite the fact that we aren't married at the present time. I can't have you talking and acting like a loose woman. You need to be more— discerning."

The floor probably had a dent from her jaw, it'd dropped so hard and fast. "You make it sound as though I'm running around town with an open for visitors sign slung over my hips."

"Remember the terms of our separation agreement. None of your visitors are permitted near Dylan without my consent."

The lid blew off her barely contained control. "I've been out a couple of times with one man. I'm not signing anybody up for stepdad duty, nor am I whoring my way through the city's bachelor population. There's nobody Dylan needs to meet." At first, she took Scott's silence as a small victory. As the seconds ticked away, she realized the opposite was true. The rat-bastard had gotten to her. She'd told him everything he wanted to know. Worse, she'd fueled his damn hope.

"For the sake of the family and our future, please be more discreet while you're working through this midlife crisis."

How could such an intelligent man be so dense? "We don't have a future. You need to accept that." The jerk, he actually had the audacity to cluck. "I honestly don't know what's worse, Scott. The way you belittled me while I was your wife, or how you think you're entitled to keep doing it now that I'm not."

The telephone diagnosis had been right. Unfortunately. The Dane's stomach was in bad shape and Mason had spent two hours doing everything in his power to correct it. In the end, the dog had needed to go to the veterinary hospital at the U of Guelph, where a team of doctors had saved the gentle giant. But it'd eaten up his entire day, because he'd driven the patient and the distraught owner. Mrs. Anderson didn't have a vehicle or a license, and the cab fare would've been one hundred and ninety-seven dollars. Each fucking way. Not a chance he'd have let them go that route.

By the time he'd gotten home last night, it'd been too late to head back to Andie's. So he'd missed out on seeing her again. But their texting, especially the late-night parts that had included a few photos, had given him plenty to smile about.

Hell, he was still smiling.

He tied the last suture on the young Doberman he'd just spayed. Monday's morning lineup of routine surgeries didn't stop him from thinking about Andie's eyes looking up at him while she sucked his cock, or her soft but strong legs wrapped around his back, urging him deeper inside her body. Fuck. Too much detail going through his cerebrum.

His assistant, Sally, shook her head as she helped him settle the pretty Dobie into a recovery stall. His distracted state hadn't gone unnoticed. Sally rolled her eyes at his grin and went about her duties. Keeping Sally had been part of the deal when he bought the clinic from a retiring vet. A lucky break for him, because she was as good as they came.

He turned and slammed into the clinic receptionist. A friendly girl he'd hired to appease his mother, Cara tended to be away from her post more than she was at it. No lucky breaks there. She'd have to be replaced. One day he'd be able to pay an office manager for stuff like that. For now, the job was his. Owning a clinic had its perks. Having to fire sub-par employees wasn't one of them.

"Oopsie. Sorry, Dr. Lang." Cara made a point of straightening any areas she may have wrinkled on his scrub shirt. Not too obvious, was she? "You have a call waiting. Andie Finkle, or was it Finley…"

"Neither, it's Finch. Excuse me." He practically sprinted down the hall to his office, shut the door and pressed the handset to his ear. "Hey."

"Not the greeting I was expecting," she said on a laugh.

"You're right. Let me try again." He waited a beat. "Hey, beautiful. I haven't stopped thinking about you for the past twenty-four hours. I'm in withdrawal here."

"Wow. Anytime I called my ex-husband at his office, he'd answer with, 'This is Scott Finch', all serious and businesslike, even though he knew it was me calling."

Mason kicked his feet up on the desk. "Glad to hear I've surpassed your ex in one area."

"Um, in more than one."

"Yeah?"

"Mm hmm. Your scrambled eggs are way better."

Anybody walking in on him right now would think he'd won the lottery or something. In a way he had. If it hadn't been for the scheduling mix-up that landed his team on that smaller diamond Friday night, he never would have met Andie. His little sister might be right about the whole fate thing.

"So, in your hurry, you left your watch. And your socks. Would it be okay if I put them in an envelope and leave them with somebody in your office?"

"As long as that somebody is me, yes. If you swing by at one, I can take you to lunch." The line went quiet. He pictured her fiddling with a piece of hair that had escaped its ponytail, biting down on her bottom lip. Her sexy, kind-of-shy look, as he was coming to think of it. "Anywhere you want, babe. Say yes."

Andie parked in front of the West End Veterinary Hospital at five minutes to one. Mason had already seen every naked inch of her, up close and extremely personal, with the lights on. So why was she a nervous wreck about visiting him at his workplace in the middle of the day, fully clothed? Because of the rest of the world, that's why. Time to suck it up. Mason had invited her here. She needed to check her insecurity about their age gap at the door.

A soft buzzer chirped her entrance. Mason stood at the reception desk with his back to the door. He wore a blue scrub shirt that accentuated his wide shoulders and faded jeans that showcased his fantastic ass.

A pretty blonde with perfect hair and even better boobs stood in profile, crowding the space beside him, her manicured hand on his lower back. Unprofessionally low. As in, practically on his butt. Sour heat curled in Andie's stomach as Mason and the girl looked in her direction. Both of them smiled, but their smiles said completely different things. Unquestionably, the young woman wanted to get her hooks in Mason. Too bad for blondie. Andie was nowhere near ready to throw him back in the pond.

"Hey, gorgeous." He ditched the blonde and strode to her, dipped his head and kissed her like he meant it. Yum. "You want a tour before we go?"

"Yes, please." Before removing her arms from his waist, she dropped her hands and gave his behind a nice, long squeeze. Take that, Miss D-cups.

Mason's clinic closed to appointments between one and two, but still had plenty going on. He introduced her to his two assistants, Sally, a quiet brunette somewhere in her mid-thirties, and Paula, a fresh-out-of-college redhead who favored hot-pink everything. Lipstick, nails, uniform scrubs. Suddenly, Andie craved a piece of bubblegum.

Mason showed her the exam rooms, the lab and x-ray areas, his office and the surgery room. Everything was immaculate. Not flashy or brand-spanking new, but impressive.

"Saved the best for last," he said as he led her into a room with small, stainless steel cages on one wall and larger stalls on another.

Four of the cages housed feline patients. Andie looked in at each one. Mason stood behind her, close enough to send her body temperature up several degrees.

"We neutered this tabby this morning. He'll go home later today. The white cat had a fatty cyst removed and the black one is here for blood work. This pretty Siamese kitty is Knight. We're giving him subcutaneous fluids because he hasn't been drinking at home." He popped the door and gently stroked Knight's head. "He has a lot of cancer and not a lot of time left."

The bottom fell out of Andie's stomach. "I don't know how you do this job. Constantly dealing with diseases and death."

"Not every day has tragedies." He shut the cage quietly and steered her across the room. Stopped in front of a large kennel and whispered in her ear, "Plus, there are always puppies."

"Oh, Mason. She's precious." A Doberman pinscher puppy lay zonked on a faded blanket. The dog looked exactly like her own Dobie, Minx, had once upon a time. Nearly a decade ago. In another lifetime, it seemed. "Please tell me she's not here because she's sick."

"Nope. Just getting fixed."

Relief forced a sigh from her, but the tension didn't disappear. "Can we go?"

"I'm an idiot." Mason stepped between her and the kennel. "I thought seeing the puppy would make you feel warm and fuzzy, but it made you miss your dog all over again. Shit."

That he realized and cared about her feelings tugged at something inside her. He was probably this considerate with everyone, though, and she'd be a fool to read too much into it. Yes, they had great chemistry. Sexual and otherwise. That didn't mean they shared some deep, meant-for-each-other type of connection. She was old enough to know those existed in books and movies. Period.

"I loved seeing the puppy. Truly. And I'm sure you can get me back to warm with next to no effort." Yup, that sinful smile of his ought to do the trick. She smoothed her hands over the blue fabric that matched his eyes. "You're aware of how hot you look in this scrub top, right?"

He laughed and shook his head, to which she issued him the whatever look. Of course he knew. She wasn't the first woman to paw him today. Probably wouldn't be the last, either. Unless she marked him as her territory.

"That's some kind of wicked smile," he said. "I haven't seen it before, but I'm pretty sure I like it."

She slipped her hands under the loose hemline and dragged her nails over his chest, enjoying the goose bumps cropping up in response. His nipples joined the club. Very nice, but she was more interested in his reaction below the belt. She snaked one hand between the denim and his flat stomach. His erection twitched in her palm.

"I think we should skip lunch and go to your house."

"I'm willing to go hungry." He clasped her wrist, preventing her from withdrawing her hand. He darted a glance at the open door. "Not yet. Stroke me first. I want to feel your hand pumping my cock."

"Here? What about your employees?" The rational side of her protested. And lost. Something about Mason brought her naughty side to the forefront. "You don't think I'll do it."

"You'll do it. I can see in your eyes how much you want to." He opened his jeans and fed his cock through the fly in his boxers.

This man she'd met only days ago already knew her sexual proclivities better than her ex ever had. She wrapped her fingers around the base and slowly slid her fist up his cock. Down and back, down and back, swirling the pad of her thumb over the slit at the top of each stroke. His eyes stayed locked with hers. His grin disappeared, becoming a line that showed his strain. She smiled. Served him right. She brought her thumb to her lips. Licked the drops of pre-come with the tip of her tongue.

His Adam's apple slid up and down his throat as he swallowed hard. "Jesus."

"I think we're all done here." She fought the urge to drop to her knees and suck him to the root. Instead, she tucked him away and took a step back. Breathing room. She needed it as badly as he did.

Mason hustled her through the hallway, past the unhappy-looking blonde at the check-in desk and into the parking lot. "You're driving." He opened her door even though she'd unlocked it with the remote.

"What a gentleman." She smiled up at him and slid into the driver's seat.

"You're gonna want to take that back." His eyes sparkled as he closed her door. Not a carefree, sunshiny sparkle. It was pure, mischievous lust. The kind that made her blood run hot.

She squeaked out, "Where to?" when he joined her, filling the passenger side of the sedan with his mass and his presence.

"Bruce Street. You know it?" He waited for her to nod and start driving, then unbuckled and adjusted his seat to make room for those long legs of his. But he didn't put the seatbelt back on. Instead he leaned over, nudged her head to the side and kissed his way down her neck.

"Mmm, that's nice. Very gentlemanly too," she said, totally baiting him.

His head ducked under her right arm. He caught her nipple in his mouth, biting it through the jersey top and bra. Hard enough to make her jerk in surprise. And send heat surging to all the good spots.

"Still think I'm a gentleman?"

She nodded, eager for him to prove otherwise.

He pushed her knees open and bunched her skirt up to her hips. "Eyes on the road," he said when she peeked down at his hand stroking the damp silk of her panties. He pushed the thin strip of fabric aside, penetrating her fully, twisting at the deepest point to bring his knuckles against her clit.

Urgent, familiar longing kicked in. All she needed was a little more friction... She thrust her hips forward and he chuckled, obliging her by using his thumb to rub circles over her bud. Her eyelids fluttered. God, she had to keep her eyes open or this would be her last orgasm ever. The steering wheel got slick under her white-knuckled grip. Her thighs shook. She could barely keep her foot on the gas pedal.

"You missed the turn." He withdrew his hand and sat back in his seat, rubbing his fingers between his lips.

What the—he was stopping—now? She gaped at him.

"Babe, I've watched you while you come. Several times. It's the sexiest thing in the world, but you'd crash the car if I let you have an orgasm while driving."

If he let her? The car's tires screeched as she took the next corner abruptly, for the sole purpose of seeing Mason slam into the passenger door. Nobody was controlling what she did or didn't do anymore. Not her wardrobe, not her behavior, and most definitely not her orgasms. She bombed up a block and careened around another corner. Then one more, putting her on the correct street. All of this only served to make him laugh out loud. Dammit. So much for staying irritated with him. Impossible with that sexy sound working its magic on her senses.

"Slow down, Danica. It's the little white bungalow up there, on the left."

"Ha ha." Though comparing her to a hot, female Indy car driver was kind of cool. "You're a horrible tease, by the way."

"Not true. I have every intention of finishing what I started."

Her stomach flip-flopped at the promise. Whether by fingers, tongue or cock, he'd certainly proven his expertise at finishing the job. She parked in his driveway and wiggled in her seat, trying to set her clothes to rights. Mason's mouth curled into a sly grin. Don't bother, it said. Fine. She shrugged and got out. Let his neighbors see her looking all rumpled.

The house was adorable. Clean white siding with dark-green shutters and trim. No gardens out front, but he did have a planter box overflowing with red and white petunias and a hanging basket to match. Not what she'd expected from a young, single guy.

The lock clicked and Mason held the door as she scooted under his outstretched arm. Once inside, he scooped up his cat and ruffled its smoky gray fur. His affection for the one-eyed kitty was obvious. The more sides she saw of Mason, the more she learned about him, the gooier her insides got. He was sweet, smart, sexy. Eye candy to the extreme. Kind. Fun to be with. Quite simply, the man was a freaking catch and a half. A total keeper.

Some stroke of luck had allowed her to catch him. She'd never be able to keep him, but she wasn't looking to. Not him or anyone. There were moments, though, like this one, when she had to remind herself of that game plan. Happily ever after still appealed to her, even though she knew it didn't exist. The idea of sharing her days and nights with somebody who made her happy...

She shook her head to clear the dangerously domestic thoughts. "Are you going to show me around?"

"Nah." Two seconds later he'd slung her over his shoulder with his hand up her skirt, working its way into her panties. He cut down a short hallway into a masculine bedroom. "No time for the home and garden tour. We've got twenty minutes.

You're gonna come twice, me once. And then I'm making us sandwiches."

She laughed as he dumped her on his bed. "It's going to be tight."

"Just how I like you." Sweet Mason, holder of doors and cuddler of kitties, vanished. The replacement Mason's pure-sex smile sent a surge of electricity between her legs. He pulled her knit top off one-handed. Tossed it to the floor. Yanked her skirt away, made short work of the pretty lingerie she'd worn, then stripped himself naked. He grabbed her ankles and pulled her to the edge of the bed. His knees thudded on the hardwood. He drew her legs over his shoulders and drove his tongue into her hot center. Did a little swirl-thrust, then headed up to her clit, where it pulsed exactly how she liked.

"Mmm, that's…" Nice, good, incredible. What was better than incredible? "Oh, oh…right there, harder." A lightning strike of pleasure hit. She jerked against his face, hips rolling and grinding upward. With every flick of his tongue she unraveled further. She clawed at the bedspread, balling it up in clenched fists. Trying to hold off a tiny bit longer. Then she was falling. Or flying. Panting, clutching his head, lost in a wave of sensation that went on and on.

The aftershocks faded, leaving every nerve ending super sensitized. Minutes—no, seconds—earlier, she couldn't get enough contact. Now she pushed at the top of his head, beat her heels on his back.

"Mason, you have to stop." She tried wriggling away, but his hands remained clamped around her thighs, his face buried between her legs. Torturing her with soft strokes of his tongue. "I can't take any more. Please."

A muffled chuckle tickled her thigh. He kissed the inside of one leg, then the other, before rising from the floor. "One down."

"That counted for my two. At least." She ogled him openly as he retrieved a condom from the bedside table and rolled it on. God, he made her mouth water. "If you come as fast as I did, we'll have plenty of time for sandwiches."

"Your priority here is lunch meat?" He stood between her legs, manmeat at the ready. "Because I can do fast." He cupped the back of her knee and rolled her onto her stomach. Smoothed his hands down her legs, made sure her feet were planted solidly on the floor. He bent over her back and whispered in her ear, "I'll come as fast as you do—this time."

Andie looked over her shoulder in time to see his face as he straightened and sank into her waiting body. The muscles in his neck and shoulders were taut. His jaw clenched. But no strain showed in his eyes, only a spark meant just for her. His mouth curled into a sexy smile. The knowing kind.

His left hand splayed on the bed beside her. She rose to her forearms, pressing her back to his hard chest, giving her breasts room to rasp against the blanket with each deep, rhythmic thrust. Her nipples tightened. She squeezed a hand between her body and the bed. Pulled back the folds of skin preventing her clit from enjoying the same hot friction. Oh yes. Much better.

"I love your soft little moans." He breathed the words in her ear. Brought his right hand under her and caressed her breast. The gentle touch ended when he reached her nipple. He plucked it, rolled it between his fingers, pinched.

Heat bloomed under his touch, shot straight to her clit. "Oh god. Harder."

Mason's lips brushed the side of her neck. "Pinch you harder, or fuck you harder?"

"Yes."

No more questions, he just acted. Clamped down on her nipple, relented, then squeezed the bud again. He drove into her harder. Ground his hips to her ass, forcing her mound to rub the edge of the mattress. His head pressed hers, his face buried in her hair. Cursing, almost growling as he held back, focusing on her. Waiting for her. Not because he had to—because he chose to.

"Now," was all she managed as her climax hit. It was enough.

"Fuck…you feel so fucking good." He ground out the words while slamming into her, taking his release hard and deep in her body.

She pancaked to the bed with him on her back. Both of them sweaty, hot and winded. As if they'd run a marathon. "I won."

"Yeah? Me too." He kissed her neck before making a quick trip to the bathroom, wherever that was, then laughing when he reentered the room. "You haven't moved."

"Can't. I think I've become one with your bed."

"So you'll be right here waiting for me when I get home from work later? Because I'm good with that scenario." He pulled his clothes on and gave her ass a playful smack. "Five minutes left for sandwiches. I have ham or peanut butter."

Yes, she ate simple sandwiches all the time. But they reminded her of lunchbox duty. That she was a mom with responsibilities, not some carefree single who could slip off to have a super-hot romp anytime she wanted.

"Babe?" Mason waited half in and half out the doorway.

"Oh. Neither, thanks."

"I'd make you something better if I didn't have appointments this afternoon."

"I know. Go feed yourself. I'll be out in a minute so we can get back." She forced a smile until he left, then buried her face in his comforter to muffle her sigh and groan. God, he was too good to be true. Why couldn't he be a few years older, or prematurely graying, at least?

"You okay?"

Andie's head snapped up to find him leaning against the doorframe, watching. But for how long? "I'm great." Mostly, sort of. She stood and dressed, one scattered piece of clothing at a time. "If you don't hustle that fine behind, you won't have time to eat."

Mason didn't move. "Fuck the sandwich."

"That'd be kind of messy, especially if it was peanut butter. Though I do like the idea of licking it off you afterward."

His lips twitched with a hint of smile. Good. They didn't have time for a serious conversation. Even if they did, talking about her issues wasn't on her agenda. She squeezed beside him, putting her hands on his chest. The muscles flexed under her palms. Just like that, she wanted to strip him down again. Run her hands over every inch of his fantastic body. For starters.

"We need to leave this room. Now, or you're going to have some upset clients this afternoon. You might have to call in."

His smile grew, spreading to his eyes. "I have a pretty solid work ethic. I'm rarely late and I'm never sick."

"It sounds like you're challenging me to corrupt you, Dr. Lang." She let her hands slide down to cup his cock and leaned into him. He moved fast, his body pinning hers to the door, his firm grip keeping her wrists above her head. Proof that she couldn't make him to do anything. Exactly the opposite, the control was all his. And sweet heaven, did she want him to use it.

"Babe, the look on your face."

She sucked her bottom lip between her teeth. Felt her cheeks heat up.

"Me holding you this way..." He stretched her arms higher, his eyes locked on hers while he did. "It turns you on."

She wasn't ashamed of her sexual fantasies. Not this one, not any. The best way to find out whether he felt the same was to lay it out there. With Scott, anytime and every time she'd suggested something other than the basics in the bedroom, her then-husband had either looked disinterested, disgusted, or he'd disappeared altogether. Sometimes all three in succession. Mason's reaction couldn't be any worse. She took a breath and crossed the fingers held high overhead.

"If you wanted to... restrain me, or..." Nervousness stole the moisture from her mouth, turning her voice into a throaty whisper. "Or do... other things, I'd..."

"You'd what?" Evidence of his interest pressed against her belly. His mouth moved closer to hers, close enough to kiss her. But he didn't. "You'd let me? If I tied your hands while I fucked you, or spanked your pretty ass until it turned pink, you'd let me?"

"It's not that I'd let you. I want you to. I want to do... everything... with you."

"Fuck." He muttered the curse as his lips sealed over hers.

Every time Mason kissed her, Andie expected her skin to burst into flames. This kiss, though, could set off fire alarms for blocks. His tongue teased in and out of her mouth. She tried to capture it and he backed off until his lips barely touched hers. He nipped and retreated, plundered and withdrew, torturing her with kisses she wanted desperately to return, but couldn't. Impossible with her arms taut overhead and pinned to the door by a six-two wall of muscle. But then, that was the point, what she'd fantasized about for so long. Not having to provide her own pleasure. Not being able to.

Mason's phone buzzed in his pocket. "Shit, I have to go, I'm already late." He dipped his head for another kiss. Longer, deeper. He released her wrists but kept his palms on the wood with his forehead pressed to hers. "I should let you corrupt me, 'cause the only place I want to be this afternoon is here with you."

There it was again. The sexy sweetness that made her heart flip and her panties wet at the same time. God, she was so gone for him already, it was scary. And thrilling. They'd shared more passion in four days than she'd experienced in all her years with Scott, even in the beginning. Maybe if she'd fallen in love with a man like Mason instead, she'd still be married today. Not actually Mason, of course. He would have been what back then—eighteen to her twenty-five, maybe? Barely legal. Truth was, as much as she wanted to know his age, the prospect terrified her. Especially since he'd avoided the question the couple of times she'd casually slipped it into conversation. For now, ignorance meant bliss, lots of it.

Ugh, she was so going to hell for this fling.

"Let's go. I don't want you to get in trouble with the boss."

"I'm sure he'll give me a pass. He thinks you're hot."

"Tell him the feeling is very mutual." She smiled and ducked under his arm, into the hall.

He grabbed her hand, keeping her close while he locked up. Then, right there on the front stoop, he pulled her in for a hug and kiss none of his neighbors would mistake as platonic. He certainly wasn't afraid to publicly display affection. Or rather, attraction. That she was obviously older than him and he didn't give a rat's ass made it even better. Mason's behavior set the bar awfully high for any men she dated in the future.

"When are you free?" he asked.

"We could do lunch again."

"Yeah, we probably should. I failed royally on taking you anywhere you want."

"Wrong. This is exactly where I wanted to go. And the service here was excellent, but..." She bit the inside of her cheek attempting to squelch a smile. "You're sort of like Chinese food."

"This I gotta hear."

"I was totally full and satisfied while I was having you, but fifteen minutes later and I'm hungry for more."

"Babe, I think that's got more to do with your appetite than what I'm serving." He laughed at the blush creeping across her face and led her to the car. "Now back to the question of when I can see you again—really see you— because I want a whole lot more than an hour."

Chapter Seven

Mason let the cool spray pound on his shoulders. Euthanizing pets didn't get easier as the number grew. Even when it was absolutely necessary, it drained him every time. Didn't matter if he'd known the client for years or was simply doing his turn at the shelter. He'd lost count about a year ago, despite promising himself he never would.

He turned his face to the water. Fumbled around for the soap and began scrubbing. Face first, working downward, ritualistically washing away the lingering sense of death and lack of control. Putting Mrs. Johnson's dog to sleep was the last thing he wanted to do an hour before seeing Andie. But loss doesn't wait for a convenient time to drop into your life. He knew that firsthand.

Ah shit, now he was thinking about Stacey and the pregnancy she'd ended against his wishes. No matter how many times he tried to sell himself the story that it hadn't been a real baby yet, he didn't buy it. Same with the line about the abortion being in the best interest of their futures. Yeah, that one sucked too. But it was the past. Five years ago and forever unchangeable. And the present looked damn fine these days. Business at his clinic was increasing steadily.

Friends and family were close by but not on top of his every move. Now he had Andie.

Yeah, it had only been a week. He wasn't stupid enough to think he was in love with her. The sex was phenomenal from the first time and it was only going to get better. Hell, she'd come to his office yesterday during lunch for the sole purpose of blowing him. Because it was all she could squeeze into her schedule and because it seemed fair, according to her, since she'd already gotten herself off that morning. Twice.

She'd walked in, announced all this, locked the door and gone to her knees. Unbuttoned her shirt to show him those perfect tits, sucked him off, then left with a smile on her face. How many women did that? None that he'd ever met. And she had a brain to go with all that sex-kitten stuff. A personality with her own likes, dislikes and interests. A self-sufficient life. Not like the twenty-something cling-ons people kept shoving in his direction.

So, yeah, he also wasn't stupid enough to think he couldn't fall in love with Andie.

He threw on cargo shorts and a t-shirt and chucked some extra stuff in a backpack. Gave Hugo half a can of real tuna and told him not to wait up.

"You brought me roses," Andie said when she answered her door. "Red ones, for Canada Day, they're beautiful. Come in while I put them in water."

"Red for passion, not patriotism, and they pale next to you in the beautiful department." He purposely stayed a couple steps behind while following her to the kitchen. The form-fitting black-and-white dress accented her small waist and the sweet curves of her body. Gorgeous, head to toe. The material ended halfway down her thigh, showing off a pair of phenomenal legs begging to be touched. The perfect length for him to get his hand under every chance he got. Like, under the patio table, or if they snuck into the bathroom…

"You're staring," she said when she turned to face the sink.

"I don't know what I was expecting to see you in today, but that dress isn't it. That's a whole lotta sexy for a house party. Definitely not the kind of thing you wear to blend into the crowd." He was going to be the envy of every man at the party with her at his side.

"Maybe you should go without me, then." She abandoned the flowers to yank off her shoes. One intensely dirty look later, she stormed out of the kitchen and up to her room.

What the hell? "Andie," he called from the bottom of the stairs. Nothing. He tried again, louder and firmer. "Andie. Come down here and t—" Slam went the bedroom door. Guess she wasn't interested in sharing whatever the fuck had set her off.

He didn't mind talking. Dealt with tears better than a lot of men. But he drew the line at drama. Not interested. Andie didn't want to go to the party—didn't want him here? No problem. He knew how to slam doors too. Starting with the fancy front one on her house.

Less than a block from his parents' place, he pulled over. Smacked his palms off the steering wheel and ripped a few curses. Maybe he wouldn't bother with the party. Going without Andie held zero appeal, and not only because there'd be questions. Today was the first day of her son's trip to the cottage—two weeks of seeing her whenever and as frequently as he wanted.

So why was he sitting here alone? It'd taken some serious sweet-talking, a healthy dose of dirty talk and a few omissions of the truth to convince her to go to the party with him.

Freaking out that way...she must've had a reason. Probably stress over meeting his friends and family. Shit, just this morning she'd told him—again—how nervous she was. He'd been an idiot back there, letting his past experiences affect what he had going with Andie. He definitely should've tried harder to put her mind at ease. Instead he'd bailed like an immature dumbass.

Enough knee-jerk reactions—on both their parts. He made a U-turn and hit the gas. They had a party to get to. If he hustled, maybe she'd still be wearing that dress.

The dress went back into the closet. She liked it too much to return it. Hopefully it wouldn't be outdated by the time she had an opportunity to wear it again.

One by one, Andie fingered the hanging clothes. Lots of colors—red, purple, orange, teal. Bold patterns, curvy tops and dresses. Jeans that showed off her body instead of hiding it. Enough high heels to stock a small boutique. Obliterated from her wardrobe were tan, blue, pastels, hideous practical shoes and anything pleated. A shiver ran down her spine from thinking about the stuffy crap she used to wear. If Mason thought she dressed too sexy for his family get-together, too bad. She shut the closet doors and walked away. Never again would she change her clothes—or anything—to pacify a man.

Agreeing to go to that party had been a mistake, one made in a moment of Mason-induced weakness. He did that to her—stripped her of sensibility and self-protection. The way her heart pounded in his presence, or even from hearing his voice...god, a simple text from Mason sent her mentally skipping through a wildflower meadow, surrounded by animated, singing forest animals. It was ridiculous and she needed to get a grip. Pronto. She had no business meeting his friends, let alone his family. That was the kind of thing real couples did. People with plans to take their relationship from casual to committed. People who didn't have an age gap that made such a thing impossible.

She flopped on the bed with a sigh. But maybe she'd overreacted a little about his comment. The dress was rather on the sexy side for a backyard barbecue, especially one where she'd be surrounded by strangers who would undoubtedly be judging her. Strangers to her, but not to Mason. In a way, she couldn't blame him for questioning her wardrobe selection. It'd just been so automatic to get defensive. Dammit.

The fist that'd tightened around her heart as he burned out of the driveway squeezed again. Anger, regret and now a pinch of guilt—the deluxe combo, the trifecta of toxic emotions. She pushed up from the bed, wandered to the closet and said goodbye to the dress. Tomorrow she'd return it. She'd never be able to wear it without thinking about their fight. But as much as today sucked, it was for the best. Being alone with Mason was wonderful. Thinking she could be part of his everyday life was crazy.

With Dylan on vacation at the cottage and Lasha out of town at a singles mixer, Andie was on her own for the rest of the holiday. She ought to go downstairs and work. The uber-frilly MacMillan bridesmaids' dresses weren't going to sew themselves. Or, she could eat the remaining half tub of heavenly hash ice cream on the deck, then nap the day away in the sunshine. Now that was a better plan for healing a grumpy heart.

She plucked the spoon from her mouth, turned to the screened french doors and sighed. Again with the doorbell. Her neighbors were sweet and well meaning, but Andie was running out of polite ways to say no. Already today, she'd turned down red-frosted cupcakes. Then maple-glazed-bean-and-back-bacon casserole. Mrs. Karnowski's Canadian-themed food creations sounded wonderful. From experience, Andie knew that no amount of Imodium combated the aftereffects of her neighbor's cooking. The memory of potato salad à la Karnowski sent a particular chill up her spine.

"Hey, babe." Mason's voice snapped her out of the stomach-churning reminiscing. He stood on one of lower steps, hands behind his back. "I tried the front door, a couple times."

"I heard it." Let him think she'd purposely ignored him, for a few minutes at least.

"Yeah, I figured." He climbed one stair. "I was deciding whether to bust it down when the old folks next door half-ran across the front lawn at me." A couple more stairs disappeared behind him. "They told me you were on the deck and I should come around back."

"Of course they did." How many times since Scott moved out had the Karnowskis asked her when she was going to get a nice, new young man in her life? She'd sure done that. Just very short term. And now that younger man was on the top step looking sheepish and sexy at the same time—a look that worked well for him and melted her resolve faster than ice cream in the hot July sunshine.

"The lady said to give you this." A small, clear bowl came from behind Mason's back.

Andie stiffened. "Oh god. That woman is trying to kill me."

"With potato salad?"

"Don't be fooled. That's the devil in disguise."

"Smells good to me." He pulled the serving spoon from the bowl, loaded to overflowing, and lifted it toward his mouth.

The ice cream container fell to the deck as she launched her body at Mason. "Stop…" She bounced off his super-solid chest, taking the vile concoction with her. As in, dumping the bulk of it down her chest. "For the record, you owe me your life." She flicked a chunk of potato off her nipple area. Disgusting. "Not to mention a load of laundry."

"Done. Should I strip you here, or take you inside first?"

Unable to cross her arms without mashing Mrs. Karnowski's mystery dressing into her tank top, she settled for rolling her eyes.

"Good thing you weren't wearing the dynamite dress."

The dress. The reason she'd flipped out. A hint of anger bubbled to the surface, only to be popped by his sexy smile and perfect…everything. She turned to survey the mess. "Oh…my ice cream…" The chocolatey mush was inching its way across the deck. A mess and a waste of sugar therapy. "Dammit."

"Guess I owe you dessert too. They'll have lots at the party."

"Great. Enjoy it."

"I will, with you."

Honestly, did he think she was that much of a pushover? Of course he did, because around him she was, or had been until now. "I'm not going."

"Yeah, I kind of got that."

"So why are you here? Again."

"To restart our long weekend together…by taking you to the party."

A glob of potato dropped from her boob onto her toe. Mason barely bit back a smile, the jerk. She cringed while crossing her arms over her chest. "You left."

"I came back."

She had to give him credit. He could've justified his exit by pointing out her hissy fit and door slamming, but he didn't.

"And I brought you a present."

"That salad is no present, it's a ticking time bomb for unsuspecting intestines." Oh lord, now her arms were flapping involuntarily. Not good.

"Not the potato salad, babe. These." A box of rosebud-shaped chocolates emerged from his cargo pocket.

"Oh. Those are my favorite." Damn him. She needed to be strong, resist the pull tugging at every cell in her body.

"I figured, since you have two jars of them in your house."

"Three." He didn't know about the one in her desk drawer.

"I stand corrected." He stepped closer, gently picked up her hand and placed the box in her palm.

The simple touch sparked a wave of electricity that shot to every inch of her Mason-addicted body. This didn't bode well for her deteriorating resolve.

Bribery—nothing new there. Scott had used it all the time, but on a larger scale, and with more pre-meditation. The dollar-something box of her favorite chocolates was charming and sincere. Scott's bribes had never been that, not even close.

"Come to the party with me." The words were a statement, not a question, but there was a hint of sweetness in his voice that was irresistible.

In the past, she'd have ended up going wherever Scott wanted out of obligation. Miserably, and to his specifications. With Mason, she didn't have to do anything. But she wanted to. That memo from her head to heart about doing what was best—mentally shoved through the shredder.

If she couldn't stop this mistake from happening, maybe she could make him do it. She tipped her chin up at him. "I'll go, but I'm not changing. If you or your family and friends don't like what I'm wearing… that's your problem."

Mason's eyebrows rose. "Okay. I'm sure Toby'll love what you're wearing, if nobody else does."

Her jaw fell. She snapped it shut, only to feel it drop again. At least he was being honest.

"I'll try to keep him away from you, but I can't guarantee it'll work. He's strong for an old guy and when he wants something, there's usually no stopping him."

The possibilities made her shudder. "Is he your lecherous uncle or something?"

"He's my parents' bloodhound." He moved in again, heat radiating off him that had nothing to do with the temperature of the July day. "And your top looks like a picnic basket exploded on it." He grinned, plucked a chunk of celery from her chest and tossed it over the railing. "It's actually making me kinda hungry. Mind if give you a lick?"

"Yes, I do mind." She pushed his head away as he lowered his head toward her filthy tank top.

"First time for everything, I suppose."

"Funny." And right, on this account. "I'm going inside to put my dress back on."

"Toby's gonna be disappointed."

And here they were, back to the subject of her wardrobe selection. Hands on her hips, she faced him down. Or rather, up. "What about you... are you going to be upset if I wear that dress?"

"Hell no."

Hmm. "So you really don't mind if I wear it? You said it was sexy. Do you think it's," she clenched her teeth and spit out the next word, "inappropriate?"

The smile on his face turned wicked as his hands snuck under her tank top. They curled around her waist, pulling her closer. "Covering your beautiful body with anything is inappropriate."

"Mason, I'm serious. I need to know." For reasons he didn't need to know.

"I know this isn't what you want to hear, but I don't care what you wear. I just want you with me."

Nope, he was wrong. That was exactly what she wanted to hear.

When Andie came down the stairs wearing that black-and-white dress again, he had to swallow a mouthful of drool.

"You're staring again," she said when she stopped in front of him.

"Get used to it. You're gorgeous and fucking hot and I can't take my eyes off you." Touching her when they had to get going would be a mistake. He did it anyway, starting with her neck, stroking downward along her shoulder and arm. Over the slippery material covering her hip. Lower, to the silky skin of her thigh.

Her eyes widened as he snagged the bottom of her dress and slowly pulled it upward.

"Your skin is so soft and warm." And bare? He explored some more. Nothing, not even a tiny string over her hip. Yup, definitely commando. His fingers twitched with the need to feel her heat surround them. His cock had the same idea.

He smiled down at her and let the dress fall back into place. "Ready to go?"

"O-okay."

Good, she wanted more too. The color of her cheeks and the way she bit into her bottom lip, kind of lopsided, told him she wanted him right here, now. And fuck, he was tempted.

"All right, let's roll." He took her hand and led her out of there. They hadn't had an opportunity to fuck since Monday. Five days didn't qualify as a drought, but knowing how amazing it felt to be balls-deep inside Andie made it seem like one. Now he had to get through the day with what would no doubt be a permanent hard-on... while surrounded by friends and family. Yeah, touching her had not been the brightest idea.

He waited until they were under way to steal another long look at her. Sunlight bounced off her hair, making it a shiny golden-brown color. Like a caramel or toffee. Definitely not blonde, but not the solid, darker brown he was used to seeing. "Your hair is different."

"I had it up earlier. I decided to let it down."

"It's nice both ways. But there's something else..."

"I got different highlights. A bit bolder." She fingered a piece nervously before thrusting her hands in her lap. "I thought maybe... I might look younger this way."

Again with the age thing. "You worry way too much."

"Women my age tend to do that."

He snorted. "That's bullshit."

"I assume that spectacular counterpoint comes from your vast experience dating women in the forty-plus bracket?"

So the lady wanted to do a little fishing, did she? No problem. "Babe, you're not plus and you don't look more than thirty-five, tops. And for the record, you're my first." If things continued to go well, maybe his last. Of any age bracket.

"Oh god, your family and friends are going to hate me for that reason alone."

"They're going to be crazy about you. Like I am." At a red light he leaned in for a kiss that lasted until honking behind him forced it to end. "So maybe they won't like you quite as much as I do."

She laughed as he shifted his erection. Women had no idea how lucky they were. Since his discomfort clearly amused her, he didn't mind. Seeing her relaxed and happy on the seat beside him felt nice. Natural.

"Did your son get to pitch last night?" He'd asked her to come watch his game and been denied. The boy took priority. As he should.

"The coach put him in for three innings. He walked two batters, struck out three and hit one. Only gave up three runs."

Pride in her kid gave her a different kind of blush. Maybe that's what people meant when they said women had a maternal glow. Whatever, it worked for her. And for him.

"And now he's off at the cottage with his dad?"

"For two weeks."

How many times and ways could he fuck her in fourteen days? Easy answer on that one—as many as she let him.

Parking had been restricted on his parents' street. Standard long-weekend pain-in-the-ass stuff. He circled the block once, found nothing, then drove over the curb onto their front lawn. Fast enough to burn tracks into the grass. Mom would have a fit when she saw them, but the jerky maneuver made Andie yelp and grab his leg, so he'd deal with the fallout. He hopped out of the truck and around to her door before she beat him to the job.

"Ready to party with the Lang clan?"

She slipped her hand into his open palm. "Not really."

"Me either." He pulled her from the truck into his arms. "If it gets awful, think about what I'm going to do to you later."

"My imagination sucks, give me a clue."

"Babe, your lying sucks." He grabbed their bags from the backseat. Wrapped his arm around her shoulders and started toward the backyard. "All right, here's one thing I've been thinking about all week. You, naked on your stomach, hands stretched above your head while I do a dot-to-dot using your freckles and my tongue. I'm gonna start with the one under your left ear."

"Where's the last dot?"

The squeaky gate drew attention. At least half a dozen pairs of eyes zoned in on their next move. He smiled at their audience. Lowered his head to whisper in her ear, "Are you aware of the little mole you have down low in the crack of your ass?" She turned her head to face him, wide-eyed. Yeah, she knew exactly where he planned to put his tongue. He couldn't hold back the smile that gave him.

He straightened as his parents steamrolled toward them. Let the crazy begin.

"Happy Birthday!" His mother's shout ensured everyone on the block heard.

Andie glared up at him. "It's your *birthday*?"

So maybe he should have told her. Too late now. "Just another day to me."

"Not to your family." His mom hugged and released him. She had that look, the weepy, sentimental one. "Especially this year."

"Mom." Trying to stop her at this point would be like trying to stop a train on the downward side of a mountain.

"It's a special one." She looked like a seal act video posted on YouTube, the way she was clapping. "A milestone."

Shit. After dancing around Andie's questions about his exact age, the answer was about to bite him in the ass. And he'd thought bringing her today was a good idea why?

"So, Mr. Secret Birthday, how old are you?"

He found her hand and laced their fingers together. Because he had the feeling she might bolt when he opened his mouth. "Thirty."

After half an hour of smiling at the end of Mason's arm, Andie excused herself to the washroom. Mason showed her into the house. Stood there while she closed the door—in his face. A juvenile action, yes, but one he totally deserved. Surely he wouldn't hang around waiting for her to come out. She gave it ten full minutes before peeking out the door. All clear. Thank god. Her purse didn't hold much, but it had her cell and wallet. All she needed for a taxi home. Her tote bag with extra clothes and other items was on a chair out back. Forget them. Just let her get the hell out of here.

"You could've asked me to take you home."

Andie froze on the front path when Mason stepped out from the carport. Dammit. "Okay. Could you please take me home?"

He crossed his arms over his chest. "Nah."

"Gee, that's helpful." If he could do the crossed-arms thing, so could she.

"Sneaking away is pretty immature."

"I guess you're an expert on maturity now that you're thirty."

"I didn't tell you because I don't care about the numbers."

"You didn't tell me because you knew that I did." Hold on, did he... oh, big mistake on his part. "You did not just roll your eyes at me."

"This age crap is pissing me off."

"Finally, you're getting it." And it really sucked.

He motioned to the truck. "Get in, I'll drive you."

She settled in the passenger seat and faced the side window, eyes closed. Safer that way. God, she was behaving like a pathetic teenager, heartbroken over losing her crush of the week. She wouldn't let him see this ridiculous, sappy side of her. No way. Even if it was her last chance to look at him. If she'd kept things private, he'd be hers for another two weeks. Stupid move, meeting his family. What was she thinking—that they had an actual relationship, or the start of one? They had an incredible physical connection. Pheromones, not emotions. She'd get over it. Nothing a few mopey days, lots of wine and a new vibrator couldn't fix.

That was a load of shit and she knew it.

Mason cursed under his breath. The truck lurched when he gunned it to pass a slow driver. She opened for a peek. What the hell were they doing on County Road Four?

"Hey..." She swiveled to face him. "This isn't the way to my house." Not by a long shot. Mason's route took them north, out of town, not toward her snooty, east-side subdivision.

"I said I'd drive you, not that I'd take you home."

"So you're abducting me?"

The man had the nerve to look cocky. "Yeah, I guess I am."

"Why—so we can do some more pointless arguing?"

"Babe, the way I see it, we can't have a rational conversation about this age bullshit until you're more relaxed."

"And since old ladies enjoy a drive in the country, this ought to calm me down?" Her irritation didn't stand a chance against his smile. And he knew it, because he flashed her his best one, the jerk. She sighed and leaned back in her seat.

"I don't know about the drive, but the rest of my plan will definitely put you in a better frame of mind." He turned off the paved road onto a bumpy gravel one. A hundred meters later he pulled into the weedy driveway of a burned-out barn, where he parked behind a monstrous stack of barn boards. "It starts with me getting you naked in the back of my truck." Two clicks later he'd unbuckled their seatbelts. "Then I'm gonna settle in between your thighs. Lick you up and down. Slide my fingers inside and suck your clit until you come against my face. I figure that'll make you more agreeable."

"That's not the worst plan I've ever heard." Need coiled low in her abdomen, spreading lower at the sound of his sexy laugh. He did dirty talk very, very well. Right now, she didn't care about the reason behind it—she just wanted the follow-through. Mason's face between her legs, his hands on her body. One more time, if nothing else.

Gravel crunched under his feet as he moved around the truck, lowering the gate, spreading a blanket he'd pulled from the backseat. Her door was next. No words, he reached in and scooped her up, kicking the door shut behind them. He carried her as if she weighed nothing. She snuggled in, savoring the hard wall of muscle against her cheek. And his scent—she could breathe him all day. He smelled better than the best cologne, just clean and…manly. Addictive. Covering that with artificial fragrance would be a crime.

"I'm still mad at you for hiding your age. And your birth date."

"Nope. We're not talking about that stuff 'til you're de-stressed." He lowered her onto the tailgate and hopped up alongside. "C'mere," he said, pulling her to her feet. Slowly, he ran his hand through her hair, letting it sift around his fingers and fall back to her shoulders before starting again.

"I like it when you do that."

"I know, I pay attention."

Again with the sexy smile. Powerless, that's what he made her. Like jelly. "What else do you know?"

"I know what'll happen when I do this…" He trailed his fingers down her arm, to the hem of her dress, and slowly—super slowly—gathered it in his fists. The soft fabric caressed her skin as he drew it upward. Over her ass, her breasts, her head, until she stood in the open air wearing nothing but heels, a bra and hundreds of goose bumps.

"Nothing happened."

"Your pink cheeks say otherwise." He thumbed her bottom lip. "And this. You bite your lip when you're turned-on. It's very cute and sexy. Then there's your nipples. I don't need x-ray vision to know what I'm going to find underneath this white lace." One-handed, he released the hooks. He took his time appraising and appreciating the view before squeezing her eager peaks and lowering his mouth to suckle them.

His mouth retreated far too quickly. "I don't like it when you stop."

"Only temporary, babe." He stripped off his t-shirt and shorts. Balled the clothes together and knelt in front of her. "For your head." Gently, he guided her to her knees. Then to her back. He bent her legs, one at a time. Kissed the inside of each thigh all the way to her ankle, where he untied the wraparound laces of her sandals. He held one up for inspection before chucking it aside. "These are nice. But this is nicer," he said, and swiped his tongue between her legs.

The man could write a book on giving oral. He was that good.

"Why can't I say no to you?" she asked as she opened wider for whatever he wanted to do. He looked up from his position on his belly. All she could see were his eyes, bluer than the sky overhead, and sexier than should be humanly possible.

"Because you don't want to."

True words, they hummed against her sensitive flesh. His lips followed, kissing her down low the same way he'd kiss her mouth. This was his thing, she knew it was. If she had a dozen lovers after Mason, none of them would taste her this way. So intimately. Lovingly.

Oh, wrong word to think. Love. Something she couldn't afford to consider when it came to Mason. She shut her eyes, blocking the bright sky and the dangerous thoughts.

The dizzy sensation remained—Mason's fault entirely. He chuckled at her dreamy sigh, then shifted gears. Faster, harder. More determined. His tongue swirled around her clit, vibrating so close to where she needed it but never hitting the spot directly. She shifted left, he adjusted. She shimmied to the right a little more subtly…damn him, he countered. He wanted her to squirm, to beg for it? With him she'd do anything.

"Please…stop teasing."

Immediately, he focused on her clit, taking her to the edge. Two fingers slid inside her, then another in her ass. Spots flashed across her eyelids. Stars in the daytime.

"That, oh god…" She clutched his head tight, coming and coming on his tongue, around his fingers, the shock rippling through every cell and nerve.

"Good?" He nipped the curve of her ass, then rose to a stand.

"Very. There's not a solid bone left in my body."

The boxer briefs came off. Got tossed aside. God, he was tall, especially from this angle. Sort of like looking up a Greek statue—only more erect. And without fig leaves.

"I'm feeling much more relaxed now. So, you wanted to…talk?"

"Babe, I'm not done with you yet."

"You didn't say there was more to your plan."

"You distracted me by looking all flushed and sexy. I didn't get to finish."

That was her cue. She moved to her knees and licked his cock from base to tip. "You absolutely need to finish. I insist." And she'd love every second of it. She took him in greedily. Reveled in the fullness, the feeling of his cock touching the back of her throat. The low groan he made.

"Not this way." He withdrew, stepped back.

"I thought you liked me sucking you."

"I fucking love it. I think about it pretty much every minute I'm not with you." The truck bounced as he jumped down. He patted the edge of the tailgate. "Get over here, gorgeous. Open up for me. Nice and wide."

No other man had ever said these kinds of things to her. Looked at her the way Mason did, as if being with her—fucking, touching, tasting—was the most important thing in his world. She'd crawl naked over broken glass to get to him when he looked at her that way. Or across the bed of his truck.

"You brought condoms." Her mouth actually watered watching him roll one on.

"When I'm with you, always."

"That's sweet." She positioned herself in front of him, legs bent, the soles of her feet barely gripping the metal.

He laughed and pulled her closer so that her ass nearly hung off the edge of the truck. He spread her feet farther apart. Wrapped his hand around his cock and guided it to her entrance, teasing her with the tip. "It's sweet that I want to fuck you every time I see you?"

"God, yes. Bring condoms, forget the flowers."

"Damn. I spent forty bucks on roses for nothing."

"The roses were beautiful, I love them. Now shut up and do me."

"Good plan." He pushed inside in one, smooth thrust. Balls-deep. He gritted his teeth and held still, savoring the clench of her muscles around him. Fuck, she felt right. Buried to the hilt, he ground against her clit the way she liked. Her soft moan, the arched back, sunshine and sweat on her skin… he'd never last. Slow and easy was going to kill him.

"Mason," her eyes opened enough to focus on his, "don't hold back."

"After you—"

"No, now. Fuck me hard. I want to watch you lose control for a change."

He wanted that too. To get lost in her. Wanted to stop thinking and ride the wave of pleasure that hit every time she surrounded him with her soft warmth, scent and sounds. Wanted it so much his balls ached. "I don't want to hurt you."

"You won't." She trailed her fingers across her nipples. She plucked them, then moved one hand lower and started circling her clit.

"Jesus." He didn't have to move. He could come from watching her play with herself, nothing more. He braced his hands on her hips and pulled back until only the head of his cock was inside her. Drove in fast and full.

"Harder," she said when he backed out again. "Harder."

She wanted it hard, wanted him to lose control? Wanted him to own her, to show her that he wasn't going to let her run away? He curled his fingers into the fleshy curve of her ass. Looked in her eyes and slammed into her. Again and again. Sweat rolled down his face, forcing his eyes closed. Sounds filled his ears—slapping skin, sharp breaths, grunts and moans… and Andie's voice, muttering single words that meant she was coming.

He hollered some single words of his own, and with one last, deep thrust, finished in a heap on her chest.

"Mason—I—can't breathe."

"Right." He eased out and off. Found his land legs after a few seconds. Blinked until the little birds and stars disappeared.

She sat, knees folded under her ass, fingering a big tangle in the back of her hair. "This gives new meaning to the term bedhead. Between the blazing sun and physical exertion, I bet I sweated half my makeup off too. Look away…"

The view of her back as she jokingly turned away curled his gut. "Andie… your back… does it hurt?"

Soulful blue eyes blinked up at him. "No, should it?"

She had no idea. But she would, as soon as she got in front of a mirror. How could he have been such a selfish, reckless dick? With her.

"You've got rug burn. Or crap-ass blanket burn. It's pretty raw."

"Guess I won't be wearing backless items for a few days." She put on her bra, then her dress. "Until I met you, I'd never even had a hickey. Now I've had scraped knees from blowing you and rug burn from you fucking me."

And… he just dropped another level, from careless jerk to total douche.

"What're you going to do to me next, I wonder." Her arms wrapped around his neck, pure mischief playing across her face.

Well, fuck him. "I can think of a few things."

"I can't wait."

"After the party?"

"Sure, I'll meet you later."

"No deal." He turned away to get dressed. The only way to hide the fact that his words were complete horseshit. He'd take a booty call if that's all he could get. But he wanted more.

"I don't get why you're so determined to have this conversation." The shoes got her full attention as she re-laced them around her ankles instead of looking at him. "Your family will flip out when they find out there's ten years between us. For the record, I thought you were in your thirties when I met you."

"And now I am."

Her head snapped up as her mouth fell open. "By a day!"

"Tomorrow it'll be two days."

"You're impossible," she said after laughing out loud. "I like spending time with you, a lot. If it were just you and me in private, our ages wouldn't matter. Other people, though... most of them will look at us and see nothing more than a cougar playing with a hot, young vet."

"Fuck most people."

"Thanks, but I'd rather not."

"Me either." Best if he dealt with the age issue in bite-sized chunks. "Today isn't about most people, it's a get-together with a bunch of my family and friends. Do you think your friends and family will judge me because of my age?"

"It's not the same, Mason."

"Sure it is. They might think I'm taking advantage of you... given that you're so old and feeble."

"Oh, that's nice." A halfhearted punch landed on his chest and stayed there as she smiled up at him. "Jerk."

That's what he wanted—Andie, relaxed and happy. He took her hand after closing the truck. Gave it a squeeze as they moved around front. "Seemed to me the people at the party so far all thought you were great. My sister hadn't shown yet when you attempted your escape. Katie'll kill me if she doesn't get to meet you."

"I don't know…" She was caving, it was in her eyes. In the softness of her voice.

Time to seal the deal. "Think of it as my birthday present, since you didn't get me anything."

"That is so unfair."

"Yeah, but did it work?"

She sighed. Rolled her eyes. Looked fucking adorable. "This time."

He held the driver's door open and followed her into the truck. "I promise not to use it again next year."

Chapter Eight

"We've been gone an hour. They're going to ask questions." Agreeing to come back to the party suddenly seemed like willingly walking the plank. "And I'm a mess. And my hairbrush and makeup are in my tote bag, out back on the deck."

"I'm on it." He pulled out his cell and whipped off a text.

Next thing Andie knew, a young woman slipped out the front door, closing it carefully behind her. "That's your sister?"

"The one and only. Katie-Kat, the little brat."

Maybe that had been the case in earlier years. By the affection in Mason's voice and the grin on his face, he clearly liked her as much as he loved her. Andie could already see why. Watching Katie make her way covertly across the yard was entertainment in itself.

"She's going to get caught simply because she's trying so hard not to."

"That's Katie."

The truck's rear door opened and Katie bounced into the middle of the backseat. "Here you go." She dropped Andie's tote bag on the front seat. "I'm not going to introduce myself, that way it'll be more authentic when we officially meet. And don't worry, I've got you guys covered." She leapt from the truck, checked for spies and sprinted to the house.

"Wow, she's got a lot of energy."

Mason pushed the fabric of Andie's dress up to her hips and lightly stroked between her legs. "You do all right in that department, yourself."

"Uh-uh. You are not starting something parked out on your parents' lawn."

He laughed when she pushed his hand away. "I bet your heart rate went up just from thinking about having an orgasm right here, right now, where anybody could see." He leaned in so his lips brushed her ear. "I bet you're so turned-on by the idea, if you relaxed against the headrest, I could make you come in less than a minute."

A few choice words and her libido shot higher than tonight's fireworks would. This, less than twenty minutes after they'd rocked the back of his truck. "I'm not taking that bet."

"I bet if I pushed my seat back, you could make me come in less than a minute."

"I'm not taking that bet, either." She located her brush and lipstick, got to work on de-sexifying her appearance. "You're a bad influence, Mason Lang."

"Meaning you seriously considered my offers." He followed with a sizzling kiss that stirred parts that should be resting up for later.

"Mints," she said breathlessly, then dug the roll from her bag and popped one. "Don't want to have dick breath while chatting up your family." She waved the package. "Want one?"

"Nah, I don't have dick breath." A wink later, he was out of the truck, coming around to open her door. As he always did. He kept her hand after helping her down. Squeezed it and put his lips to her knuckles.

Sweet actions like that gave her a little fit of butterflies. The stunning roses he'd brought, the words that came with them. Making her breakfast. Holding her hand every chance he got. Not trying to control what she wore or how she acted... she'd sure misinterpreted his comments about her dress earlier. He'd let her bratty moment slide without question, but she really needed to get a handle on her baggage before she scared Mason off permanently—a prospect that made her stomach clench. Bit by bit he was worming his way into her heart. And that was dangerous, because he couldn't stay there. In the end, there'd be a big hole.

"What did your sister mean by having us covered?"

"Go along with whatever she says. Katie's good at managing things."

Oh, sure. Agree with whatever a total stranger made up about her. No problem.

The house was empty when they went in the front door. A miracle, given the amount of noise coming from out back. Andie deposited her purse and tote bag by the door in case she needed to grab it and run again.

Mason shook his head. "I don't think so, babe," he said, moving them to a cupboard in the kitchen. She stuck out her tongue and he laughed as they rejoined the party on the deck.

"Well, there you are. I was about to send out a search party, see if you'd gone down and fallen in the lake. Without telling anybody where you were going." Mason's mother added a dose of stern to her last words.

Enter Katie, waving her cell. "My bad, Mom. I forgot to tell you when Mason texted me a while ago." And cue Katie's cover story. "Andie thought she'd left the iron plugged in, so they had to cruise back to her place. Make sure her house didn't burn to the ground."

All the huff disappeared from Mary Lang's demeanor. Not only did Katie lie convincingly, she'd chosen the perfect excuse. Women don't take the threat of an unattended iron lightly. And it could've been true. Andie had hurried home on more than one occasion because of that nagging feeling that some appliance might still be on, plotting to overheat and throw itself at a flammable surface.

Easy as that, everybody resumed party mode. The official introduction to Mason's sister. Another to her handsome fiancé. Talking, eating and a generous amount of drinking followed. Nobody leered or made insinuating remarks. That she and Mason had argued, gone off to make up with incredibly intense sex, then snuck back in, didn't occur to anybody. Other than Katie, perhaps. If she knew what they'd gotten up to, she didn't let on. Maybe she was used to covering for her brother and his dates. Not a good place for Andie's mind to go since she had no business being possessive or jealous.

By evening, the Lang's backyard had fifty people in it, maybe more. There were people everywhere—in the pool, filling every chair, hanging out on the lawn with plates of food. Every branch of his family had representation. Aunts, uncles, cousins, nieces, nephews. Even Mason's last surviving grandparent, Grandma Millie, who'd proven she could down firecracker shooters faster than Katie's fiancé. Several times. Friends and neighbors rounded out the crowd. Not one of them seemed fazed that Mason's girlfriend, as she'd repeatedly been called, was clearly older than the popular vet. Kind of gave her hope.

"Sooo, Andie," Katie called as she hauled Logan away from the makeshift bar and his eighty-six-year-old nemesis. "Mason tells me that you're a fabulous dressmaker."

"Fabulous? Really?" She eyed Mason. All he did was shrug.

"No, he's not that good with words." Katie snorted. "What he said is that you're super busy making a bunch of wedding dresses and stuff. Not so eloquent, my brother. I added the fabulous part because I'm sure that's what he meant. Right?"

"You know it." Again, the affectionate tone of voice. Plus, he wrapped his arm around Andie's waist and squeezed. Here was a man who knew how to keep all his ladies happy.

"Did he mention my wedding? Probably not, he's been pretty grumpy about anything love-related... until recently." Katie gave them a completely over-the-top wink. "Anyway, it's a New Year's Eve ceremony. Formal but not traditional. Trendy, but easy on the bling. I'd love to get something unique instead of off-the-rack, for me and my girls."

Wow, Katie could talk. Fast. Like, impossible-to-interrupt fast. But after the comment about her bridal party, which sounded rather like she was referring to her ample endowments, Mason and Logan broke into laughter. Logan even tweaked the side of her boob.

"You guys are pigs." Katie gave both men a shove. They used this as an excuse to put distance between their testosterone and talk of taffeta.

Andie envied them. Mixing business with socializing had the same effect on her stomach as finding out her regular lady doctor had been replaced with a hot male gyno—after the nurse had her gowned up and waiting in the stirrups.

Mary drifted over to fill the gap left by her son and future son-in-law. "I heard wedding. Whadid I misss?" Not the bar, apparently. She slurred as much as she swayed. She'd probably tip the scales on a breathalyzer machine before getting close enough to blow.

"Andie might do the dresses," Katie said. "We just have to work out the details."

Oh god. How'd they make that jump? "I'd be happy to meet with you sometime and show you samples of my work, references and a rough pricelist, though I'd need to work up a firm quote based on the intricacy of your designs." Mentioning money scared off most acquaintances who thought she'd either work for free or at some secret, discounted rate.

"Can you drop some names of bigger weddings you've done?" This from Katie. Mary was too busy trying to focus on Andie's face to speak.

"Sure. I did the bridal parties for the Almeida-Halliday wedding and the Jenner-Barrey wedding. I made all the dresses for the Paton-Thaler wedding, including the bride's gown and both mothers." Yes, she was boasting a bit, but Katie'd been the one to ask. Those jobs were the jewels in her business crown. Well-known families with enough money to buy the best of the best, and they'd chosen her to do custom work. Katie looked impressed. Mary, not so much.

"I remember you..." Mary aimed a pointed finger at Andie, but it wavered as much as its inebriated owner. "That liddle housse on Buller Street."

"Years ago, yes. I'm on Paradise Avenue now. The address is on my card, I'll run inside and get one from my purse." Anything to get away from the wild-eyed stare.

Mary stopped her with a drunken grab on the forearm. "You hem pants."

"Some. Less than I used to." Where was this tangent coming from—or headed to—for that matter?

"Mason's filled out since you first met him, hasn't he?" Mary's speech was getting clearer and her grip tighter. She gave an unfriendly laugh that turned most heads in their direction, Mason's included.

"Excuse me?" Andie asked, trying unsuccessfully to free her arm.

Mason appeared beside her, gently prying his mother's fingers loose. "Mom, what the hell? Let go of her." He stood between them, one hand on each woman. Like a referee.

Andie's stomach rolled. She'd let Mason—and her heart—talk her into coming back to the party. What a mistake.

"Mom needs a big glass of water and some food," Mason said to his dad after he made his way through the party-goers. "And to walk away before she says something she'll regret later." Those words were directed at his mother.

"I'm jusstalking." The hostess shook off the helping hands. And the advice. "Your baby cried the whole time you were pinning Mason's pants. When was that…?"

"Mom, let's go inside and make coffee," Katie pitched in, her arm firmly around her mother's shoulders.

But Mary wasn't quite finished. Her eyes bulged as Katie hauled her toward the house. And her voice got louder—much louder. "His senior prom… twelve years ago…"

An acidic burn rose from Andie's stomach. Up her throat, threatening vomit at the top. She looked up at Mason. Saw the shadow of the cute, gangly eighteen-year-old he'd been before becoming the handsome, muscular man of today. And she remembered. He'd stood in her little workroom, probably thinking about sneaking booze into the dance or getting laid in the backseat of a borrowed car. Her mind would've been on whether her baby would sleep more than four hours at a stretch, if her milk would wait for the clients to leave before it let down and if her husband would touch her again before she hit thirty.

The years between her and Mason suddenly seemed like an eternity.

"I remember those pants. They fit great." Dozens of his friends and family goggling and he didn't balk. Just smiled and took her hand. "Now we fit great."

Andie woke to a face full of fur. "Good morning, pretty kitty." Hugo purred his reply from his position above her head, his tail swishing across her cheek to tickle her nose. "Where's your master?" And hers, for that matter.

Thanks to Mary's alcohol-induced temporary insanity, they'd left the party before the fireworks display over the lake. After listening to the cracks and booms from his back deck last night, he'd suggested a shower before bed. She'd climbed in first. Mason had followed, carrying the tie from his bathrobe, with which he'd promptly secured her to the showerhead on the wall. First he'd used the handheld sprayer to make her come. He'd barely let her recover from the first orgasm before driving his tongue over her clit for a second. Then, hands still tied above her head and surrounded by mist and steam, he'd scooped her legs around his waist and fucked her against the tile wall. And it wasn't even her birthday.

She reached across the empty half of the bed, smiling as she grabbed for the clock. He'd flipped the face away when she pointed out that at half past twelve his birthday privileges had expired. They both knew the calendar date had nothing to do with her willingness.

Her arm brushed over a piece of paper, a note tucked under the edge of his pillow. A note with her name on it. She already knew he was at the clinic. They hadn't given in to exhaustion until close to two, and he'd chosen then to tell her he had to be at work at seven. To tend to patients and boarders, a job his tech usually did. But being the incredible person that he was, he'd offered to fill in so she could go away for the long weekend. Even though it was his birthday.

Andie righted the clock and groaned. Quarter after eight. She glared at the uncovered window and the shafts of sunlight hitting the bed. Bare naked, he didn't even have a curtain rod mounted. There had to be time in her schedule to make Mason some bedroom curtains. Whoa…that tangent needed reining in. The man was a morning person. He got up early and didn't require window coverings. Staying over once did not mean redecorating. Hell, she could sleep over every night for the next two weeks and it still wasn't her place to make changes to Mason's house. Because fourteen days from now she'd be gone. Back to her regularly scheduled life as a responsible, single mother. Sleeping in her own bed in a properly darkened room—alone.

She pushed the crappy thought away. Goose bumps rose as she dragged the edge of the note across her breasts, enjoying the scrape and tickle of the thick, stiff paper. Two words that also described Mason's cock quite nicely. Every muscle ached, but it didn't stop her needy parts from humming while thinking about him. Mason had mentioned spending a lazy Sunday together. By lazy she hoped he meant lying on his back while she rode him three different ways. There were still plenty of things she wanted to try. She unfolded the note—maybe it'd tell her what time he'd be back, so they could get to work on that list.

Good Morning, Beautiful.

Leaving you alone in a bed is a tragedy.

XXO

(Is there a symbol for fucking? If not, there should be, so I can add it to every note I'm going to write you.)

"Oh god." She pressed the paper to her chest, then read it again. And six more times before having a squealing fit between Mason's sheets that sent Hugo running. Call her a hopelessly romantic sixteen-year-old…this note was going in her keeper box.

Chapter Nine

Andie opened the door expecting to find Katie on the other side. Alone, or maybe with a bridesmaid or two in tow. Instead she got Katie and Mary—and the urge to sneak a shot of Frangelico into her coffee.

"Please, come on in." She ushered them through the house to the basement, where her dressmaking shop lived. The route bypassed most of the main-floor rooms, but she didn't miss the way Mary gaped at the parts she could see. Including the lower level as they made their way down. Scott had insisted that every inch of the house be top-notch. Appropriate for a family of their standing. Gag.

Andie had two rooms in the walkout basement—one for client meetings and one for sewing. Both had large windows overlooking the professionally landscaped yard. The place was impressive, embarrassingly so.

The client area had a small sofa and a couple of chairs. Her visitors sat together, one relaxed and the other stiff. No big surprise there. Katie had stopped by Mason's last Sunday afternoon, embarrassed and apologizing for her mother's drunken behavior. When questioned by her big brother, she'd admitted that the sorry didn't come from her mother. In the four days since, Mary hadn't attempted to contact Andie. In a way, Andie respected that. An insincere apology was worse than no apology.

But today's visit was business. Andie's business, and she excelled at it. For the time being they were prospective customers, nothing more. She set a few albums on the table and pulled a chair across from them. Flipped open the first book and starting the walk-through, beginning with her most impressive jobs. She had Katie hooked after the first page. Mary appeared to be on board by the second set of shots. They discussed styles and fabrics. Looked at swatches, pattern catalogues and bridal magazines. Andie sketched a couple of details from her head as the creative buzz took over. The gowns Katie wanted would be stunning once Andie had finished with them.

"You've come a long way from hemming pants in that single, tiny room." Mary surveyed the upscale furniture and plush carpeting, her eyes landing on Andie's desk and the framed photos there.

Back to that again, were they? "You're right. It took a lot of hard work and commitment to get to this point."

"And a wealthy husband."

"Mom." Katie leapt from the couch. "Stop being a bitch. Andie's been nothing but nice to you. I like her. Mason really likes her. What's your problem?"

Mary's mouth tightened to a thin line. The gesture added years to her appearance. Andie made a mental note never to allow that expression to cross her face, especially ten to fifteen years from now, when she'd be Mary's age.

"Katie, go easy on your mom. She's upset because I'm not the ideal woman for Mason. I understand her concern." She scooped the photo albums into her arms like a security blanket. "But Mary, you're worried over nothing. I'm only dating him. It's casual, not permanent."

"So you're using him."

"That's not what I meant at all." Which didn't make it any less true. She needed a new tactic. One that didn't focus on her. "He likes me, yes, and I like him. We're enjoying each other's company right now, but I have no long-term expectations. I'm mature enough to know he's not about to fall in love with me or get down on one knee." She finished with a light laugh that neither woman returned.

"You don't know him very well," Mary said.

Andie moved about, straightening the books and samples. Anything to avoid Mary's eyes. "No, I don't. As I said, we're not serious."

"Meaning, you're not serious. Don't assume on my son's behalf. Katie, tell her I'm right."

"Mom. Whatever happens between Mason and Andie, it's none of our business."

Mary tsked, waving her daughter's comment away. "He wants to settle down, have a family. Do you want that... is it a possibility, or have you had your tubes tied?"

Katie grabbed her mom by the back of the shoulders and directed her toward the door. "Holy shit, Mom. I can't believe I have to send you out to the car. I'll be right back, Andie."

Andie fell into her desk chair. She needed a drink, a double at least. She reached for a photo of Dylan and traced her finger over his face. Her baby boy. Would she be as aggressive as Mary if he dated somebody Andie didn't deem good enough? God, she hoped not. She replaced the picture and sighed. Probably she'd be worse.

"I'm so sorry about that," Katie said as she re-entered the room. "She's really great most of the time."

"I believe you. I know what it's like to be a lioness with a cub. Sometimes the claws come out. But honestly, I doubt

Mason would appreciate his mother rushing him toward fathering my children."

Katie dropped into the chair opposite Andie. "Well, her cub is a thirty-year-old man. It's time she retires the claws, even if she is right."

What the huh…not Katie too. "You agree with her—you think I'm using Mason?"

"No, no, no. Anybody with eyes can see that you care about him. But she's right about you not knowing him very well and…" Katie picked up the small snow globe from Andie's desktop, shook it and watched the snow settle before setting it back down. "Can I ask a question?"

"Okay."

"Has he let you sleep over at his house? Has he spent the whole night here?"

"That's a pretty personal question."

Katie shrugged. "I already know that you've stayed there, and him at your house."

True, they'd spent every night together since Saturday, some in her bed, the others in his. They'd shared meals. Phone calls, emails, texts. Every free minute they'd had, each one incredible. "Then I'll answer yes, since you're already in the loop."

"Mason and I are more than siblings, we're friends too. He's very open with me."

Andie doubted the extent of that openness. She couldn't picture Mason in a tête-à-tête with his little sister, sharing detailed stories about his sex life.

"My brother's not a player, but he's had his fair share of dates and hook-ups—I hope it doesn't bother you to hear that."

"Of course not," Andie cut in, casually rifling through papers that all looked green at the moment. If Katie bought that load of bullshit, Andie should go into politics.

"Sure. So, those women, they never spent the night, or vice-versa. Mason always called it a night before they got too comfy. He doesn't do sleepovers."

This was more information than Andie cared to have. "Just because Mason is changing his game doesn't mean I'm special." There was nothing left to fiddle with. She turned on the monitor and opened a blank Excel file. "It's going to take me a while to work up your quote, but I think I have all the details I need. I'll email it to you later, if that's all right."

"You're kicking a customer out the door?"

"Yes. Yes, I am."

"And you're going to claim it's because you have work to do."

"Probably."

"That's not your real reason for booting me."

"Nope."

"You want me to shut up about Mason."

"Well, as enlightening as it's been…" Andie walked to the doorway and made an exaggerated, sweeping arm gesture. "I don't think my ears can take much more."

Katie laughed and grabbed her purse. "In that case, I'm talking all the way to your front door."

"Oh, goodie."

"You're not afraid to say what's on your mind, that's cool. I can see why Mason's so smitten."

Andie snorted at that one. Mason, smitten with her? Ha. "Mason and I have great chemistry. Lots of it. That's why I got to be his first sleepover friend. No other reason." A few more steps and she could file this conversation under the never-to-be-replayed heading.

Katie paused with her hand on the knob. "Oh, you're not the first woman to sleep over, just the first since he split with his fiancée, after the shitty episode involving the baby." She opened the door and looked out at her mother standing next to the passenger door, arms crossed and blowing smoke from her ears. "Guess I should've given her the keys," she said with a snicker.

Andie's head was reeling from the fiancée and baby comments. Mary looking royally pissed off on her driveway amplified the effect. God, if that woman marched back to the house, Andie would lose it for sure. As soon as she put a closed door between Katie and herself, she was calling Lasha for drinks. The big, slushy kind with several shots of alcohol, a plastic sword and a bartender named Juan serving them. So what if it was barely noon?

Katie gave her mom the one-minute sign. Andie's jaw dropped. What more could Katie have to say after those bombshells?

"Okay, roundup time. You guys are having a ton of sex and according to you, that's the extent of your relationship. I say you're wrong, at least on Mason's side of the equation."

Andie choked on air. This girl knew no boundaries. "Did you even see the line before you crossed it?"

Katie flapped her hand. "Put our theories to the test. Next time you get together, tell him your monthly friend showed up, or that you have a yeast infection—whatever—but take sex off the menu. Then encourage him to go and do his own thing." Two steps down the walk she turned around. "And no blowjobs, etcetera, either!" This, at top volume, in front of her mother and the world.

Andie waved at Mr. Karnowski, her retiree neighbor, whose attention they'd caught. Please let this be a day when he'd opted not to wear his hearing aids. She slinked inside and slid down the closed door. Working for Katie Lang would be a loud, in-your-face experience. Or not—it wasn't too late to pad the estimate.

The doorbell made Andie jump off the couch. Not a good thing. Her brain thumped against the inside of her skull, initiating a monster headache. Since an excessive amount of alcohol was at the root, she ought to go ahead and call it what it really was—a hangover. At seven in the evening. The sun had two hours of life left, a hot man was knocking on her door and she was a wreck from her unintentional afternoon bender. Those Long Island iced teas had gone down a little too easily.

"Whoa. You okay?" Mason asked when he walked through the door.

So she looked as shitty as she felt. Awesome. "I fell asleep on the couch. Rough afternoon."

"Are you sick?" He did the palm on the forehead thing.

"As a mom, I can tell you—that's not an effective way to check for fever." But it was sweet that he tried.

"As a doctor, I can show you the most accurate method of checking for a fever." His eyebrows went up and down. The grin came out full force. "My emergency bag is in the truck."

"Oh, no. You are not sticking a thermometer up my ass."

"How about something else?"

"That'll raise my temperature, not measure it."

With his fingers hooked in her belt loops, he walked her backward until she hit the wall, pinning her there. "The endorphin release it'll give you will fix whatever's wrong."

"Is that your professional, medical opinion?"

"Nah, strictly personal."

She splayed her hands over his chest. Solid, warm. She ventured lower, over the flat plane of his stomach. God, she couldn't help herself. Whenever he touched her, especially from a dominant position, her libido revved higher than high.

Her hand stopped at his waist. More than anything, she wanted to pop the button, push his shorts down. Beg him to release her so she could drop to her knees and suck him until he verged on climaxing, then bend over and let him give her that endorphin rush. Heat swirled between her legs. How could she be so desperate for him again? He'd made her come three times yesterday. They'd had more sex—all of it fantastic—in this one week than she'd had in her life. And she had eleven more days to enjoy him thoroughly, except...

Damn Katie and her theory, her test. The words replayed in Andie's head. She didn't know who she wanted to be right, only that she wanted to know. This had mistake written all over it.

"I can't go any further tonight."

"You're really not feeling well?" He stepped back, now holding her waist gently while surveying her from head to toe. "What are your symptoms—do you want me to take you to the walk-in clinic?"

One point for Katie. Mason's concern could be related to his doctoral instincts, though. She had to step up the stupid test she'd begun, let him know she didn't need his help. Give him the green light to clear out. She hated to lose precious time with him. More than that, she hated lying.

"I'm not sick, it's my—" An acidic burn inched its way up from her stomach. "I got my period, unexpectedly, meaning

I'm out of commission for a few days. I'll be good to go by Sunday. Maybe we can get together after that."

"Of course we will."

"All right, call me then." She touched him one more time. Reluctantly, she let her arms drop to her sides.

"Did you give me a buddy pat?"

"I don't know what that is."

"Like this…" He gave her a firm yet easygoing slap on the shoulder. "Hey, buddy."

"Mine wasn't like that." Too much. "I was just letting you know I don't expect you to hang around while we can't have fun. Seriously, you should go out with your friends for a few days—they've probably been missing you this week."

"Babe, I don't care that you have your period."

Faking or not, she automatically scrunched her nose at that idea. "I guess we found a sex act we don't agree on, because I'm not interested in period sex, period—pardon the pun."

"It's not my favorite kind, either."

"Great, we agree." Not that she'd ever had sex during her period. Scott would sooner have passed a giant kidney stone than do anything dirty. Conversely, Mason based his preferences on his experience with god-knew-how-many women. A more than mildly nauseating thought. She ducked out of his arms and opened the front door.

"Are we going somewhere?" he asked, not moving.

"You are."

"Only if you're sending me out for supplies."

He had to be joking. "You'd go to the pharmacy and buy me tampons?"

"Actually, I'd go to the superstore. That way I could pick up snacks and a movie for us too. Unless you'd rather do something else tonight."

"You don't have to go to the store for me. I have everything I need in the house."

"Then so do I." He did a slow walk that looked like sex sliding across the floor. Closed the door. Locked it. Smiled down at her. "Do you allow kissing while you have your period?"

"Yes."

His head dipped toward hers. "Open-mouthed?"

"It is the best kind."

"With tongue?" he asked, his lips almost touching hers.

Taste and smell collided as she took in faded mint mixed with his natural, yummy essence. "Maybe a little bit."

"As in, only the tip?" He kissed her softly, slipping said tip between the seam of her lips.

"Oh god, you're killing me." So was this stupid, pointless test.

"Sorry." He kissed her again. Longer, with more than the tip.

"You are so not sorry."

"You're right, I lied."

No, what Mason was doing amounted to teasing. What she was doing was lying. And it tasted terrible.

"You should go. Do fun things. Be with fun people." She put a shoulder to his chest, but he didn't budge. He only laughed.

Mason checked his watch while the movie credits rolled up the screen.

"Yes, you've done your time, and then some. You're free to go." Big blue eyes blinked up at him from Andie's resting place on his chest.

"Not happening. It's ten-thirty, you want to watch another?"

"After I totally tortured you with that chick flick? It had no nudity, no sex, no humor, nothing got blown up and I soaked your shirt twice."

"Exactly. I figure we have nowhere to go but up after that disaster." He'd seen a lot of movies, and that was definitely the worst. The crying parts weren't bad, actually, because she'd snuggled tight to his chest when the tears started.

"It was pretty awful. I can't believe you stayed to watch it."

"You had me pinned."

"This from the guy who's tossed me over his shoulder like a caveman how many times?"

"Not enough. I like going Neanderthal with you. I like having that fine ass by my face." The shitty movie had kept him in check. This line of conversation, not so much. That's all it took. Fifteen seconds of thinking about Andie squirming and he was getting hard. Her eyes widened. Yeah, she felt the bulge growing under her stomach. "It'll go away." He nudged her—with his groin. Stupid mistake, his cock mistook the action for thrusting. "Throw in another of those movie recommendations you found on the back of a tampon box and it'll be gone in seconds."

"Ha ha." She rolled off him, padded to the TV and leaned over to grab the movie binder from the floor. The stretchy pants she'd changed into hugged her ass perfectly.

"That view—not helping matters."

She peeked back at him, all smiley as she wiggled it. "I have both of the Crank movies. Or 300. Want to watch one of those?"

"Hell no."

"Why not, they're totally guy movies." She pulled a disc from its sleeve and tapped her finger on the metal. "It says here, rated MT, maximum testosterone."

Yeah, that's exactly what he didn't need on a night when touching Andie—really touching her—was off-limits. "Give me another option."

She covered a yawn with the back of her hand. "I think I'm done. I'm going to put on my comfy jammies and catch up on some sleep. Somebody's been keeping me up past my bedtime lately."

"A solid eight does sound good."

"Come on, I'll walk you out."

He took the hand she offered, but didn't get up, pulling her on top of him instead. "I could stay. We could...cuddle."

"Voluntary cuddling, without sex first? Isn't that a major violation of the guy code?"

"I have my own code."

"I'm starting to realize that." That, and Katie was right. Mason had passed the sex test with ease, proving he had more than his dick invested in their relationship. Not fling, relationship. She was in a relationship with Mason. Scary how much she liked the sound of that. She hadn't meant for it to happen and it surely wouldn't last. Right now, though, it gave her a tingle inside as well as out.

"Okay. Let's go to bed."

Nerves swirled in her stomach while she worked through a slightly amended bedtime routine. She skipped the heavy moisturizer and put on a hint of fresh eyeliner and mascara. A little bit of vanity, but not enough to clog the pores. Next came the body-hugging, sheer black camisole and panty set. A touch of pale-pink lip gloss. Hopefully when she admitted to fibbing, he'd be distracted enough not to be angry. Much.

Or maybe he'd have fallen asleep already. She peeked out from the en suite. No, definitely not sleeping. He was propped up against the headboard, bare-chested, one knee raised with the white sheet covering only his most intimate parts. No sports highlights spewing from the TV... he was reading. He was the finest poster boy for literacy she'd ever seen. Oh god, he had the novel from her bedside table in his hand. And she'd put it aside at a good part—a really good part.

"Enjoying the book?"

"Yeah, it's pretty hot. I should read more often." A quick glance in her direction and the book slapped shut. "When you said comfy pajamas, I was picturing a lot more material."

She crawled up the bed, pushed his leg flat and straddled him above the sheet.

His eyes roved over her body. "And less temptation."

"This is actually very comfortable." She ran her hands over the skimpy top, spending extra time and attention on the fabric covering her nipples. "You should feel how soft it is."

"No, I really shouldn't," he said, groaning when she scooped up his hands and cupped his palms over her breasts. "Babe, you have great tits."

"Thanks, they like you too." She leaned forward. "They like it when you suck them... even more when you bite them."

"What about your period?"

"Tip about the female anatomy—we don't menstruate from our boobs."

"Thanks, I'll make a note of that in my health binder," he said before catching one lace-covered nipple between his lips, then his teeth.

The pressure sent a spike of need straight between her legs. "Now I really want to come."

"I respect you, and I'd like to think my self-control is above average, but you're pushing it close to the limit."

"Then I'll push a little more. Just because we're not going to fuck doesn't mean we can't get off." She ground down on the steel rod under the sheet. Back and forth, the friction causing a pre-orgasmic wave to bloom between her legs. "You're so hard and feel so good, I'm going to come like this, from rubbing on you." She rocked harder, smiling when he cursed under his breath and began thrusting up to meet her. "Mmm, right there, god, I'm so close…"

"Fuck, babe. Me too."

"Stop—I don't want you to come on the sheets."

"Seriously?"

"Well, they're my best set and…" The tortured look on his face when she scrambled off him was priceless. A giggle slipped out, ruining her act. "I don't care about the sheets, but I want you to come in my mouth."

He let out a long breath. "I won't turn that offer down." He snagged her hip and pulled her back into place. "But you first. Use me. Rub your sweet clit against me. I want to watch you come."

"Then you'll have to look down while I'm sucking you, because I'm going to come while your cock is in my mouth." She shimmied down, taking the sheet with her. Knowing he'd been naked and hard under there didn't diminish his impressiveness. "I never get tired of looking at your pretty cock. Or devouring it. Now, be a good stud-muffin and open the lower nightstand drawer."

"Feeling a little objectified here." He laughed, then leaned out of the bed. "Holy shit, look at it all. I don't even know what you'd do with some of this stuff." He held up a sample. "Like these."

"Vaginal balls, you—"

He held up a hand. "Stop. That just sounds…wrong." He returned them, fished through the drawer and held up another item. When she didn't answer, he rolled up onto the bed. Examined the toy's shape, texture and…flexibility. "And this?"

"Come on, you know what it's for."

"No, but from the look on your face, I can't wait to find out."

She tried to snatch it away. He sat, stretching to dangle it several inches beyond her reach. Laughing. Smiling. Annoying the crap out of her by looking uber-hot while totally embarrassing her.

"Babe, I've never seen you blush this much. It's cute. And fucking sexy."

She gave up the fight she didn't have a chance of winning. "They're anal beads." Of course he grinned wider. And inspected them again. Thoroughly, including pulling them back and forth through the tight hole he'd made with his thumb and index finger. Yup, he had them figured out, all right.

He whistled low and appreciatively. "You've used these?"

"Yes. But only solo." Like everything else in her collection.

"Any chance this is what you wanted from the drawer?" he asked, and she shook her head. "Damn. Too bad. Next time?"

"Sure. Your ass or mine?" The shock value from that question was worth any embarrassment. She reclaimed the silicone caterpillar while his jaw was on the floor and traded it for a small, pink vibrator. "This is what I wanted."

"Lipstick?"

"Not quite."

His eyebrows rose as she dragged it smoothly across his balls. "That feels kind of good."

"Too bad, this toy is for me alone. Now, on your back. I want you in my mouth."

"Not gonna argue with that." He leaned against the pillows, still in an upright position.

One of the many hot things about Mason—he liked to watch. Lights on, eyes open, whenever possible. Tonight, his eyes followed every movement. The slide of his cock between her lips. How she gripped him at the base, holding him at her preferred angle for sucking. Her other hand—with accessory—slipping inside her panties.

She'd always wanted to try this. In itself, giving head turned her on. Touching herself while she sucked Mason's cock took her to the edge, but she could never tip over. It required too much coordination—one style of rubbing with her right hand, a completely different motion with the left. With her toy handling the hard work, she could think less. Just feel.

She moaned around his cock as the vibe did its magic—a little too fast. A couple of clicks changed the vibrations from the ten-second-orgasm setting to a slow, escalating pulse. Perfect. It took her up, up, up…then back to the beginning. She sucked him deep, relaxing her jaw to take him all the way. She breathed him in, the heady scent of skin, sweat and arousal. Let him slide out. His cock throbbed, pre-come beading on the tip. She swirled her tongue around the head and slit, licking it away.

"Jesus." That curse meant he was barely holding on to the edge.

She looked up at him and licked her lips, knowing the sight drove him crazy. More, she needed more sensation on her clit. She clicked to a more intense setting. Climax hit her immediately. She filled her mouth with his cock, holding it deep, sucking and swallowing while he came. And she came. And came, and came.

"Babe... Andie..." Two fingers tapped her on top of the head. Then again, hard. "Teeth."

Oh, no. No, no, no. She tossed the vibe aside. "Oh my god, I hurt you."

"It's fine—now."

"Let me check... I don't see any blood. Oh god, there are tooth marks. I'm so, so sorry."

He quickly inspected things for himself. "No permanent damage." He shrugged and smiled. "You definitely have to do that again."

She shook her head vigorously. "Mason, I bit your cock. What are you, a masochist?"

"It only hurt for a couple of seconds at the end, while you were milking that orgasm for all it's worth." He laughed out loud, presumably at her affronted intake of air. "I can take a little pain for something sexy-as-hell like that." One-handed, he stopped her escape and had her underneath him. Kissing her the way only he knew how to kiss.

"It's jabbing me in the back," she said while catching some oxygen.

The vibrator was still humming away when he removed it from beneath her. "You were wrong about this. I enjoyed it as much as you did."

She waited until the lights were out and Mason's breathing had its distinctive, pre-sleep rhythm. Twelve hours ago, she would've sworn she didn't care if he stayed or went— temporarily or permanently. Now, the idea he might get angry and leave gave her a stomachache. One in the heart too.

She liked him. As in, really, really liked him. Not only in bed—or the alley, or his truck—but anywhere, doing anything. Doing nothing but being together. Somehow, she'd gone from enjoying him carnally to pining for him on a deeper, more personal level. A dangerous place to be—but it was too late to rein the feelings in.

"Are you awake?" she whispered. "I have to tell you something."

"What… yeah… go ahead."

"I don't have my period."

"Hmm… yeah, okay," he said in a slow, sleepy voice.

Telling him the rest now was cheating. "It was a stupid test, to see if you're only with me for sex. I lied, I wish I hadn't." No reply, just breathing. "Mason?"

He merely hummed in acknowledgement. Crap, he hadn't absorbed a word of it, meaning she'd have to admit the whole thing while they were both wide awake and face-to-face. She swallowed the lump in her throat and snuggled closer. His strong, easy heartbeat calmed her, made her feel secure—even if only for tonight.

Since he wasn't registering anything she said, "I didn't mean to fall so hard for you," she whispered into his warm, firm chest. "Please, don't be too mad at me."

Chapter Ten

Mason winced as the drive-thru coffee burned his tongue. He'd rather be sitting in Andie's kitchen with a mug of her instant, or better yet, propped up in bed, sipping while watching her sleep. But after her lie, or game, whatever it was—he needed space.

The only reason he hadn't taken off after she fell asleep last night was her safety. He wouldn't leave her alone and unconscious in an unlocked house. Now, at six-thirty in the morning, he was fine with it. Not really. But fuck it, he was still pissed off. He didn't want to hear the daytime version of last night's confession, not right now, and he really didn't want to hear it while looking at her big, pleading eyes. So, yeah, he was gone. At least until he sorted through the crap from last night.

Hugo wrapped around Mason's legs when he walked through the front door, practically tripping him as he made his way to the kitchen. Mason tossed more kibble in the half-full bowl, but the disgruntled feline turned his nose up at the offering.

"Yeah, I know, buddy. I haven't been around enough lately. That might be changing—effective immediately."

He headed into the bathroom and cranked the taps in the shower, setting the water as hot as his skin would tolerate. Thick steam and soap scent surrounded him, cleaning his body but doing nothing to clear his mind. He just didn't get it. Testing him to see if he was using her for sex… what the hell was that about? He'd never treated her that way—the opposite, from where he was standing. He'd taken her to meet his family, for crissake, and it'd taken a hell of a lot of convincing to get her there. Not the kind of thing he'd do if he only wanted her for a booty call. Yeah, they had a lot of sex. Fucking amazing sex that neither of them could get enough of. But he wanted more than that and he'd made that pretty damn clear.

First her insecurity about the age difference, now this. Having to constantly reassure her wasn't his idea of quality time, especially when he hadn't given her any reason to worry. And having a girlfriend who lied to him… he wouldn't go there again. If he couldn't trust Andie, if she wasn't capable of trusting him, he'd have to let go. No matter how much he liked her.

Too little sleep and too much bullshit made the doctor a grumpy jerk. After repeatedly barking at his assistant during morning surgeries, he holed up in his office. Clients wouldn't be as forgiving. Canine, feline or human.

"Your sister's on line one," Cara's voice informed him when he got tired of watching the light on his phone blink.

"Tell her I'm in surgery. Or an appointment. Whatever. I'm not available."

"Is that how you'd like me to handle all of your personal calls?"

Nobody was around to see him roll his eyes, but he still did it. Could she get any more obvious? She'd been coming on stronger than ever since he'd started seeing Andie. It had gotten so bad—her copping a feel of his ass, or crotch, whenever he got within reach—he was actually considering suing her for sexual harassment in the workplace.

"No, just this one."

"I noticed you're in a foul mood this morning. Have a fight with your girlfriend?"

"Everything's fine." And Cara would be the last one to hear otherwise. Ever.

"Your schedule is open for the next fifteen minutes—I could come back there and cheer you up. All the way up, if you know what I mean."

Only an idiot wouldn't know what she meant. "No thanks. Deal with the call on the other line, then go file something. And I don't mean your nails." He hung up immediately. A bit harsh maybe, but necessary.

And by the knocking on his door two minutes later, ineffective. "Cara, that's it—you're fired. I'll pay your two weeks' severance, but you can clear out now."

"Did you just fire your moron receptionist through a door?" Katie asked as she peeked around it. "That's awesome. And way too long coming. That girl is a bimbo and an airhead. She's a bimhead."

"Don't I fucking know it? I've got ten minutes before a hypochondriac Pug gets here. What's up?"

"Dogs can be hypochondriacs? That is so cool. How can you tell?"

"Did you rub up against Cara on your way back here, because I think you caught the airhead bug."

"Meanie." Katie stuck out her tongue. "Why so cranky, big brother? I prefer the new, improved Mason, the guy who smiles all the time. And whistles. The one whose girlfriend will be making my wedding dresses."

"Shit, Katie-Kat. Hiring Andie isn't the greatest idea."

"It's a spectacular idea. She's crazy talented."

"What if we break up, won't it be awkward?"

Katie pushed his feet off the desk and plopped in front of him. "A couple of days ago you're gushing about her—"

"I was not gushing. Guys don't gush."

"Fine, expressing your heartfelt affection, and—"

Mason cringed. "Stop, please, before they come and take my balls away."

"Loser," she said with a laugh. "Whatever. Now you're talking breakup?"

If he didn't tell her, she'd continue to poke him, verbally and physically, until he kicked her out, then she'd call and text incessantly. He didn't stand a chance.

"One of the things I liked about Andie was her openness. Honesty, no bullshit."

"Uh-oh. You said liked and was, as in, past tense."

"This'll sound low, but I didn't expect a woman her age to play games or fuck with my head."

"Oh boy."

"Yeah. She called it a stupid little test, but a lie is a lie, and I'm not going there again." It was a rare day when Katie sat still. Or shut up instead of pumping him for information. Both at once—major red flag territory.

"Um, if the stupid little test happened yesterday, it's probably my fault."

"Your fault?" He checked his watch. Five minutes 'til Mrs. Cleary got here. Fuck. "Talk fast, bullet-point form is good."

"We went to her house for a consult. Mom was a bitch. Andie tried to reassure her by insisting the thing between you is a casual, short-term fling. Both Mom and I interpreted it to mean fuck-buddies. After kicking Mom out, I disagreed and suggested Andie test our two theories. Take sex off the table."

"You disagreed. And how the hell would you know what our relationship is really like?"

"Because you totally gushed." Katie jumped off the desk before he could get her. "And you keep calling it a relationship. Not seeing each other, not dating. A relationship."

Shit, two minutes left. "So you advised the woman you think I'm gushy about to lie to me and trick me, because it's worked so well for me in the past." Katie turned a shade of red she didn't sport very often. Yeah, she hadn't thought about his experience with Stacey when she came up with that stupid suggestion for Andie.

"Don't blame Andie," Katie said as she slunk toward his office door. "She went through with the test, that means she cares about you."

Psycho woman logic if he ever heard it. He shooed her out and prepared himself mentally for Mrs. Cleary and her pug. Poor, tormented dog had to be sick and tired of Mason shoving a thermometer up his ass during their totally unnecessary weekly visits. With any luck, that's all he'd be sticking up there today.

He pasted on a smile as he reached the exam room door. First thing he saw... Mrs. Cleary holding up a plastic baggie of shit. So much for his luck—and the pug's.

"And you told me fucking my boss was a bad idea," Lasha said by way of greeting when Andie answered the front door. "It allows me the freedom to ditch work when you have a love-life crisis—two days in a row. So, lay it on me, sista."

"I took Katie's advice and faked my period."

"I bet that was a lot less messy than the real thing." Lasha helped herself to a beer from the fridge and hoisted her butt onto the counter. "I'm all ears, did he pass the stupid-ass test?"

"He was great. He—" Andie started to tell her the details, but suddenly what happened between her and Mason seemed too intimate to share. "He got an A-plus." And several bonus pluses for what went down in her bedroom afterward. "I told him the truth, but I thought he was too far asleep to hear it, except...when I woke up, he was gone. He usually stays for breakfast. And when he can't, he leaves a note. He, um, didn't this time." This newsflash didn't move her best friend. Lasha would gag if a guy she'd taken to bed left a cute, sappy note like the ones Mason had been leaving her all week. Knowing Lasha, she'd prefer gift cards.

"Shame he didn't last your full two weeks of kidlessness." She shrugged. "We'll hit the strip later and find you a new bed-warmer. Now that you're back in the game, men will be lining up to be on your team." Lasha took another long drink before hopping off the counter. "Pick you up around seven-thirty? We'll grab some dinner and drinks before hitting the dance floor."

For years, Andie had envied Lasha's free-spirited lifestyle. The conveyor belt of men passing through her bedroom. All the stories about hot, wild sex—Andie had believed the thrill came from the variety of partners. And maybe for Lasha, it did.

Sex with Mason got better every day. Same or different, wild or tame, all of it rocked her world. Even when they weren't naked, or on their way to being naked, he excited her. On the skin and all the way through. She'd rather keep him than trade him, if she had the option.

"I'm supposed to be going to Mason's baseball game tonight. At minimum, I want to talk to him before I run off for a night of slutting around." The idea of which gave her a nauseated twinge. "I'm not sure where things stand."

"Honey, I can see the hearts and stars in your eyes from ten feet away. Remember your game plan for after the divorce? Freedom, fun and fucking. This little crush on rebound boy will fade as soon as there's a fresh, hot body to rub against. Trust me."

"I'm sure you're right," she said, feeling her nose grow about three inches. "But I don't like loose ends."

"Do what you need to do." Lasha sounded bored as she stopped at the mirror to refresh her lipstick and pop a breath mint. "Text me when you're done. Oh, and wear those red fuck-me shoes you got online. Every guy with a working cock will be yours for the choosing."

Mason's game started in twenty minutes. The diamond his team was scheduled on tonight was a fifteen-minute drive from her house. From experience, Andie knew he liked to arrive early for some warm-up throws. Easy math, this. No calls, no texts, no show, plus no breakfast together and no note. The sum of those things was one blow-off breakup.

She should cut her losses and go out dancing with her man-magnet best friend. Perhaps find a hard man to get slippery with. But no, she was going to crash a Friday night rec-league ball game. Wearing the red fuck-me shoes. Such was the extent of her plan.

The game was underway and his team was in the field when she arrived. Small blessing, since it meant she didn't have to walk right up and get communicative. She found a spot on the end of a bleacher, close to the backstop, putting the first move in his hands. He could easily come talk to her, wave, nod, etcetera. And if he chose option D, to ignore her, she could escape without leaving too much of her dignity in foul territory.

She knew immediately that he'd seen her. Okay, so she was hard to miss in this particular red t-shirt, skintight black capris and the shoes. More than that, though, she'd caught the jerk of his head as soon as her heels had hit the grassy area beside the fence, sensed the heat of his eyes as they followed her to her seat. But when she looked back at him, standing tall and strong at first base, his focus returned to home plate. As for everyone else assembled to watch the game... she had their full attention.

His opponents couldn't buy their way on base, and Mason's team soon came in from the field. Minus Mason, who had the first at-bat. His line drive into the gap for a double was powerful and exciting. Like him. He stole third, then tagged up on a deep fly ball. She cheered for him openly with each play. If he had a problem with that, he'd have to come over here and tell her so. Only he didn't. After slapping a few hands—hers not included—he took over as third-base coach.

A woman bouncing a baby on her knee slid across the bench. "Don't take this as terribly catty, but I think he's avoiding you."

"Thanks, I was wondering." The woman's mouth opened and closed silently. Oops, that hadn't come out quite how Andie intended. "Oh, I didn't mean it sarcastically. Really. Any input is appreciated. I'm Andie, by the way."

"We figured. Carrie," she said, sneaking a couple of fingertips out from the stranglehold she had on the baby. "And this is T.J. His dad is the shortstop."

No missing the we in Carrie's statement. So Mason had mentioned her, at least. Hopefully before tonight's game.

"The team's been bugging the crap out of him since the game a couple of weeks ago. The one where he threw the ball at you to get your attention? Mason's never gone after a female before, they always come to him, so the guys are milking the fact that he's walking around with Cupid's arrow stuck in his butt."

Some good news, at least. "Do you think that's why he's avoiding me, because he's embarrassed?"

"I've only known him a couple of years, since he moved back from Guelph…" Carrie hesitated. Mason was staring directly at them now. Glaring would be a better description. "But I've never seen him embarrassed. Not about anything. Sorry, that's not the answer you wanted, I'm sure."

"An honest one is always the one I want." Except when it ripped a chunk off her heart.

"You're eyeballing the right guy for that. Mason has a rep for telling it like it is." T.J. thrashed on her knee, so Carrie stood and hiked him onto her hip. "Not even a year old and he already hates listening to women talk." She shook her head in frustration while searching her pockets for something to amuse the boy. "I hope when Mason comes over, he says what you want to hear, because whatever he says is the real deal. Good luck."

Andie endured stares from strangers and zero attention from Mason for the next hour. When the ump called last inning, she smiled politely at the heads turned her way and made her exit. Being a decent guy, he'd probably feel obligated to talk to her after the game. Or maybe he wouldn't. She wasn't putting either of them in that situation.

Once she cleared the parking lot, she pulled over and slumped against the steering wheel. Lasha would be happy to take on the challenge of distracting her, but it would involve flirting at minimum, if not bumping, grinding and possibly more, with men other than Mason. Nope, not tonight. Maybe tomorrow. Or next week, month, whatever. Her best friend wouldn't understand, but she'd have to take no for an answer tonight.

Apparently Lasha wasn't in the mood for no. As if texting Andie every five minutes wasn't enough harassment, now she was out front, ringing the bell.

"Not tonight, Lash, I've got a—" The sight of Mason looking dusty and sexy on her doorstep stopped all movement and ability to speak.

"Headache?"

No, that would be an easy fix. Take two Advil and start fresh in the morning. "Heartache."

"Extra-strength Tums works for that."

"For heartburn, yes. Not the same affliction, but thanks for the medical advice."

"You came to my game."

Sarcastic comebacks licked the inside of her lips. No, she was a mature forty-year-old... "I did, since you neglected to un-invite me." Okay, that was slightly immature, but he deserved it. "It was a good game. You were very impressive offensively and in the field." There, maturity restored.

"Can I come in—I'm pretty sure the old folks next door have their Whisper2000 pressed to the bay window."

She shrugged in an attempt to look indifferent. By his smile she assumed it looked more like a klutzy, spastic tic. "Are you planning to say something that's not rated for a geriatric audience?"

"Maybe." His version of the casual shrug was perfect. Damn him. "Depends how the apology part goes over."

Oh, he was gooood. He still wasn't getting in, though. If he broke her heart out here, in full view of her nosey neighbors, she wouldn't cry. In the house she'd be a blubbering fool. She'd also be in close, private proximity to his tight pants and unbuttoned jersey. Thinking straight while he half-wore his baseball uniform was pretty much impossible.

"I think the Karnowskis would love to hear what you have to say."

"I acted like an ass at the baseball game. And when I left this morning and late last night…" He turned his head toward the neighbors' house and increased his volume. "After you deep-throated my cock while getting yourself off with that pink—"

"Shh! Get in the house," she said, jerking him forward by his uniform shirt. "There's no cock talk on the front lawns of Paradise Avenue."

"Doesn't sound like paradise to me."

"Ugh. You're in, you win." And she was no longer in charge of her tear ducts or the color of her complexion.

"How about farther than the front hall?"

"No way, I can't allow it."

"You don't trust me?"

"I don't trust myself."

"Worried you'll get all worked up while you've got your period?"

"You know I don't have my period."

"Yeah, I heard everything last night." And he hadn't uttered a single word in reply.

"I am sorry that I lied. It was stupid. I screwed up."

"I'm the one who felt stupid. I wasn't expecting lies or bullshit from you."

Oh god, the lump was starting in her throat. Dammit, she hated crying in front of anybody. Doing it with Mason looking on would be worse. He'd either pity her, which she didn't want, or he wouldn't, which she also didn't want. She leaned against the wall and slid to the floor, hugged her knees and squeezed her eyes shut until it was safe to open them. Nope, still no good. She closed them again, and stayed that way until he started talking.

"I was engaged to a girl I met during veterinary school. We planned to graduate together, start a clinic, get married and have kids eventually, when the time was right."

Acid curled in her stomach. Just when she thought she couldn't feel worse.

"Stacey got pregnant summer before our final year. Accident." He shrugged. "I thought we'd make the best of it. She hated the idea of postponing her graduation and career. It made for lots of serious talks and crying. Then she lost the baby."

The bottom fell out of her stomach. "Mason, I'm so sorry, I know—" She stopped in the nick of time. "That's a hard thing to deal with, for both people."

"Yeah, it was. Especially when I found out she'd had an abortion, not a miscarriage, like she'd told me."

What a bitch. A selfish, manipulative, lying bitch. "Where is she now?"

"Don't know." He dropped to the floor opposite her, pushing his hands through his hair. "Katie wasn't using her brain when she gave you relationship advice. Not for one with me, anyway. I fucking hate lying and head games. She feels shitty about it, she really likes you."

No mention of his feelings for her. Of course he wasn't forking that detail over. "I'd like to blame your sister, but I'm the one who took her suggestion." Sometimes being mature sucked. And the big-girl panties she just pulled up—they sucked too.

They sat in heavy silence for what felt like an hour, at least to her ass. Mason didn't squirm once. The cold ceramic tile probably didn't bother his firm, muscular behind. Thinking about his butt reminded her of Carrie's comment about Cupid's arrow. For a second, she smiled. He smiled back. Warm, genuine. Suddenly she didn't feel so chilled.

His head cocked to the side. "Did you really think I was only seeing you for sex?"

"No, not really. Mind you, it was nice to know for sure. And when we first hooked up, I thought that's what we were both doing. After all, it'd been well over two years for me, and gah, you're like a walking orgasm machine."

"Two years? You went without sex for more than two years?" The eyes went wide first. The huge grin followed immediately. "You gotta be kidding me."

"Nope. Until you overthrew your way into my life, it'd been nothing but habitual masturbation for me for a very long time. Even before the separation. That's why I got all the toys—I was developing carpal tunnel syndrome in my right wrist."

The hallway came alive with the sound of Mason's whooping laughter. "No wonder you're such a horndog. Making up for lost time."

"There may be some truth in those statements, but—"

"Some truth?" He laughed until he had to wipe away tears. "You're insatiable."

"Funny, you never complained before."

"I'm not complaining now." He pushed to a stand, crossed the hallway and pulled her up, sandwiching her between the wall and his hot, uniform-clad body. "Come home with me tonight."

"I... I don't think I can do the casual-sex thing. Not... with you."

His lips skimmed the shell of her ear. "Babe, I've never had casual sex with you. I wasn't planning to start now."

Oh god, her heart. "So it'd be…?"

"Make-up sex. A mutual, physical apology for acting like idiots." His mouth progressed to her shoulder as he hooked the t-shirt aside. "You look hot in this outfit. Where are the shoes?"

"In my bedroom." Immediately, he had her walking backward down the hall. "I've never had make-up sex. Is it better than regular sex?"

"Can be. How can you never have had make-up sex in all those years of marriage?"

The marriage had operated under Scott's rules since the beginning. They hadn't fought because Scott wouldn't, simple as that. If she told Mason how it'd been, he'd think she was a spineless wallflower. Or he'd pity her, which would be worse.

"We didn't argue. No fights—no need to make up."

"He's a lawyer. They argue for a living."

"Let's just say that Scott was more passionate about his cases than his wife."

He turned her forward facing, keeping his body close behind hers as they mounted the stairs. His breath tickled her ear. "If you were my wife, I'd be picking fights about stupid shit all the time, for the excuse of making up with you."

This conversation had definitely taken a turn for the better. She knew better than to read too much into his last statement. Making up was one thing. Marrying Mason—that was a never-going-to-happen thing. No harm in enjoying the sentiment, though.

The shoes were next to the bed, where she'd kicked them off before flinging herself facedown on the mattress. She had one in her hand when he spoke.

"Take your time." He was leaning against the wall, focused completely on her. The comment either meant she didn't have to rush, or that he wanted her to slow down.

She'd put money on the latter. With one hand on the mattress, she bent at the waist, giving him a view of her backside in the tight pants as she slipped each foot into the heels ever so slowly. His eyes followed the movements, making an appreciative sweep of her entire body. Stripping for him always sent a wave of need straight to her hot spots. Getting dressed was having a similar effect.

"You have a lot of shoes," he said when she opened the closet. From his vantage point he could see a dozen or so pairs of assorted heels. Tip of the iceberg.

"It's a weakness. They're my sexy treat to myself."

"More than the stuff in your nightstand drawer?"

"Okay, maybe I have a few weaknesses…"

"Shoes and sex toys, that's two. What else?"

"I don't think I should point out any more of my quirks until you're sufficiently drained from make-up sex. You might change your mind."

"About you, or this?" His arms slid around her waist from behind. "Not likely." His lips grazed her neck. His hands snuck under her shirt, seeking her nipples. Found them.

She pressed against him—ass to his pelvis, breasts to his palms. "We could start the make-up sex here…"

His talented fingers migrated south. Popped the button on her pants, eased the zipper down. Snuck under the lacy thong and found a wet, needy target. He circled her clit until she was panting and desperate. Then withdrew his hand.

"Grab whatever clothes and stuff you'll need for the weekend."

"W-what?"

"Unless you want to spend it naked, which I'm totally on board with."

"But… you were just… I thought… what about the make-up sex?"

"You wanted to start the make-up sex here, so we started. This one?" He grabbed a tote bag from the shelf in her closet, a sexy and completely mischievous grin plastered on his face as she nodded.

When she didn't take the bag—because she was too busy picking her jaw up off the floor—he turned to the closet and started grabbing items. Mason's selections for her weekend wardrobe—slinky sundresses and high-heeled shoes. A million miles from the kinds of things Scott would've packed for her, and yet the muscles in her stomach clenched at the sight. The urge to snatch the bag and dump the items Mason had chosen, even though she loved every single one of them, overwhelmed her. She squeezed her eyes shut. Took a deep breath and focused on letting it out slowly.

Mason's wolf whistle yanked her out of her attempted panic control session. "Damn. Maybe we should take a drive to Grand Bend, hit the beach." A black bikini with red paisleys dangled from his finger, looking startlingly small in comparison to his large, strong hands. "Better yet, I'll run the sprinkler in my backyard. That way I won't have to behave myself when I see you wearing this."

The knot unraveled and breathing got easier. Mason wasn't Scott. They weren't alike in any way. She needed to get a grip, and maybe some therapy. For the moment, that included calmly watching—and letting—a man pack for her.

"Aren't you going to pack me a bra?" she asked when he added several pair of tiny panties from her lingerie drawer, but nothing else.

"Nah."

She plucked one from the drawer and tried to stuff it in the bag, but he jerked it away. "Mason. If we're going anywhere public, I need this."

"I like that scolding tone, it's hot." The tote went up above his head while she waved the bra at him. "I like seeing your hard nipples poking at the material. No bra for you this weekend."

That's what he thought. She hooked her fingers under each strap at her shoulder and snapped. So what if it was red lace and would show under some of the dresses he'd chosen. She snapped again—and stuck out her tongue.

This proved to be a mistake.

"Let me have it."

She shook her head and crossed her arms over her chest. The tote bag dropped to the floor. Goose bumps popped up all over her body when he gave her the come-hither motion. The urge to give in to him and give it up almost won. But the brat beat it down.

"You're not getting it."

"I'm gonna enjoy this," he said, stalking toward her.

Baseball pants don't hide much. Chicken legs, scrawny butts or giant erections. Mason didn't have the first two, but he sure had the third.

The inner brat screamed at her to run for it. Easier said than done wearing three-inch heels on plush carpet. By some freakish luck, she deked right and got past him. Out of the bedroom, down the stairs and through the kitchen without breaking her neck. The living room was her demise. One way in meant only one way out. And he had it blocked.

"I should have ditched the shoes."

"Wouldn't have mattered." One step into the room for him.

"You're not really planning on taking my bra." A sidestep around the coffee table for her.

"Oh, I really am."

No luck getting around him this time. He caught, maneuvered and pinned her on the couch—all with one hand and a massive grin on his face. The cool leather squeaked under her back as she squirmed. He was large, warm and hard on top of her, making her wriggling more about rubbing against him than escaping.

"Front or back hook?"

"I'll never tell."

"You're hot when you're being bratty."

"I thought I was hot when I was scolding you."

"Yeah, then too. And when you moan, say dirty words, wash dishes at my kitchen sink…pretty much always." His free hand shoved her t-shirt above her breasts, revealing a lacy red demi-bra with handy front closure. "Very nice."

For a big man with ample strength, he had the lightest touch—when he chose to. Like now. She shivered as he traced the scalloped detail along the swell of her breast, dipping his finger slightly under the edge, teasing her nipples with a mere hint of contact. Any other time, her cleavage refused to stay put in this barely there bra. Because she wanted them to pop out, they didn't budge. She'd gone from fighting to keep the bra, to wishing he'd snap to it and take the damn thing away.

"You win. What're you waiting for?"

He toyed with the clasp, clicking it between his thumb and index finger, obviously considering his options. He released her arms from above her head. "I want you to give it to me. Or beg me to take it off. Either way, a willing surrender."

"No. No way. I guess you don't win, after all." Having the use of both hands didn't make him any easier to move. No amount of shifting or shoving got her free. And he didn't have a ticklish spot to weaken him, not that she'd found yet, anyway, and she was on a first name basis with every inch of his body.

"Then the game isn't over yet."

The soft kiss surprised her. She expected something more playful or assertive, given the moment. Another kiss followed, soft as the first, but deeper, longer. His tongue teased its way in. She sighed into his mouth, twined her arms around his neck. Gave back as good as she was getting. Playing was fun, but passion was better.

His hips nudged her legs apart. He settled solidly between them and rocked. The hard bulge of his cock rubbed her clit despite the layers of clothing. Slowly, repeatedly, rekindling the need to come he'd created with his fingers not so many minutes ago. He cupped one breast and thumbed the peak of her nipple through the lace. Heat spread through her body, sparking at the pleasure points, but not igniting the release she wanted desperately.

He swallowed her frustrated groan, dipped his head to her breast and caught the edge of her bra between his teeth. Finally. A nip or maybe a suckle, skin on skin, enough to push her over. She held her breath. Held his head. And he held the lace in his mouth, giving her hot breath on skin, nothing more.

"Touch me, bite me... I need something..." She moaned as he added a twist to his grinding motion, forcing her that much closer to the edge.

"Can't." He forced the word through his teeth. Sweat beaded on his forehead. His jaw clenched as he bit out another single word. "Bra."

"Then take it off!"

He snapped the clasp. Shoved the bra off and clamped down on her nipple... as he lifted his hips from her body, leaving her high and dry... and horny as hell.

Chapter Eleven

Between the moon and streetlights, Mason had a clear view of Andie's face. If he dared sneak a glance. Yeah, he might've taken the teasing a bit too far. But playing around had wiped away the last of the tension, plus she was damn cute when she was sexually frustrated. The way her cheeks went all flush, the pouty set her lips got. Thinking about how she'd felt wiggling and writhing under him... Maybe he wouldn't wait until they got to his place.

"I'm gonna get some drive-thru. Want something?" Only to maim him and eat his still-beating heart, by the look on her face. Shit. He had to change that expression to a satisfied smile, and fast.

The line for assembly-line burgers and heavily salted fries reached the street. Perfect for what he had in mind. He signaled and waited, hooking into the driveway a few minutes later.

"This is insane. It's going to take you five minutes to reach the speaker." Her hands waved wildly at the windshield, another sign that she needed immediate de-stressing. "Park and go inside. Or send me in. The restaurant's air-conditioned—I'm sure the counter clerks would enjoy seeing my nipples through this flimsy t-shirt."

"I'm sure they would, but we're staying in line." Five minutes should be enough, unless ice had formed an impenetrable layer over her hot spots. Her toy box was on the seat between them, tucked under his elbow. He popped the lid open and poked through the contents.

"What the fuck are you doing?"

He bit back a laugh. Couldn't stop himself from smiling. Andie used the f-word for dirty talk, but he'd never heard her use it as a curse. "You're hot when you're mad."

"Then I must be really fucking hot right now." The seatbelt came off and she laid a fist into his arm. Probably full strength. She shook off the sting and curled the fingers to her lips to blow on them. "Dammit, why do you have to be so hard?"

Now he laughed. She did not look impressed. "Hit me in the face." He tapped the bridge of his nose. "It's been broken before, a couple times, so it'll be easy to break again. And it'll hurt like a son-of-a-bitch, which I deserve, so give it your best shot." He cringed when she leaned toward him, hand in the air.

"I'm not messing up this handsome face." The hand landed on his cheek, soft and gentle. "Plus, you wouldn't be able to go down on me if your nose was broken. Eventually I'm going to forgive you for your wretched teasing, at which point I'll be collecting on the orgasms you owe me from earlier."

"A broken nose wouldn't keep me from burying my face between your legs." He hadn't been there for over forty-eight hours. Way too fucking long. "It'd be worth a little pain to lick you up and down, suck your clit, feel you grind against me as you explode under my mouth."

The idiot behind them honked, jerking them out of the moment. He cursed under his breath as he pulled forward. A car length. Shit, they'd lost about two minutes already. But her grumpy face was gone. Her cheeks were pink, her eyes glassy. Most important, her bottom lip was tucked between her teeth. Time to make his move.

"Slide closer, babe." She did, and he kissed her, stopping only after she melted into it. "Undo your pants and push them down a bit."

"What—why?"

He picked out the pink lipstick-esque vibrator and moved the box to the backseat. "I want you to come."

"I want that too, as soon as we get to your house."

"Too long to wait." He reassessed the line of vehicles. Nodded at her lap. "Pants. Open. Now." Either she'd do it, or she'd decide that breaking his nose sounded like a good idea. She startled him by reaching into his lap and squeezing, smiling the naughtiest smile he'd seen on her yet. Oh fuck. Yeah, she'd do it, all right.

Her hands worked her button and zipper. Shimmied the pants and lacy thong past her hips. She offered her hand, palm up, but he shook his head.

"I want to do it. Show me how."

She wrapped her hand around his and guided it to her mouth, where she sucked the toy in a way that made his balls throb and tighten. "That was for you. I know I'm nice and wet already." She clicked the button on the vibrator. It hummed against his palm as she cycled through the different settings. Another quick check of their surroundings and she clicked twice more. "Fastest way to get the job done."

"Jesus," he said when she fingered herself, pulling the soft flesh aside to reveal her clit. Thank god for excessive parking lot lighting. He couldn't decide what to look at first—her eyes, mouth, or the slice of heaven he'd come to think of as his.

He didn't know where to begin with the buzzing lipstick. "I wasn't exactly taking technical notes when I watched you using this thing."

"Pretend it's your finger."

Easy enough. Using the tip, he circled her clit. Lightly at first, increasing the pressure when her lips parted and she sighed, low and long.

"More pressure." Her hips arched up from the seat. "Now flatten it out…"

What the fuck did that mean? He moved it around—obviously the wrong way—before her hand clapped onto his, angling the vibrator lengthwise along her clit. Now he got it.

"Jiggle it a little, like you do with your tongue…"

"This way?"

"Uh-huh, yes…just…harder…" Her legs shook as she bucked against the little vibe and his hand, filling the truck with gasps and moaning. Then giddy giggling and panting as she caught her breath.

All the blood in his body raced to his cock. If he even moved the wrong way, he'd lose it. "That was fucking hot. I'm gonna smile every time I drive past here."

"Me too. And anytime I hear someone mention a Happy Meal." She had a huge smile going on. His was probably a mirror image.

The windows had steamed solid. Add that to the tints and he couldn't see jack. He dropped his window and stuck his head out so he could see to move up. They were almost to the menu board. Fuck it. Food wasn't what he needed most. She was. He jerked out of the line, out of the parking lot and headed west with the most addictive woman he'd ever met.

Too many excruciatingly long red lights later, he killed the engine in his driveway. She'd kept her hand in his lap the entire drive. They'd passed a couple of choice-looking parking lots and he'd almost stopped and fucked her right then. But it would've been cramped and awkward. Not good enough given the state he was in.

"I'll come back for the stuff." He pulled her out his side, kicking the truck door shut behind them, needing to keep the contact between them. Clothes got tugged off as they stumbled to his bedroom. "No," he growled when she went to her knees in front of him. "I need to fuck you. Right now."

She scrambled onto the bed. Assumed the doggy position, her favorite. His too, but not what he had in mind. He did the condom thing, then flipped her over. Yeah, this way. Face-to-face.

"It's gonna be fast," he said, poised at her entrance.

"As long as it's deep."

"Always." He pushed inside. She was tight, hot and he'd been on the edge since the first time he touched her tonight. He could speed to the end, she wouldn't be upset, but now that she surrounded him, filling his senses, he didn't want to rush. He lowered his body until her tits pressed flat against his chest. Her arms and legs folded around him, urging him closer, deeper. Exactly where he wanted to be.

He stroked into her slowly, savoring the sensation. Rubbed his face in the softness of her hair. Her neck. "I love the way you smell." He swirled his tongue on the sensitive spot where her neck met her shoulder. Moved upward, lapping at her skin. Sweet, with something more he couldn't describe. "And your taste…I can never get enough." Here, behind her ear. The pulse spot on her temple. Her mouth—the plump bottom lip and that wicked tongue. All the other places he wished he could lick while fucking her.

She broke their kiss, moaning near his ear when he thrust deep enough to brush her clit with his body. Yeah, he loved that too. "I love the sounds you make. Your voice, your laugh. How you feel…" He wanted every part of her, every way, all at once. And he didn't want it to end. Not tonight, not ever. "I want to get lost in you… I love you."

Nails bit into his skull as she dragged his mouth onto hers. His head filled with the sounds of heavy breathing and desperate kissing. The clap of suction from their skin separating and reconnecting. Words, parts of words, his and hers, jumbled together. Harder words spurred by their fucking. Softer, sweeter ones from a deeper place.

The scent of their sex filled his head, made him dizzy, made his cock pulse harder. His balls tightened mercilessly. Not yet, not fucking yet. Her hips jerked against his grinding motion. Knowing she was coming—feeling every ripple of her climax—stripped him of that last thread of control. Deep, he needed to be deeper than any time before. He covered her with his entire body, buried himself and let go. Yeah, he was lost. And part of him never wanted to find his way back.

"Now I get the hype about make-up sex," she said, whimpering a little when he pulled out and left the bed.

He didn't answer. His head was a mess, still processing what'd happened between them. "Have to hit the bathroom, babe. You need anything?"

"You to hurry back." Her voice was already heavy with the onset of sleep. She'd be out within minutes. Exhaustion didn't stop her from smiling fully when he kissed her, though. She really was beautiful.

He planted his hands on the porcelain and stared into the mirror. "What the fuck did you do?" His reflection blinked back, offering no explanation. In the midst of their intense… lovemaking… he'd gone and done it. Told her that he loved her. Not just things about her. He'd said the three words, straight up.

Definitely not part of the plan. Make up from their sort-of fight, yes. Enjoy each other all weekend, in and out of bed, yes. Confess to loving her—uh, hell no. At least she hadn't called him on it. Come to think of it, she hadn't even acknowledged it. Maybe, in the heat of the moment, in that tangle of words and moans, she hadn't heard the specifics. Or she might be ignoring it. Maybe love wasn't high on Andie's list. He shook off the shitty thought. Maybe she was just as scared by the words as he was.

He splashed cold water on his face. Gave himself a good slap, physically and mentally. Yeah, he'd thought about falling in love with Andie. He'd felt it building, simmering in the corner of his heart. But saying it changed things. Love led to commitment, or it was supposed to. He didn't want their relationship to end, but he hadn't considered anything permanent, either. Not seriously. Ah, fuck it. Staring at his reflection wasn't going to make the answer magically appear. He'd figure it out later—or not.

A sandwich and some sports highlights later, he hit the sack. No snuggling up to her, though, even if she was soft and warm and still smelled fucking incredible. He needed to get his head straight, not blindly follow his heart and his cock. This guy was sticking to his side of the bed tonight. His side. He gritted his teeth. It was his fucking bed—both sides belonged to him. Hell, he might as well crack open the laptop and order an engagement ring online. Tomorrow they could rearrange the house, make room for her stuff, paint a room for her son…

"Fuck." The curse slipped as he shot upright in his urge to get the hell out of there.

She followed him up, groggy from being startled awake. "What's wrong?"

No escaping now. Shit. "Stupid leg cramp. Roll over and go back to sleep." Emphasis on the roll over part.

"Those are nasty. Let me rub it out for you."

He half-laughed. In her sleepy state, it took her a few seconds to catch up. Once she had, she gave him this cute little shove that wouldn't tip over an empty highball glass, but he let it knock him to his back. His stressed-out mood—gone.

He found her hand and arranged it around his cock, perpetually at half-mast since she'd come into his life. "If you insist."

"Let me deal with your leg cramp first, you bad, bad boy," she said as she crawled to the end of the bed, between his legs. "Right or left, and which muscle?"

"It's good now. Probably just dehydration."

"I'll get you a drink of water." She slid off the end of the bed. Padded across the room wearing nothing but the moonlight. "When I come back I'll give you that other rub you're in need of."

Down the hall, a cupboard door opened and closed. The water cooler glugged. The kitchen light didn't come on, because she knew her way around his house. He waited, but the earlier panic didn't hit him again. He propped up on his elbows when he heard whispering. The scrape of metal followed, then something tinkling against glass. Cat food.

"Thanks." He made a show of draining the glass she offered. Lie upheld. "And thanks for feeding Hugo. Can't believe I forgot to do it."

"My pleasure. And on the subject of pleasure…"

For half a minute he stayed still, enjoying the tight slide of her fist on his cock. But he'd be a total dick to let her keep going. "You should still be asleep—I was kidding about the hand job."

"I'm awake now, and I definitely don't mind. Unless…I'm not doing it right?"

"Babe, you do everything right." Including occupying one side of his bed. He rolled her over top of him, so they lay side by side, facing each other. A couple small adjustments later, his quadriceps was wedged up against her clit.

"I can't do much for you in this position," she said, demonstrating her limited stroking range.

He nudged her with his thigh. "Yeah, you can. Use my body, rub on me until you come."

"That's for me, not for you."

"Watching you get off is the sexiest thing I've ever seen. It makes me rock hard, makes me want to come on the spot." The dirty talk was working. She started moving against his leg. The moon lit the room well enough for him to see her bottom lip caught between her teeth. "Feel how hard I am, fucking your hand? You do that to me." His cock was like a steel rod. Talking dirty to her worked for him too. "Yeah, that…rub your clit nice and hard, come all over me." The squeezing and grinding, her panting in his ear…much more and he was gonna lose it before she got to the finish.

She moaned, a low sound that shot through him like electricity. Her hold on his cock tightened almost to pain. Then she bit him. On the side of the neck and hard enough to make him curse. All worth it when she bucked desperately against his skin.

"I need inside you." So much, it almost hurt. He dragged her leg over his hip. Pushed against her, entering a little. "You're so wet." Something he never got to feel wearing a condom. "And hot. Soft." He slid deeper. Close to halfway. What the fuck was he doing? Yeah, they'd had the talk. Both of them were up to date on tests and clear, but she didn't take the Pill. This was stupid. Neither of them were stupid people. "I can't…" He battled for control as her body tempted him farther inside. "You gotta tell me to stop."

"You should…should…"

Shit, she was going to say it. He slid his hand over her silky skin, stopping to rub the spot at the base of her tailbone that made her shiver, trailing his fingers lower to tease her ass by circling the rim. Her hips jerked and rolled. Offering all, begging for more. The selfish bastard in him knew how to weaken her defenses. To get what he wanted.

"Please..." The word rode a desperate moan.

"Please what?" He used her juices as lube and breached her with the tip of one finger. "Stop?" He was the biggest douche in history, manipulating her this way.

She pulled him in. All the way in. "Never stop."

"Jesus..." Nothing compared to this. Skin to skin, no barriers. Her body squeezing him, drawing him deeper. Everything was more, better. As if he were high. He crushed into her. Cupped her ass and brought her up to meet his strokes. "You feel too good, I'm not gonna last long and I don't want to come yet." He took her mouth, kissed her deep and long. "I'm close... I should—" *Pull out, idiot, pull out!*

"Not yet, please... more. More fingers, deeper..."

Holy hell yeah, he'd wait on that request. He eased the single out, slid a second finger alongside. "You're so fucking sexy—I love your sweet ass, so tight around me. I think about it all the time, filling it with my fingers, my cock."

Long nails dug into his butt. Her chin jutted upward. Her breathing shifted to low-pitched moaning and everything tightened around him.

Andie coming pulled his trigger big time. His balls clenched high and tight. Every drop of blood he owned must've rushed to his cock, because he felt hung like a giant as he came and then came some more. Drained in the true physical sense, he crashed, still deep inside her. For once he didn't have to jump up and deal with a condom. Perfect, because he didn't want to move.

"What I said earlier, the first time..." The words were right there, and this time, his head was clear. "I, uh..."

She focused on him. Heating him up all over, impossible as that should be. Even in the dim lighting of the moon, her eyes sparkled. Crazy beautiful. And he wanted to say it. To see her reaction, to hear her return the words. Fuck, where were his balls now, when he needed them for something other than sex?

One small, delicate hand moved to his chest. "It was sex talk, don't worry about it."

"No, it wasn't."

"Oh." Her bottom lip dropped, ever so slightly, before she sucked it between her teeth. "It's okay. We don't need to talk about... anything you said. Really."

"I want to." And still, he kept her hanging. Shit, why couldn't he say it? "Yeah, I suck with words. This..." He captured that delicious mouth of hers. Took it over. Kissed her, softly yet thoroughly, hoping she got the message. Trying to pour three important words into a minute of lip work.

"Me too," she whispered after they came up for air.

He smiled into space as she snuggled under his chin. Incredible.

A face full of sunshine woke Andie. The no-blinds thing would drive her crazy if she slept here on a regular basis. Which she had been, the past week and a half, but wouldn't be, less than a week from now. Once Dylan got home from Scott's cottage in Gravenhurst, she'd only get the opportunity to sleep with Mason—in the literal sense—on weekends. If they lasted after the reality of her day-to-day life set in. And there was a good chance he wouldn't be interested in sticking around for that. He was gorgeous, fun, successful... and thirty. Why would he settle for an older woman with a divorce decree and a child?

Because he'd said he loved her during some very passionate sex? Pfft. That was then, and maybe even now, but next week would be entirely different. Something she had to keep in mind so she didn't get her hopes up. Right... a bit too late on that aspiration.

Sunny day outside, cloudy mood inside. On a happier note, Mason was still in the bed. A first, and a fine one, at that. Having the opportunity to admire him while he slept made things a bit better. The negative reality crap could take a backseat for a few minutes.

She propped up on one arm. Where to start the ogle-fest? She pulled the sheet away carefully, exposing every naked inch of him for her viewing pleasure. God, he had long legs. Just hairy enough to be rough when they brushed against her skin. Like last night, when she humped his thigh like a horny dog. Shameless, that's what he made her. Her libido hadn't dipped below zoom since they met. Awake less than ten minutes and her body was revving up for action.

Checking out Mason's morning glory made it worse. His cock stretched high across his flat abdomen, begging her to suck it to the back of her throat. Sweet heaven, her mouth was actually watering. Maybe she had a hormonal imbalance or something, to be jonesing for him around the clock.

She shook her head and forced her eyes above belt level. Arms strong enough to swing from—check. Perfect chiseled chest with its tattoo of the Franciscan cross that honored the patron saint of animals—yup, her nipples were getting hard simply from looking at it. Sexy hands—check and double check. Who'd have thought men's hands could be sexy? Knowing the pleasure Mason's hands delivered gave her the warm and tinglies every time she looked at them.

She slipped her hand under the sheet. One touch and her clit ached for her to finish the job. She'd masturbated in stealth mode plenty of times lying beside Scott. Completely silent, her body rigid on the mattress as she rubbed herself with furious efficiency. Could she pull it off with a naked sex god spread out in front of her? Not likely. Maybe it was time to wake him up.

Sunlight covered the bed. It had disturbed her sleep, but apparently had no effect on Mason, despite the brilliant glow hitting him in the face. His lips were a relaxed, straight line. She leaned in and kissed them delicately. He didn't so much as twitch. She traced the set of his jaw. Put her fingers through his hair. No movement, the man was a log. His eyelids remained closed, covering the most mesmerizing blues she couldn't say no to.

Not that she wanted to say no to Mason. Ever. Last night, though, no would've been the smarter answer. Sex without a condom. They'd discussed it one night after a rush trip to the pharmacy for yet another box. No risk of diseases, they were both doctor-approved. His disappointment that she wasn't on the Pill had been clearer than this morning's sky. And she could be on it. Should be, now that she was back in the saddle and currently riding a virile stud.

Forty, single and pregnant wasn't part of her plan. Now that she thought about it, though… Okay, she still harbored a smidgeon of baby lust. Maybe the possibility of an accidental pregnancy gave her a bit of a thrill, not chills. And Mason would be a great dad, she could tell. Ugh, what was she thinking? Babies didn't equal happily ever after. If last night had consequences, she'd deal with them on her own.

"Morning, beautiful." Mason scrubbed at his jaw, cracked his neck once on each side. "What's with the big sigh? You disappointed that I let my lazy ass linger in bed instead of getting up and making you an omelet?"

God, he was incredible. Outside. Inside. Her heart did another flip-flop. "That's exactly what it is. I'm hungry and you've spoiled me for cold cereal."

He hooked her by the knee and pulled her on top of him. "Yeah? Well, you've spoiled me for other things."

Ditto and double ditto on that. Not so long ago, she fantasized about assorted random men on a regular basis. Now she couldn't imagine being with anybody but Mason. She was in sooo deep. If she didn't detour left or right in the next ten seconds, he was going to be in deep too. And they needed to talk when their bodies weren't joined in all the good spots before they took any more chances.

"I'll go start the coffee," she said, scrambling off and away from temptation.

She detoured into the bathroom to clean up. Yikes. Mirror—so not her friend this morning. Mason must've had the sun in his eyes, calling her beautiful with this bed head and the raccoon rings from last night's purple eyeliner. She scrubbed her face until it shone. Washed the other areas requiring attention more gently. The frequency and intensity of their sex life kept her on cloud nine, but it also made things a bit tender on occasion. A trade she happily accepted.

One of Mason's t-shirts hung on the back of the door. She brought it to her nose, eyes closed, inhaling him. The worn fabric tickled her nipples as it dropped into place, the scent of him wafting over her as she shook it down, over her hips. Weak in the knees from a t-shirt—those pheromones of his packed a mean punch. She instructed her feet to take her to the kitchen, instead of sprinting back to the bedroom and jumping him. Coffee first, then a shower. With an orgasm. Maybe more than one if he joined her.

"I guess you're waiting on me to cook those eggs," Mason said as walked into the kitchen. "I'm starving too. You drained me last night."

She glanced up from measuring coffee into the pot. He hadn't bothered to cover up, bare windows be damned. Seventy-four inches of walking naked glory. Her mouth fell open at the sight of his erection. Morning wood, still? No way.

He must've shown it some extra attention before coming out of the bedroom. Either way, giddy up.

While finishing with the coffeemaker, she saw Mason's neighbor on her stoop, checking her mailbox. And rechecking it, while looking this way. Andie didn't blame her one bit. "Your hotness is spiking the neighbor lady's blood pressure this morning."

He laughed while transferring items from the fridge to the counter. Eggs, cheese, asparagus. "You're biased about the hotness, babe, and this is no different from any other day."

"I wish you were my neighbor." She pitched in by rinsing the asparagus. This required she squeeze in front of him to get to the sink. And back again—extra slowly.

He slapped her ass, then started cracking eggs into a bowl. "I'd never go to work if you were that easily accessible. I'd go bankrupt and have to live in a cardboard box on your front lawn."

"You wouldn't be out there long. Hordes of women would happily take you in."

"Yeah? How about you?" Muscles bulged as he whisked. "Would you take me in?"

"Only if you agreed to be my sex slave."

"Pretty sure I already signed on for that job." He quit prepping food to kiss her. Open mouth, little bit of tongue, whole lot of sparks. "Best career move I ever made." He returned to the chopping board, leaving her in a heightened state of botherdom.

Breakfast could wait. She climbed onto the small oak table. Plunked her naked ass down on the edge closest to him and lay back, pulling the t-shirt high over her breasts as she did. He clocked every second of it in his peripheral vision. Some crazy sex juju must've taken over her brain to be doing this.

"Forget the eggs—eat me." She pushed a chair with her toe, only it didn't slide out from the table in the sexy, welcoming way she'd imagined. It crashed to the floor, echoing off the ceramic and missing Mason's feet only because he jumped to avoid it. "Oh crap."

"Nice move," he said, grinning ear-to-ear.

"It went a lot smoother in my head."

"Worked fine for me the way it was." The chair stayed overturned. It didn't get another blink of his attention.

"Everything works for you—you're so easy."

"When I want to be." He cupped one of her feet in his hand, placed it on the table, repeating the process with the other.

This position left her completely exposed. As in, feet-in-the-stirrups exposed. At the doctor's office, she had to force herself to keep her knees apart. Under Mason's heady gaze, she couldn't spread them wide enough.

He lowered himself to his knees and slid his finger inside her. No, not his finger—he had one hand wrapped around each thigh. Oh god, it was his tongue. And since it wasn't his tongue teasing her clit, or his fingers, it had to be his nose. How could he breathe? If she got too enthusiastic, as she always did with his mouth between her legs, she'd suffocate him. She tried backing away, but he clamped down on her legs and bore deeper. Insistent. Relentlessly pushing her toward climax. She grabbed the sides of the table and let him have it.

He came up smiling. Not the usual, hot-stud smile. More like the amused kind. "Why'd you tell me to breathe?"

"Oh god, I said that out loud?"

"Twice."

Oops. Escaped internal thought. "Well, you had your whole face jammed in there. Imagine the headline in the newspaper if I'd suffocated you with my cootchie... Veterinarian Killed by Pussy."

"I can only think of one better way to go." The chair got righted and under him in two seconds. "C'mere, killer. Ride me."

Every room now had a stash of condoms. Some had multiple stashes. Her waiting stallion raised his eyebrows as she scooped a foil package from the bottom of the dishtowel basket. "Last night, without the condom, was..." She refused to call it a mistake.

"My fault.

"A mutual lapse in good judgment."

He slung one arm over the back of the chair, making his muscles flex and dance. "Last night was fucking incredible." He wrapped the other hand around his cock and started strumming. Bad boy, he knew that would flip her nympho switch.

"It was. It really was." Autopilot had placed her over him, straddling his lap.

His fingers snuck under the long t-shirt. "My shit judgment wants me to corrupt you again."

Her pitiful resolve deteriorated more with each teasing stroke along her slit. "Mason..." Oh god, now he was finger-fucking her. And looking up at her with those devastating eyes. Caving really seemed like the way to go.

"I'll pull out." He caressed her hips, her ass, a physical plea to go with his words.

"You'll try, but it'll feel so good I won't let you go... and I could end up... pregnant." The word had sounded a lot more romantic in her silent fantasy.

"Yeah." His big hand closed around hers. Squeezed lightly before taking the condom package. "We don't want that."

Chapter Twelve

As Saturday mornings went, it was brutally slow. Only three appointments booked between ten and twelve, and the middle one hadn't shown. He'd checked email, read a few sports blogs. Played a stupid video game on his phone. A couple of times he'd almost texted Katie, but stopped short of hitting send. He needed someone with balls to bounce this shit off of.

"Hey, man," Logan said, stepping into his office. "Where's your crazy guard-bimbo today, getting her roots bleached?"

"Day off, thank god. It's as if she's got eight hands lately, and all of them want in my pants."

"You got it rough, doc. Busty blonde chasing you at work, hot girlfriend after hours…" Logan straddled a steno chair and crossed his arms on the backrest. "Or are you a minus one in the girlfriend department after last night's ball game freeze out?"

Yeah, he'd acted like quite the dick. Not a proud moment. "I convinced her to keep me around."

Logan grunted his understanding. "Good. Katie'd be pissed if you screwed up her wedding dress plans. And I don't like when she's pissed at the outside world. Messes with our personal time."

Meaning her focus drifted from Logan, her Master. Mason still had trouble wrapping his head around Katie, his spitfire of a sister, living as a submissive behind closed doors. But she was happily in love, and Logan felt the same, but from the top. So whatever.

"I told Andie I love her."

"No shit," Logan said on a laugh. "That's all right."

"You think? It's only been a couple of weeks. And with her being older, having a kid...am I fucking crazy even considering getting serious?"

"Truth?"

"That's why I called you. I just need to bounce this shit off somebody who'll tell me how they see it, not what they think I want to hear. If I wanted sugar coating, I'd have called my sister."

"All right," Logan said, rubbing a hand over his usual scruff. "I think you won't know 'til you meet her kid. He might hate you, make your life a living hell. Or, maybe he's a little shithead and you'll want to pummel him. I think that'd kill the love pretty fast."

Good points. In Mason's head, he'd already decided Andie's boy was awesome and that they'd get along great, but who knew? "Yeah. But let's say it's all good with the kid."

"Remember, you asked for this." Logan rolled back from Mason's desk, out of reach. "She's got ten years on you. Ten. She looks great now, but what about five, ten or twenty years down the road. Have you checked out any fifty- or sixty-year-old women lately? It's mostly scary, saggy shit. Look at your mom, man. Nice lady, but I'm betting your dad keeps the lights off."

"First, that's disgusting. Second, I'm not some TV show vampire, I won't be thirty forever. When Andie's sixty—and still hot," he chucked a pen at Logan, who deflected it with a thick forearm, "I'll be fifty. Nobody'll give a crap about the ten years then."

"And now, or a couple years from now, what about kids?"

"Don't know."

"You don't know if you want them, or if she does?"

"Yeah." Mason kept the answer vague. No need to rehash the past—Logan knew how excited Mason had been about Stacey's accidental pregnancy. How low he'd been when it ended. A family was definitely part of his future plans. He'd just forced the subject to the back of his mind for the past few years.

"Man, you might want to squeeze some talking in with the balling. From where I'm sitting, you're in love with her magic pussy. Nothing wrong with that kind of love, either, and it doesn't require you meet her kid." Logan pushed up from the chair. "I'm gone, unless you need some advice in the pussy department too?"

"Get gone, Brenner. And thanks."

"Anytime, brother."

"Hey, one more thing," Mason said as Logan approached the door. "Katie's gonna look just like her mother one day... I hope you enjoy fucking with the lights off."

The truck pulled in at half past twelve. As soon as Mason stepped out onto the asphalt, butterflies flew into action in Andie's stomach. Likewise, her heart rate kicked up a few notches. She backed away from the window before he spotted her. Added a quick swipe of lip gloss and waited.

"I'm home," he called from the entryway.

Wow, she liked the sound of that. Too much. "In here, with your lunch."

"Smells gr—wow. Nice… apron."

She ran her fingers under the straps at the top of her bare breasts. "It's yours." Electricity sparked through her body as his eyes ate her up, head to high-heeled toes and back again.

"Damn right it is." The bulge in his jeans told her he wasn't referring to the apron.

She turned her back to him and bent to retrieve the chicken from the oven. Mason appreciated her whole body, but at the core, she knew he was an ass man. The view she was giving him, thrusting her ass upward and sporting the world's tiniest black thong, elicited a testosterone-fueled groan.

"Sounds as though you're starving," she said as she straightened.

"I am, and I don't know what to eat first." He stepped forward and started with her neck, sweeping her hair aside and nibble-kissing his way down the side. His mouth followed her spine, past the apron ties at her waist, right down the valley of her ass. "Think I'm gonna go with dessert. Hands on the sink and bend over."

"Yes sir." He groaned again as she assumed the position, legs spread, hips rotating in a figure eight. "Anything else, sir?"

"Look out the window, to your left. The Martins are out front weeding their garden. Make sure they know when you come."

She glanced out. Yup, there they were. A couple, late twenties to early thirties, crouched on the grass, definitely within earshot. And they were dead silent. No music playing, zero conversation happening. Neither of them looking thrilled with their activity. With the kitchen screen wide open, they'd hear anything louder or more distinctive than a normal speaking voice. Oh god.

A smack landed across her ass. She looked over her shoulder in time to see him deliver another. The heat spread from her backside, swirling low in her abdomen and stretching up to her nipples. She'd started the game by addressing him as sir. Now he expected her to answer, to comply. But playing the brat was so much better.

"No, I don't want them to hear me." To be extra rebellious, she reached to close the inner slider. His hand closed around her wrist immediately. If anybody else grabbed her this firmly, she'd cry out or hoof them, maybe both. Mason doing it just made her more eager for what was to come.

He guided her hand back to the stainless steel. Brushed the denim-covered ridge of his cock against her ass while he breathed in her ear. "They're either gonna hear you through this window or the front storm door. And if I take you there, it'll be with your naked body pressed up against the glass for their viewing pleasure."

Forget about remote control panties, Mason had her primed to explode with a simple touch and a few select suggestions. He knew a dozen different ways to turn her on. Right now he was using a few of the big ones to great effect.

"I promise to be loud for you... sir."

A chuckle tickled her ear. He stretched, tipped the basket of dishrags and dug through the pile for a condom. "Yeah, I'm gonna make sure of that." The scrub top came off, then the jeans and boxer briefs. This time, he even removed his socks. He sat his naked butt on the cool tile, wedged himself sideways between her legs and grinned up at her.

That smile was equal parts bad boy and genuine affection. It zinged her. She pinched her eyes shut to banish the gooey thoughts. Focused on his fingers sliding the teeny, tiny thong to one side. The parting of her folds as the pleasure began.

"Open your eyes. Watch me tasting you."

The view from this angle was beyond erotic. "I wish I could record this... I'd watch it every time I want to get myself off."

He stopped to chuckle lightly. "You're the only female porn-a-holic I've ever heard of."

"I'm comfortable with my addiction."

"Me too." He went back to work, lapping at her with long, broad strokes. Her clit got extra attention from the tip of his tongue, pitching her closer to the edge. When she could've tipped over, he eased off. Covered her with his lips and sucked, intentionally keeping her from coming. His eyes, dark and expectant, stayed locked on hers. This man loved giving oral, and he was in no hurry. Especially since she wasn't obeying his command. He'd torture her as long as it took and love every minute of it.

So good, the pressure, the spiral tugging at her clit. "I want to come... please, I need to come..." She said the words louder than necessary. Much louder. Mason's growl against her flesh told her he was pleased. Tremors shook her legs, the muscles straining with tension. He wrapped his right arm around one thigh. Extended the left up, over her ass, to the small of her back, supporting her weight while urging her down, onto his face. Yes, that's exactly what she needed. "Oh god... right there... harder... more, more... oh god, yessss..."

She'd closed her eyes at the end—it was impossible not to—and now that they were open again, she had a view of the front yard. The neighbors were on their feet. The guy had his hands on his wife's hips with his groin tight to her backside, whispering in her ear. And they were looking this way. Oh, they'd heard, all right.

"Good girl," Mason said, now standing behind her. "I've lived here over a year. Those two are always miserable around each other, but look at them now. Your sexy noises turned them on, babe."

"Does that make me a porn star, or a marriage counselor?" She laughed, then shivered from his kiss on the erogenous spot behind her ear.

"It makes you my porn star." Two tugs later, the apron fell away. He cupped her breasts, rolled the nipples between his fingers. Let his right hand cruise lower and nestle between her legs. "It's crazy how much I need you after only a few hours."

Need. He'd said need, not want. She swallowed a mouthful of sappy words better left in her head. "Then I'm crazy too. Take me to the bedroom."

He swung her into the cradle of his arms. "Anything you want."

The walk to his room was short, but he took it slow. Used those seconds to capture her lower lip, then turn that gentle nipping into a sensual kiss. One that continued as he wrangled them into position on top of the bed.

With his sexy smoothness, he'd hitched her thigh over his hip and angled his cock between her legs. He rocked against her, bumping her clit through the thin strip of black satin with each forward motion. Hands slithered everywhere. He softly traced the side of her body, past the dip of her waist, around the curves of her ass, pulling her closer. Her grip was firmer, along the line of his shoulder, splaying across the solid expanse of his back. His tongue slid alongside hers in perfect rhythm. And her heart—it threatened to leap up her throat and bare all her impossible feelings. Pointless things she needed to keep inside.

"Anything I want, you said?" After his smile, she rolled away, waved her ass in his face. Bull, meet red flag. "This is what I want."

"Damn, it's my lucky day, that's what I want too." All of his muscles rippled as he stretched toward the bedside table for a condom. Since he caught her ogling, he paused to flex a few. Six-pack of abs first, then the biceps as hard and round as five-pin bowling balls.

"Very nice." So was his ridiculously sexy grin. "Want to do a naked pose down for me?"

"Sure, if you oil me up first."

"That could get messy."

"And slippery," he said, sliding his hand between her thighs.

The screaming orgasm from ten minutes ago meant nothing to her body. Heat curled low in her abdomen. Her thighs quivered, wanting him between them any and every way possible. "Direct me to the oil."

"Kitchen. Cupboard to the left of the stove."

"You want me to rub you down with vegetable oil?"

"I was thinking up, not down." To demonstrate his point, he began stroking his cock.

Having sex with Mason was like erotic truth or dare, minus the truth part. He seemed to take great pleasure in testing her boundaries. She certainly enjoyed proving how far she'd go.

Currently, that was to the kitchen and back. "On your feet, beefcake." He flexed and stretched while getting off the bed. "Yes, yes, you're pretty. Save the show for after I grease you."

"Don't forget to grease the monkey," he said, tap-tapping her belly with the monkey.

"I'd rather watch you grease it." Again with the familiar tingling between her legs. She swallowed hard, met his eyes. Dare time. "Can I? Will you let me watch you sometime?"

"You've seen me stroke myself lots of times. Like now..." Each pull brought his hand against her naked body.

"You know what I mean. I want to sit at your feet and watch you finish the job."

His eyes got darker, his smile more mischievous. "There'd be conditions."

"Yes to all."

He laughed, a sexy, low sound that turned her nipples diamond hard. "An automatic yes, without hearing what I want?"

"And here I thought you knew me..." She squirted a dollop of sunflower oil into her palm. A brisk rub warmed it between her hands before she flattened them on his chest. That's where they stayed. Mason circled each wrist, preventing her from slicking him up—or down. The dirty-boy smile downgraded to something one step above a straight line. Her stomach did an uncomfortable twist, even though the hard ridge of his cock remained pressed against her belly. At least she hadn't killed his hard-on like she'd somehow killed his playful mood.

"I want to."

"To jerk off for me?" she asked tentatively, but he shook his head.

"To know you. All of you."

"You already do. Intimately. Better than anybody ever has in that department."

"I'm interested in your other departments too."

"The rest is so... serious."

"I'm up for serious."

"But it's only been a couple of weeks." What the hell was she doing, trying to talk him out of liking her too much?

"Guess I should have checked the relationship playbook. What's the requisite amount of time to put in before starting to fall in love with someone?"

Oh god. He said it. Well, he almost said it—close enough, anyway. And not while under the effect of orgasmic pheromones. "Around six months, though the process can be accelerated by incidents involving rogue fastballs."

"Love at first strike."

"That'd be a great movie title for a romantic comedy. Not very realistic, though."

"Ouch, cynical."

"Rational. I've accepted that happily ever after doesn't exist. The average marriage is hanging at around eleven years. Forget about the 'til death do us part, unless one of the spouses murders the other."

A smile tugged at the corner of his mouth. Despite his obvious attempt to hold it back, it still showed in his eyes. "How'd we get from me telling you I'm falling in love with you, to you informing me we'll never need a double plot at the cemetery?"

Heat spread across her cheeks. "How'd we get from me slicking you up with oil so we can have slippery, doggy-style sex, to talking about…about…love stuff?" He tossed his head back and whooped until he turned a shade of red that probably mirrored hers. If he wasn't holding her in place, she'd stomp her bare feet out of there.

He recovered himself and looked down at her. "I've never been with anyone like you."

"Old and jaded?" That comment earned her a scolding headshake.

"A woman who'd rather fuck than talk."

"Sex has a happy ending. Talking, on the other hand…" She wrenched her hands free so she could throw them up in the air. Wave them around in front of his face. "Does this to people."

"Babe, I think it just does that to you."

Yup, he was still calm, cool, sexy and in full control of his extremities. She returned to the bed with a flop and a sigh. "I have issues."

He propped alongside, looking down and making no attempt to hide his amusement. "Yeah, I got that."

"Bet you're rethinking that request to know me better."

"Nah." The grin turned softer, sweeter. His index finger moved randomly over her body. Or not so randomly. He was connecting the dots again, working his relaxation magic. The trail ended at the mole under her jawline. His next stop was her hair, fanning it out on the navy-blue comforter, then sifting his fingers through it. Another of her favorite things. "Better now?"

"You know I am. Every time you do that, it's as if you're the Andie-whisperer."

"See, knowing stuff is good." He leaned over, close enough to kiss her, but didn't. "I know some other things too."

Ooh, she liked where this was going. "Such as?"

"You hate all the shortcuts people use in texts."

"I never told you that." A fact that didn't make it untrue. She refused to dumb down perfectly good words for the sake of convenience. Texts from Lasha hurt her brain, they carved the English language so badly. Not Mason's, though. The man could spell and he wasn't afraid to use long words in his messages. Double penetration, for example.

"You brush your teeth when you get up in the middle of the night."

How did he know that? She used a regular toothbrush, not the powered one, and she closed the door. A weird habit, yes, but sleep-mouth felt so disgusting, and the breath that went with it... not appetizing.

He didn't ask for confirmation, just grinned. Then closed her gaping mouth by inviting it to join with his in a steamy tangle of tongues.

"Here's one more thing I know..." He leaned over the edge of the bed. The lid on the bottle clicked and snapped. He nudged her onto her stomach, straddling the backs of her thighs. Strong, warm palms slid effortlessly over her back. His well-oiled hands wasted no time working lower to massage the curves of her ass. One hand dipped into the valley, rubbing the sweet spot at the base of her tailbone before venturing lower to a much spicier spot. His other hand teased the crease where the meat of her ass-cheek joined the leg. Ever so slowly, he let those fingers wander into the needy zone between her legs.

The dual assault had her writhing and moaning. One second she wanted to grind down on the hand teasing her clit—the next she wanted to thrust her hips higher to better enjoy his fingers rimming her ass. Much more of this and she'd hyperventilate instead of coming.

She angled her head for a better view of the sexy man driving her crazy. Every visible inch of him was taut and focused. On her. His eyes flicked up to meet hers. Hunger burned in his gaze, but more than that. All of the feelings he'd claimed were right there, clear as the blues looking back at her. He didn't need to say a word.

"I need you inside me. Right now."

"On it," he said, stretching to snag a condom from under the pillow. Seconds later he knelt behind her again. Hands on her hips, he thrust inside, then stilled. "Shit, this is gonna be fast."

"In that case, get out." She wiggled forward, almost fully dislodging him.

"Seriously?"

"Yes." Poor guy, he actually groaned when he pulled out. But she planned to make it up to him. "Mason…"

"Yeah?"

Face half-pressed to the blanket, she smiled up at him. Reached around and caressed her oil-slicked skin. First, with her palms, then by dragging her nails across the round mounds of flesh. "Do you like this?"

His eyes tracked her movements while his hand milked his cock. "You've got a great ass."

"Do you like it when I do this?" She slid one hand down the valley and massaged the ring with her middle finger.

"Fuck. You know I do." More cursing followed when she snuck the tip inside. He barely stifled a moan when she added another finger all the way to the first knuckle.

"Mason…"

"Yeah?" Poor guy could barely choke out the word.

"Get the oil and my toy box." The bed shook from his hasty retreat and return. "I'll take the little purple one… yes, that one… for the front." She smiled at him as he handed her the pint-sized device. "As for the back… it's all yours."

The tortured desperation vanished from Mason's face, replaced by a wicked glint in his eyes and a lust-filled smile. He squirted oil into his left palm and dragged his right fingertips through it.

"My turn," he said, drizzling the oil over her body. He smoothed it with practiced expertise, using circles to tease her until she writhed in anticipation. The head of his cock pressed against her at last, rocking, stretching her. Breaching her bit by bit with slow, determined strokes.

She clicked on the vibrator and touched it to her clit. Instant relaxation. Instant need to come.

"Babe," he groaned as he gained deeper access. "You're so tight. So…fuck…hot. I need to be…" A couple adjustments and her legs were between his, straight and nearly flat to the bed. The angle perfected, he pushed farther, until his hips pressed up against the meaty part of her ass. All the way inside. "Jesus, Andie…"

Her breath caught as he moved inside her.

He stopped, brushed wisps of hair from her ear to tickle it with his deep, leathery voice. "You okay? Is this too much?"

"God, no…keep going…deeper, it feels sooo good when you're deep." The strokes got longer, easier. Faster. The spiral of need between her legs built each time he thrust, with each flicker of vibration across her clit. Guttural, raw moaning filled the room—mostly hers, some his—each time he stroked into her with his full length. None of her toys came close to the sensation of Mason's cock filling her ass. "Oh god, that's so good…"

"You're gonna make me come with those sounds." He caught her earlobe between his teeth. Nibbled it while breathing hot and hard on her neck.

Every cell in her body wanted to come with him. "Do it…" She tipped over instantly, bombarded by the urgent, tingling need radiating inside and out, front and back.

He hollered her name and a string of beautiful curses, then collapsed on her back, huffing as if he'd run ten miles, uphill.

Together they made one sweaty, greasy heap of satisfaction.

"You were right," she said between breaths. "Knowing stuff about each other is good."

"That it is, babe." He laughed, then kissed her thoroughly before rolling away to take care of business.

She didn't try to hide the giddy smile. Yes, he knew how to turn her on, how to make her frantic with need, and how to satisfy her in ways she'd never thought possible. Maybe…he'd be able to make her believe in love again too.

Chapter Thirteen

"So much for our lunch."

Mason looked from the demolished casserole to the cat, then to Andie. The guilty feline sat on a kitchen chair, serenely cleaning his face. Andie stood, hands on her hips, glaring at the furry glutton.

"Looks like Hugo enjoyed it." The glare turned on him. Shit, wrong thing to say. "I bet there's enough left for a couple of small servings if we," he poked at it with a fork, "scrape away the parts with the gnaw marks."

"Not helping."

With that combination of fire in her eyes and sex-mussed everything else, she was adorable. He wrapped his arms around her waist from behind and bent his head to her ear. "I'd give up any meal for what we just did." Less than ten minutes ago he'd had her every which way and come like a fucking volcano, and already his cock perked up at the mere mention. "I'd live on bread and water if it meant fucking you that way every day."

"Okay, that's helping," she said, sounding a little breathless.

"I wanted to take you out this afternoon anyway, so we'll start with lunch on the way. Go get ready." He released her with a light smack on her silky robe-covered ass. "Put on the red dress I packed for you." She stiffened, stared up at him, unmoving as the seconds ticked by. "Babe, you okay?"

"You're telling me what to wear."

"I like you in red." Such as that red bra and panties she'd had on last night, or the red sexy-as-hell shoes. "Yeah, definitely wear the red dress." Her hair called to him, so he twirled a section of it around his finger. Soft and silky. If he got closer, it'd smell fresh as a spring day, like it always did. "And leave your hair down." Easy access while they were out and about. Her expression whenever he played with her hair made him feel like king of the world.

The glare she gave him as she pushed his hand away, not so much. What the fuck…? Chin in the air, she huffed out of the room. Shut his bedroom door with enough gusto to rattle the house. Apparently slamming doors when pissed was Andie's thing. Could be worse. It'd sure be nice to know what had set her off, though. Women.

Some of the chicken was salvageable. He dealt with the casserole, left the dish for Hugo and took his chances knocking on the bedroom door. "Can I come in?"

"It's your house."

He grunted. She'd sure treated it like her own when the mystery tantrum came on. He turned the knob and found her standing by his bed, hands on those curvy hips, toe tapping on the hardwood. Call him fucked-up, but her fiery stance did it for him. Act on it, though? He wasn't that stupid.

Her eyes followed every step as he moved around the room. Burned a hole through him would be more accurate. He dared to smile at her while throwing on some clothes. No return on that investment.

"You chose the purple dress," he said, stopping in front of her.

The hand he offered got a disgusted glance, one that quickly moved to his face. "And I put my hair up."

"I noticed." Aside from a few wavy escapees at the back, her neck was bare. Long and sexy, begging to be stroked and kissed. Or bitten. Like while he bent her over the bed, slippery dress pushed to the waist so he could fuck her hard and in a hurry.

"That's it? You're not going to say anything else?"

Shit. Dumbass, standing here with his tongue hanging out instead of complimenting the lady. "Yeah, I am. You distracted me, that's all."

"By going against your wishes."

"By looking fucking incredible. I knew I liked that dress when I saw it in your closet, but seeing it on you is like winning the lottery. The way it shows off your nice little waist, your sexy legs... I want to put my hands all over you, lick every inch of you, starting with your beautiful, sweet-smelling neck—which is what I was thinking about a minute ago."

Her bottom lip fell open. The bracelets on her wrist jingled as her hands dropped to her sides. "You're not mad?"

"No. Should I be?" Technically, scientifically, he knew how the brain worked. But understanding women's thought processes... no clue.

"Scott would've been," she whispered, focusing on the group of metal bangles on her right wrist. "He insisted on choosing what I wore outside the house. Pretty much always. I hated the stuff he bought for me." She spun the bracelets a few more times. When she met his eyes, hers were full of tension. "I resent being dressed like some mindless doll."

Andie, voluntarily opening up to him...hell must've frozen over. He finally had her talking, yet he couldn't think of a single right thing to say in return. Shit.

"So I freaked out a little when you told me what to wear." Her head jerked to one side in a nervous shrug.

He captured one soft hand and brought it to his lips. He could've reassured her that he wasn't like her ex, but that wasn't really the problem. Everybody had hot-buttons—he sure as hell did—and now that he knew one of hers, he'd try not to trip it. Part of him did want to point out that she'd bought everything he stuffed in her weekend bag, but he kept his mouth zipped on that one.

"Thank you," seemed like a wiser choice.

"For what? Being a psycho bitch with issues?"

"For sharing why you acted like one."

"Jerk," she said, halfheartedly trying to regain possession of her hand.

From the smile on her face and in her voice, he'd said exactly the right thing.

After watching Andie's nipples press against the clingy purple dress during lunch, Mason had almost ditched their afternoon plans so he could take her home to bed. Instead, he'd summoned his last speck of willpower and hit the highway. Then, on the way to St. Jacob's, she'd slid into the middle spot so she could snuggle up beside him. That'd led to his discovery that she'd omitted panties. He'd been this close to turning the truck around.

It wasn't the first time she'd gone commando around him. It didn't matter that he'd fucked her twice today already, and very well at that. Following her up the stairs now, watching that ass sway and knowing explicitly what treasures were bare beneath the thin, single layer of material... his head was crowded with images. And his shorts were crowded with a non-stop, raging hard-on.

The market's mezzanine area was packed with people, forcing him closer. No more visual appreciation of her body, but direct contact suited him fine too. When she tilted her head to smile up at him, he caught her lips for a kiss.

"My breath has to be horrible after everything we sampled downstairs," she said after cutting it short.

"I only taste you."

"I have a flavor?"

"Yeah, Andielicious."

"God, you're smooth." The tone of her voice might be sarcastic, but her pretty smile lit her whole face. "It's congested and stifling up here. Want to go back down, walk around outside?"

"There's one place I have to hit first. Pawprints something or other. Then we'll get out of here."

Once Andie got a glimpse of all the shops, the elbow-to-elbow crush of bodies didn't seem to faze her anymore. She squeezed between people and pillars to reach the booths that caught her eye. Pottery, pillows, stained glass. Through it all, she kept her fingers laced with his. The crowd meant staying tight behind her, the perfect place for soaking in the naturally sweet smell of her skin.

He whispered in her ear, some things innocent, others, not so much. *She's mine*, the actions said to anyone watching. Given Andie's natural beauty and shapely figure, that was a lot. Let them look. When he caught guys checking her out, his chest swelled to what felt like twice its normal size. They could ogle her all they wanted—Andie belonged to him.

"This must be it." He nudged her toward one of the larger booths, stocked floor to ceiling with brightly colored clothing. Miniature clothing.

She looked up at the hand-painted wooden sign. "Pawprints Clothing Company. When you said paw prints, I thought you meant pet products for the clinic."

"Yeah, weird name. Shopping for the clinic would be easier. No, one of my buddies has a boy turning one. Apparently his wife loves this stuff and you can only get it here." The salesgirl smiled at him, so he nodded, then pulled his girl into a proper hug. "Help me pick something, since the gift'll be from both of us."

The nod wasn't enough to keep the young blonde clerk at bay, and she promptly floated over and hit them up with a pitch about quality and uniqueness, yada, yada, yada.

"And if you're looking for the newborn items, they're mixed in the racks by style, rather than being grouped by size. Most of our things are unisex, though we do have a few gender-specific fabrics if you know what you're having."

Mason kept his arm tight around Andie, who looked as if she'd been caught on one of those practical joke-type reality shows. "Thanks, but we're shopping for a one-year-old, not a newborn, and not ours."

"Oh—oh gosh, I'm sorry." The girl's fair skin turned solid pink. "I assumed you were expecting…" At Andie's wide eyes, the pink changed to beet red. "Oh no, that didn't come out right. You don't look pregnant at all, it's just that you're obviously in love and you're practically glowing, I thought you must be in your first trimester and… I'm going to sit over there behind the counter and hide until you need some help with sizes or patterns." Walking away, she shook her head and mumbled something about how her boss was going to kill her.

Mason glanced around at what had to be hundreds of little outfits. "So, what do you think?"

"About having a baby?"

Whoa. Not the question he'd been asking. Still, this was a perfect opportunity to find out where she stood on having more kids. Specifically, with him. "Yeah."

She fingered through a rack of puppy- and kitten-printed overalls, pausing at a tiny pair. "I'd love another child. I always wanted more, but..." She didn't look at him while answering. For the first time since arriving at the farmer's market, she let go of his hand and moved away.

No psychology degree needed to read between those lines. The more Mason learned about Scott, the less respect he had for the guy. Anybody who'd let Andie down in such a huge way deserved divorce papers. The day would come when they'd meet, he and Scott Finch. Not punching the fuckwad in the face was going to take effort.

For now, he shelved the baby conversation. They'd pick it up another time, privately. "What do you think of this stuff, see anything good for a rowdy one-year-old who eats sand and dog kibble?" he asked, joining her in front of a bunch of clothes displayed on an oversized wooden crate.

"Plenty." Her smile returned. Smaller than before, but better than nothing. "Something with dogs on it, you think? An appropriate gift from the best vet in town."

"And his girlfriend. Grab a couple of things so I can pay and we can get out of here."

"So we can pay. If it's from both of us..."

"You do the choosing and the wrapping. I'm paying." Shit, she had her feisty face brewing. "This time, babe. By the next party you'll know Josh and Jane and both their wild things better than you'll ever want to. You can chip in for that one, if you want to."

Apparently appeased, she shifted her attention to the clothes. "How old is their other child, should we pick up that present while we're here?"

"Nah, we'll come back another time." Like next May, a week before that party rolled around.

"Anything to get out of here faster, right?" A couple of minutes later, she held up two hangers. "These okay?"

"Great."

"You didn't even look at them." She laughed as he snagged them with one finger.

"Nope. I'm a guy."

"Try a six-foot tower of solid testosterone."

"Yeah?" He dropped Andie's picks on the counter with a credit card on top. "What are the other two inches made of?" The blushing clerk kept her head down while tallying their receipt. Unlikely she was missing a beat of his conversation with Andie, though, or the fact that he was caressing Andie's incredible ass through the clingy dress.

Her hand snuck under his t-shirt. The long, perfect fingernails crossing his stomach made him shudder. "Cream and sugar, of course."

A squeak slipped out of the salesgirl. Her eyes flitted everywhere except directly on them as she handed over his card and the bag. "Thank you, and uh, sorry if I offended either of you before...but you're absolutely the sweetest couple to ever come in here."

To hell with courtesy. He draped his arm over Andie's shoulders and pulled her alongside him as they hit the aisle way again, smiling down at her when she slid her arm around his waist. Exactly how it should be.

"That's a bad-boy grin."

"I was thinking that the salesgirl back there wouldn't call us sweet if she knew the things I did to you a couple of hours ago."

"I don't know... I came three times. That was pretty sweet."

"Three? I thought it was only twice."

She pulled him inside a booth filled with leatherwork. "Two and three sort of ran together. You were, um..." She glanced at the shopkeeper, then back to him. "Enthusiastically distracted at that point."

"Understatement of the year, babe." Yeah, he'd never forget that part. Fucking her oil-slicked ass from behind while she used a vibrator on her clit... it was a miracle he'd had awareness at all. "I'm getting lightheaded thinking about it."

Six feet or so away from the guy working the booth, Andie stuck her free hand inside the front of his shorts. Copped a giant, lingering feel. "That's because all of your blood has gone to your cock, honey."

Honey? She'd never called him anything like that. Whatever the reason, she could do it again, anytime. Ditto with the way she continued to surprise him. "You keep your hand down there much longer, I'm gonna buy a few of these sheepskins and take you out to my truck."

The man buzzing away at his crazy-looking sewing machine didn't look up, but snorted openly. "For you two, no tax. Oh, and they're machine washable, which might come in handy."

"Good to know, thanks." Albeit unnecessary, since Andie'd already removed her hand and moved off to look at a shelf of moccasins and sheepskin slippers. Not her usual type of footwear. "Moving to Nunavut?"

"It's the sewing. My feet become blocks of ice when I work for hours at a stretch, even in summer." She paused with her hand on his elbow, halfway through the process of slipping off her sexy sandals. "Do you think it's okay for me to try them on with bare feet?"

"Ask."

"I can't talk to him now. Not after..." Her face went from sun-bronzed to deep pink. "Will you ask?"

"Anything for you." Those three words were becoming reflex. Every time he said them, he might as well have been saying the other three words, because they meant the same thing.

The blush receded from Andie's face when the man chose to speak to them from behind his equipment. In the end, she had two pairs in her hands. Purple slippers bursting with white fuzz—those he could see her wearing. The boring, brown mocs, not so much.

"For Dylan," she said, answering his unasked question.

Of course. The kid was twelve. Twelve-year-old boys had adult-sized feet. They shopped in the men's section, ate a ton of food and if memory served, got the sheets sticky on occasion.

Twelve. Almost a teenager. Shit, it'd been so easy to forget that since he'd gone up north with his dad. Not to forget about Dylan himself. Andie talked about her son often, spoke to him on the phone every day. She'd made no attempt to hide that part of her life or its importance. A couple of times, while she'd been chatting away to the boy, Mason had gotten this picture in his head. What it might be like, hanging out with Andie and her boy, doing normal, family-type stuff. But in those imagined scenarios, Dylan was smaller, younger. Like six or seven. It was the age part Mason had forgotten. Or blocked out.

"Nothing for the big man of the house today?"

Instantly red-faced again, Andie began stammering an explanation at the vendor as he bagged her purchases.

"I'm good," Mason cut in, "but if you have another pair of the fuzzy ones in my beautiful lady's size, I'll take them, in r—" Shit. He almost told the guy what color to get. At least he'd stopped in time instead of nicking her old wounds again. "Is there another color you like, babe?"

"Red." The appreciative smile she gave him shot straight to his heart. "I like the red ones."

He wanted to kiss her so damn bad. Soon. He swallowed hard and nodded at the shopkeeper. "Red, if you've got it."

The man winked and left them to rummage through his stock.

"Why?"

"To keep at my house. The floors are damn cold in the winter."

"Mason… winter's at least three months away."

"Yeah. And?" The requested goods appeared on the desk in front of them. He slapped a bunch of twenties on top as payment. "You planning to dump me before the snow flies?" Even the salesman paused to hear her answer.

"Not if you're buying me these wonderful ruby slippers, no."

Most of the booths had closed for the day by the time they loaded a heap of bags into the backseat and hopped in the front of the truck. "The woman working the jewelry booth said the stores in the village are open later."

"Would you be disappointed if we skip it?"

"Hell no. I'd rather be home, with you all to myself." The smile she gave him was weak, and she followed it up by staring at the window while he drove. For ten long, silent minutes, her restless hands fiddled with her dress while she looked at the side of the expressway.

Then it clicked. "How about we go out dancing tonight? Or grab a bite and some drinks with friends?" Now that he had her attention again, he caught her hand and kissed each knuckle. "I've been monopolizing every minute of your free time. I don't mind sharing you... a little."

"You shouldn't have bought me the slippers."

Where the hell had that come from? Because he'd spent too much, or it was too practical to be romantic?

"It's not going to work out—us—being a real couple."

"Shit, is this the age thing again?"

"No, the single mom thing. You joke about sharing me with people, but after Dylan comes home, he's the one that'll have the monopoly. Our sleepovers, sexcapades, spontaneous day trips... they'll only be an option when he's at his dad's. This time we're spending together, it's a fairytale for me. But a week from now my coach is going to turn into a pumpkin, and all of this," she waved her hands around, "will cease to be my reality."

The steering wheel squeaked under his clenched grip. "You've got a pretty low opinion of me."

"What... I do not. I think you're amazing."

"To fuck. Or blow, or generally spread your legs for." Yeah, it was crude and cruel. Too bad. "But I'm not capable of standing next to you while you tolerate your ex, or participating in your day-to-day life." The jump from irritated to fully pissed off was a short one. "And I'm obviously nowhere near good enough to meet your son."

"Oh my god, you've got it all wrong. I just didn't think that you'd... when you could..." Her words came on sobs as she wiped at the corners of her eyes. "Why would you want to do any of those things?"

"Remember when I told you that I'm falling in love with you?" He took his eyes off the road long enough to see her nod. "Yeah, that's why."

"Okay," she said, and dug her cell out of her purse.

That's it? No apology, no kiss or cuddle? Not even a little stammering to show some remorse for judging him unfairly? He snorted. Of all the women he could've taken a header for, he'd found one who had shittier communication skills than he did. What were the odds?

"There." The phone went back into her bag. "I emailed Scott. You are officially my boyfriend. After Scott cross-examines you and I get clearance, I'll introduce you to Dylan."

Maybe it was inappropriate, but he grinned. He hadn't missed the hint of challenge in her voice. "Great. Looking forward to both of those meetings."

"I have no doubt that Dylan will like you. You're great, plus he's been pushing for me to…get a life, as he puts it." Up, down, up, down, went the zipper on her purse. "As for Scott…you can expect him to be a well-mannered asshole."

"I can deal with that. If the tables were turned, I'd be an ill-mannered asshole, to say the least."

She scooted over to the middle spot and leaned against his arm. "You're so sweet."

It took a sec for his brain to register the lack of sarcasm. He laughed so hard, actual tears almost rolled. "I say I'm falling in love with you—more than once—and you ignore it. I imply that I'd rough up any guy who had your affection when I didn't and you call me sweet. You're an unusual woman, Andie." His unusual woman. A fact he couldn't wait to rub in Scott Finch's lawyer-smug face.

Chapter Fourteen

"Mmm, that's nice..." Andie murmured when Mason's fingers glided from her shoulder to her wrist, making a small pit stop to circle her nipple. "A girl could get used to this kind of wakeup call." She shimmied closer to the hot mass of male behind her in the bed. Make that hard mass, or even more accurately, massively hard. She reached back to stroke his glorious erection. Now that was something she'd like to wake up to every morning.

His hand slid down to cup her sex, one finger testing and teasing. "How's this for a wakeup call?"

"Even better."

"Yeah? Let's try the third option."

She pouted audibly when he rolled away, making him chuckle. The nightstand drawer opened and closed. For a condom, obviously. They'd been vigilant since that one time. That one, mind-blowingly wonderful time when he moved inside her, skin-to-skin. The sheets crinkled as he slid between them again. His cock nestled against her ass. Her hips angled toward him involuntarily, a magnet to his steel. Awake less than five minutes and she was more than ready for him.

211

"Wake up, beautiful." He breathed the words in her ear as his arm wrapped over top of her. Low buzzing followed a soft click and his hand settled between her legs once more, this time with an accessory.

"Oh... I like option number three." She didn't need to see it to know what he'd chosen from her toy box. The curved, black unit had been her go-to favorite for a long time, with good reason. Perfect fit against her clit, perfect amount of vibrations. Mason holding it against her body just made it more so. He found her hot spot easily. Slid the magic little machine into place and maneuvered it like a pro, immediately taking her to the edge. "Somebody's been... ooh... taking notes..."

"Am I teacher's pet?"

"Yes..." Little bursts of color flashed behind her eyelids. Sweat dampened her skin, yet goose bumps struck out all over. The need to come tugged urgently at her clit. Almost there... the edge was so close and she desperately wanted to dive over. "Inside me. Now."

Fuck her right then he did, in one slick stroke.

"Sweet motherfucking Jesus."

He barely moved, but it didn't matter. The size of him, seated deep inside her—filling her, hitting that spot inside while he rocked the vibe back and forth across her hungry clit—was enough.

"Oh, god, that. That..." A swirling, tightening explosion hit inside and out. Merciless with the vibe, Mason held it against her body, forcing a second shuddering orgasm from her sensitive clit, leaving her squirming and barely able to catch her breath. He growled a mixture of curses and endearments while pushing deeper inside for his own release.

She grumbled softly when he pulled out soon after. Damn condoms. Watching him cross the room, though, not a bad thing. Honestly, he had the finest male butt she'd ever seen.

Sure, she hadn't seen many up close and for real, but she'd seen plenty in the sexy videos she liked to watch. Mason's backside beat them all, hands down.

"Mmm…I want to go back to sleep, so you can give me that wakeup call again."

"In that case, I'll go throw back a few energy drinks while I make breakfast."

"You spoil me. And you've got the best ass."

"Back at you, babe. On both counts."

She burrowed into the down pillows and warm sheets that smelled of Mason and sex. Spending a lazy Sunday in this bed with her now-official boyfriend—that was a plan she was on board with.

Her cell buzzed on the nightstand. Then again. A call, not a text or an email notification. At this time of day it could be only one of two people. She dragged herself to the edge of the bed and grabbed the phone. Scott's cell number lit the display, but please, please, let it be Dylan's voice on the other end of the call.

No such luck.

"I got your email," Scott said, skipping the basic courtesies of hello, and so on.

"Good to know."

"I think you're rushing things, And."

She grimaced at the shortening of her name. Bit her tongue and waited for the rest of the speech he'd likely practiced multiple times before making this call.

"Introducing our son to some man you're dating will force Dylan to give up hope of reconciliation for his family."

And there it was…the truth, veiled as concerned parenting. "Scott, we're legally divorced. We've been apart for two years. Dylan's old enough to understand what that

213

means…he isn't pining for us to get back together." She squeezed her eyes shut and tried for her kindest, most understanding voice. "You should stop waiting for that too."

Scott's end of the line stayed silent long enough that she almost asked if he was still there. But this was Scott, a man who used silence to its calculated effect on a daily basis. Not on her, though. Not anymore.

"We're cutting the cottage visit short," Scott said after enough time had passed to dry a coat of paint. "There are important cases requiring my attention at the office, so I'll be dropping Dylan at the house on Wednesday afternoon. Tell Mr. Lang I'll be contacting him directly once I'm back in town." Then it was dead air.

Nothing killed a blissful mood like interacting with Scott. Andie made her way to the kitchen, reaching it in time to see Mason—still naked, of course—scooping today's breakfast concoction onto two plates. Beautiful sunshine filled the room. Mason was whistling to some song in his head. He spotted her standing in the doorway and quit making music to give her one of his sexiest smiles. A little bit of the bliss squeaked its way back into the day.

"You've got cold feet already?"

"What…no, not at all. I just wish we had the full week to ourselves before you meet Dylan and we test drive our real-life relationship. God, I feel like the most selfish, worst mother in the world for saying that."

"Uh…" Mason's looked from her face to her feet. "I meant, you're wearing the sheepskin slippers…in July."

"Oh. Yes." That kind of cold feet. "I really like them, that's all."

"Good. I like seeing you wear them around here." He signaled her to the chair he'd pulled out. Poured their coffee, kissed the side of her neck, then sat next to her. "Now what the hell were you talking about?"

"Scott called. He's cutting this cottage trip short under the guise of work, but it's really his way of being pissy about the email."

"He doesn't want you getting some with another man."

"He didn't want me getting some when I was with him."

Mason nearly choked on his mouthful of food. "I can't wait to meet your ex."

"You can't say anything…"

A big, warm hand landed on top of her fidgety one. "Babe, I won't have to. It's a given. People talk shit about their exes."

"You don't." Aside from explaining his trust issues by telling her that his ex-fiancée lied about getting an abortion, Mason hadn't said two words about the woman, good or bad.

He shrugged. "Neither do you, not really. But, the right expression on my face and he'll think I know every complaint you ever had about him."

"Tempting, but not a good idea. He might… retaliate… and involve Dylan."

"Babe, don't worry." Strong fingers brushed her cheek softly. "Doctors can do blank faces as well as lawyers do."

"Thank you." If Scott thought Mason—or anybody—knew the intimate details of their marriage, he'd be infuriated. Maybe enough to become a jerk about Dylan. He could pull a few legal strings and take over primary custody… simply because he was embarrassed. A chance she couldn't take.

"You gonna eat those eggs, or just organize them into rows of bite-sized piles and drive your fork around them?" His plate was empty. The man was a pit, but she'd bet he wasn't really after her breakfast. Not by the tender smile that went all the way to his eyes.

Sure enough, she'd readied the food for easy feeding. An old habit brought to life by the recent rash of baby thoughts, most likely. "It's been years, but let's see if I've still got the knack." She loaded one pile onto her fork and steered it toward Mason's mouth. "Here it comes…open up for some nom-noms." Like a good baby, he took the offering. "Yup. Works every time."

He barely chewed before swallowing. Waggled his eyebrows and grinned. "Yeah? Then I'm using that line on you later."

"It only works if you use a cutsie-wootsie voice."

"No problem."

The trouble with issuing that challenge was the images it conjured up. Mason, engaged in a one-sided conversation with an adorable infant. The deep, leathery voice that made her tingle all over would work soothing magic on a baby. One with blue eyes, like both parents had. Bad train of thought, bad. Her ovaries were humming just thinking about it.

"Later, when you use that line… " She shook her head to clear the fantasy away. "Skip the baby talk part."

"You think I can't do it? I'm good with babies. Kids love me."

Oh god. So not helping with her ovary issue. They'd better double up on the condoms later. At this moment, her eggs were probably lying in wait, microscopic whips and handcuffs at the ready. Any escapee sperm didn't stand a chance.

"You'll see when we go to that birthday party next weekend," he said, clearly oblivious to the loud ticking coming from her biological clock.

She hugged herself below the waist, but it was pointless. Every cell in her reproductive system was on alert. National security had its code red. Baby lust came in code pink and blue.

"You okay?" He leaned closer and touched her face so, so sweetly.

"Yes." No. Make that a big, fat no. More accurately, a big, she-wished-she-was-fat-because-she-was-pregnant fat, with dill pickles dipped in Cheez Whiz, no. "I'm fine."

"You look kind of freaked out."

"Maybe I'm a little bit stressed."

"Because I'm meeting your ex, or Dylan? Don't be. I can handle Scott and I'll do whatever it takes to win your son's approval."

How had she managed to snag this amazing man, even temporarily? "I have no doubt about either of those things."

"Good." He smiled, and the room got brighter.

"And I'll try to relax." While she was at it, she'd try not to think about making babies and playing house.

"Even better." A kiss followed the smile, one that made her lightheaded to the point of almost tipping out of the chair. "I think you'd better finish those eggs before you pass out." He offered her the empty fork, taunting her by pulling it back when she reached for it. "Unless you'd rather I show you my excellent spoon-feeding abilities."

"No!" She snatched the utensil. Her eggs couldn't take that kind of demonstration.

Her arm swept across the other side of the bed Wednesday morning. Empty. And cold. As the sleepy fog dissipated, the memory returned. Mason's pager going off at an ungodly hour, his irritated cursing as he fumbled around in the dark for his phone. Then a softer curse as he slid out of bed to head for the clinic. An emergency call. Never a happy thing.

That had been around two-thirty in the morning. According to the clock finally coming into focus, that was nearly four hours ago. He was probably exhausted and starving. Not much she could do about the first issue. The second problem, though—she was all over that one.

His truck stood alone in front of the clinic. Normally, he parked out back. The clients with the emergency must've been waiting when he pulled in. And now they were gone.

The buzzer over the main door chirped when she pushed through it, but Mason didn't appear. Fluorescent lights hummed overhead, the sole noise in the building. No water running or equipment operating, no footsteps. Most notably, no animal sounds. More than a little foreboding. Her feet wanted to turn around and walk out the door.

The feet didn't win, she forced them to make their way to his office instead. The blinds were closed and the lights off. Only the glow from the computer screen lit the room. Mason's chair faced the monitor, but he wasn't working. He sat in a reclined position, arms folded behind his head, eyes closed. Good thing she hadn't called out to him from the reception area. She set the bag of food on the edge of his desk, cringing at the too-loud, synthetic crinkle. Right now, he needed sleep more than breakfast.

"Don't go." His voice stopped her withdrawal from the room as effectively as a physical restraint.

"Sorry, I didn't mean to disturb you."

"You didn't." Slowly, he swiveled to face her and patted his lap. "C'mere. I need you."

That kind of invitation usually worked like a match to dynamite, setting off one giant charge between her legs. Something about his tone made this different. The overwhelming pull was the same, just focused higher. She went to him. Eased onto his knee, only to be pulled higher, closer. Tighter, enough to make breathing difficult—and she let him.

He spoke with his face buried in her hair. "I wanted to call you so bad."

"Why didn't you?"

"You need your sleep."

"I need you more. Mason, I—" The words spilled out, evading her guard. An automatic response to his raw emotional state. But she reined her tongue before the last two words escaped. "I'm here for you, always."

"It was fucking horrible."

Anything that upset him this much, she didn't want to know. But for him, she was willing to hear it. "You want to talk about it?"

"I've seen a lot of cruelty, working at the shelters. Beatings, stabbings, worse shit than you could imagine. Never in my practice, though."

"Somebody hurt their pet then brought it in for treatment?"

"No, nothing like that. This was a calculated attack. Somebody coaxed their dog to ingest... objects. Probably fed them to her wrapped in pieces of meat or cheese. The x-ray was," he shook his head against her neck, "horrible. There was too much internal damage. Fuck. Fuck."

Andie's mouth went dry. The picture Mason painted stung the backs of her eyes as though she'd been right there to witness it firsthand. "What kind of monster would do such a thing?"

"They had a doggie door for while they were at work. Fenced yard, but chain link. Could've been anybody, so nobody'll get charged, but they have good reason to believe it was the neighbor. They'd had issues with him."

"So he killed their dog?"

"No, just tortured her until the injuries were irreparable. I'm the one who had to end her life. Hers and five unborn puppies."

"Oh, Mason…" What could she say to ease his burden? Nothing. All she could do was try to comfort and distract him. She brushed her lips along his ear, over his cheek, softly working lower, to his mouth.

At first, he sat back, accepting her kisses as the gentle caress she intended them to be. When her tongue dipped into his mouth, though, everything changed. His lips engaged hers. His tongue returned the favor, touching hers and igniting a fire low in her belly. Hands that had been still on her back roved lower. They slid under the elastic waistband of her yoga pants to cup her ass, to steal between her legs and stroke her with a slow intensity that sparked more than her compassion.

"I need you." His voice was low and husky, almost desperate.

"You have me. For anything you need. Everything. I'm yours."

"I don't have a condom."

"I don't care." The words tumbled out. Wrong or right, it was the truth. "Take what you need—I want you to."

His mouth found hers again, searing her to the core with soul-deep kisses. Hands fumbled with clothes. Metal jingled and cloth rumpled as her yoga pants hit the floor and his jeans were shoved down to the knee. The hard length of his cock teased her from beneath, sliding along her slit. An aching heat roared between her legs. He stroked again, the tip of his erection bumping her clit before retreating, only to repeat the torture again.

She shifted—in vain. He leaned forward in the office chair and maneuvered her legs around his waist. Cramped, but it'd work. All she had to do now was lift her hips and…god, yes… slide down, down, down his cock. His skin inside her skin. Hot, slick, perfect—it should always be this way.

He held her tight when she hit bottom. Rocked his hips upward while guiding her body into a slow, circular grind. "Come for me," he said with his lips still touching hers. "I need to feel it. To hear your noises. To see your face when you let go."

Oh god. She loved him. With her heart and soul, she loved him.

Buried to the balls, he moved inside her. Never withdrawing, just a slow rhythm that dragged her clit across his pelvis again and again. The first, soft wave of pleasure washed over her and she moaned against his mouth.

"You're so beautiful." He pulled her closer, as close as possible in their position, adding more sensuous friction exactly where she needed it. He pressed his lips to her neck, kissing, licking, nipping and murmuring. Naughty things. Sweet things.

She could barely breathe. Every inch of her skin sang as she writhed against him, stars—no, hearts—flashing behind her eyelids.

"Fuck… you feel too good…" His fingers dug into her hips, forcing her down and wide open. He groaned as his cock swelled, pulsing deep inside her. Shuddering, he wrapped his arms around her and pressed his forehead to hers. "Andie, I—"

"Shh, it's okay." She covered his lips with two fingers. "I told you to, I wanted you to."

He kissed the tips, then guided them away. "Not that. Well, that too, but first this…" He pulled back enough to look into her eyes. "I love you. I wanted to say it when I'm not fucking you, so you know I mean it when I say it while I am."

This was where she was supposed to say it back. And she wanted to. God, did she want to. Hints of sunlight crept around the blinds, giving light to the room. Enough to see his eyes clearly. The expectation there dimmed as she remained silent, despite opening her mouth several times. Here she was, impaled on the cock of a gorgeous, near-perfect man who'd just told her he loved her, and she couldn't get one out in return. What the hell was wrong with her?

"About the no condom..." Gently, he helped untangle her limbs from the chair. As soon as she withdrew from his lap, he pulled up his jeans and zipped.

The moment was past. Her opportunity—gone.

"If my irresponsibility gets you pregnant, I'll support you any way you want me to. All I ask is that you're honest with me."

"Mason, I... I..."

This time it was his fingers on her lips. "It's okay. It doesn't have to go both ways." The front door chirped, snapping both their attention to his open office door. "Might want to put your pants back on. I have to go take care of..." He rubbed his temples and shook his head. "I have to finish cleaning the operating room before our morning surgeries."

She threw her arms around his neck, clutching him as if her life depended on it. "You didn't eat anything and you've barely slept."

His arms closed around her—thank god—and he chuckled in her ear. "I'll eat soon, and I'll try to rearrange things so I can catch a nap at lunch." He nuzzled her hair briefly. "Thank you for taking care of me."

He left before she had a chance to answer, closing the door behind him.

"I love you," she said to the empty room. She tried the words a few more times. Not so hard without Mason standing in front of her. That's what she could do—leave a message on his answering machine. Or text him. Ooh, a handwritten note. Juvenile ideas, the lot of them. He'd had the courage to tell her face-to-face, with no guarantee she'd reciprocate. Which she hadn't...

She needed therapy. Luckily, she had the perfect person for the job.

"Are you exclusively sleeping with your boss?" Andie asked between bites of a chicken panini. She'd have been happy eating at a coffee shop, but Lasha had insisted on a restaurant where everything cost three times as much. For an accountant, Lasha wasn't budget-minded.

"Hell, no. If I was willing to settle for fucking just one man," Lasha mock-retched beside their table, "it sure as hell wouldn't be him. He has a monster cock and he knows how to plow, but he won't shave because it'll raise questions with his wife. I generally prefer my men on the smoother side."

"I've seen him in a golf shirt, he's not that furry."

"Below the belt, sweetheart." Lasha threw back half a glass of Cabernet in one swig. "Ever blown a cock that's surrounded by bush? It's no joy. He likes me to suck his balls too, and they're hairier than a yeti's must be. And you don't even want to know how nasty it is rimming that asshole. When I can find it through the tangle, that is."

Strangled gasps came from the neighboring table. Lasha didn't acknowledge them, just resumed picking at her overpriced salad. Nothing fazed her, ever.

In contrast, Andie's cheeks burned with embarrassment. She had zero issue with the content of their conversation. The audience they'd garnered was another thing.

"So why do it?" Boinking the boss wasn't going to get Lasha a promotion or more money. A relationship wasn't in the cards, nor did Lasha want one. "Seems like a lot of fuzz to deal with for some extended lunch breaks."

"Did I mention his girth? The anal is crazy wild, it's like having two in there at once. Since his wife won't even let him finger her ass, let alone fuck it, he's a very eager puppy. And I do expense the lunches," Lasha said with a wink.

The puppy comment gave her away. For Lasha, sex was about control—getting it, having it, keeping it. The day her boss stopped being desperate for her, Lasha would dump his hairy ass—and balls—and move on. For the sake of her best friend's tongue, Andie hoped that day wasn't too far off.

Lasha pushed her dishes aside and crossed her arms on the table. Today her eyes were bright green—thanks to contacts—and they bored into Andie's face. "I'll never complain about a lunch invitation from my bestie, but I think I got the call for a reason. Summarize."

"I'm a little stressed. Mason wants a serious relationship. I emailed Scott, who got his tighty-whiteys in a bunch and cut their vacation short, but whatever. They'll be back today. Scott has to approve Mason first, then I can introduce him to Dylan."

"So, that'll be never."

"Scott has no grounds to turn down my request."

"Other than wanting you back." Lasha's long, violet nails drummed on the tabletop. "Back to the stressed part. I hate to be the voice of reason, so shame on you for making me go there. Maybe deep down, you're not so sure about this step, or this guy."

"I'm sure about both. Especially the guy."

"What if he only wants to meet your kid so he gets more booty time once Dylan is back in the picture?"

"I don't think that's his motivation."

"Hmm. He's young and mouthwateringly hot. I doubt he's itching for family games night with somebody else's twelve-year-old boy."

Andie winced at that little dart of probability. "He told me he loves me."

"Was he drunk?"

"No. But thanks for your multiple votes of confidence."

Lasha shrugged. "Were you fucking, or more to the point, was he coming at the time of the big reveal?"

"Not the last time he said it, no."

"Good. Because you can't count on the shit they spew out when they're under the influence of alcohol or orgasm." One perfectly manicured hand snuck across the table and snatched Andie's half-full glass of wine. Two swallows later, it joined her empty dishes.

"Mason's not the bullshitting type."

"Looks, brains and a soul? I didn't think any of them came that fully equipped. Go ahead, tell me all the romantic details—the where, what and how of your big lovey-dovey exchange. I promise not to gag. Too much."

"I, uh, didn't say it back."

Totally inappropriate whooping broke the cultured silence in the restaurant. "There's hope for you yet, girlfriend."

"I didn't say that I don't love him, only that I didn't tell him."

"And why didn't you?"

"Nerves. I was chicken."

"What a load of crap. He said it first, you had nothing to be afraid of."

This is why she'd called Lasha for lunch. Her friend might not have much experience in the love department, but she knew Andie to the core. Lasha never sugarcoated her opinions—which seldom meshed with Andie's—but she supported whatever choices Andie made. And that's why Lasha was her best friend.

All traces of sarcasm and raunchy humor disappeared as Lasha reached for Andie's hand. "Honey, being tightlipped with your feelings won't make it hurt less if things don't work out. You know that better than anybody."

Andie managed a little nod and a whispered, "Thanks."

"For reminding you of the miscarriages? Sure. What are friends for, if not to dredge up your most painful memories?"

"I haven't forgotten…in fact, I've been thinking about them a lot lately."

"Oh, shit. Tell me you're not knocked up."

"I'm not." Not that she knew of, anyway.

"Thank god—you've been through enough hell in that department." Lasha's phone vibrated on the table, its blaring ringtone treating the restaurant patrons to explicit song lyrics. Typical Lasha, she let the entire chorus play through before hitting the mute button and shoving it back in her purse.

They were the center of attention once again. "We're going to be blacklisted from this place."

"Don't worry, I'm on very friendly terms with the manager," Lasha said as she exchanged the check for three crisp twenties.

Andie looked around for a manager-type as they headed for the exit. "Is he in the current rotation, or have you already cut him from the roster?"

"Current all-star, but you've got the wrong team." Lasha's nod indicated a gorgeous redhead standing behind the bar.

"Wow, she's beautiful. Nice boobs too."

"You should see them in the flesh."

Okay, so this was a new vein of conversation—and lifestyle, even for Lasha.

"Um, since when are you bisexual?"

"Since when are you a cougar?" Lasha asked, hand on hip, smile on her face.

"Point taken."

Her friend doled out the usual hug and cheek-smooch before folding herself into a sporty two-seater better suited to an exotic dancer than an accountant at a livestock feed plant. "So. You going to tell the hunky veterinarian that you love him, be all conventional and stuff?"

"First chance I get."

Chapter Fifteen

"What?" Not the nicest way to answer Cara's page from the front desk, but he was sick of politely dodging her sexually laced offers every time he turned around.

"There's somebody here to see you. Scott Finch, he doesn't have an appointment. Do you have time—I told him you're swamped today."

Ah, fuck. What a day for this visit. "Yeah, send him back." At least this once, his receptionist was using a part of her brain that wasn't focused on getting at his cock. "Hey, Cara—thanks."

"Oh, my pleasure, Dr. Lang. If there's anything else I can do for you, buzz me."

So much for the reprieve. The longest, worst day in the history of having his own clinic, and now he got to deal with Andie's bitter ex-husband. Fucking great.

He turned his chair toward the knock. The only glimpse of Scott he'd had was from a distance, the day he'd first met Andie at the ballpark. The man standing in his open doorway wasn't a geeky dad in a golf shirt. Not even close. Eighty-dollar button-down tucked into name-brand, wrinkle-free, belted khakis. Wire-frame glasses over wary eyes. Yeah, he was being a judgmental jerk, but he didn't like Scott Finch.

Mason forced a smile into submission when he stood. Finch came up to his chin. If they were buddies, height wouldn't mean a damn thing. Towering over Andie's ex, however—that was all right.

"Dr. Lang," Finch said, extending a hand. "Scott Finch, Andie's husband."

Husband? Think again, pal. So the ex wanted to play games. No problem. "Call me Mason, unless you brought Andie's dog in for a check-up."

"We have an excellent veterinarian with whom we're very satisfied."

First the husband thing, now referring to them as we? This guy was either delusional or he thought Mason was an idiot. Probably the latter. Wrong day to fuck with him, Finch.

"Your ex-wife is very satisfied with her new veterinarian."

Surprisingly, Scott didn't slug him. Self-restraint, or lack of balls? Again, Mason put his bet on the latter.

"Thank you for bringing us to the heart of the matter. Let's have a seat."

"Help yourself." He motioned to the assortment of chairs in his office, waited for Scott to choose one, then leaned against his desk. "I'm good to stand." His legs would have to fall off before he'd let this weasel control the show. Knowing what he did about how Scott had controlled Andie, Mason wasn't giving up an inch.

Scott's jaw clenched as he looked up at Mason. "I'm aware that you're having a physical relationship with my former wife. She's a beautiful woman with a particularly healthy and diverse sex drive."

The words, no shit and understatement of the year, came to mind, but he held back. "Andie agreed to let you screen any man she wants to introduce to Dylan. I know she didn't intend for us to discuss her libido or sexual preferences."

"Nobly said. It sounds as though you care about her."

"Of course I do, she's incredible. Excuse my lack of nobility here, but you were an idiot to let her get away. Whatever she wants, I plan to give it to her."

"And she wants you to meet her child, so you're doing that."

"Don't jump to conclusions, barrister. Meeting Dylan was my idea, one hundred percent."

"Why bother? You're already reaping the benefits of her midlife crisis. Why get tangled up with the rest of her life?"

Finch thought Andie was having a midlife crisis? She'd ended their marriage two years ago, for chrissake, and not gone on a single date until recently. This guy was delusional.

"So I should keep having sex with your ex, but stay away from your son, is that it?"

"I see no reason to subject him to this."

This conversation was getting surreal. "Subject him to what—his mother moving on with her life? Forget it, Finch. Run a background check on me or whatever. Aside from wanting to assault you because you're aggravating the shit out of me, I'm a decent guy. Ties to the community and the rest of it." Mason stalked to the door and shut it in Cara's nosy face. "Maybe Dylan will like me, maybe he won't. But it'll be his decision."

"He'll like you. He'll probably even think you're cool."

"So what—you're worried I'm going to steal your son from you?" For that, Mason managed to feel a little compassion for the man sitting in front of him.

"If I died tomorrow and Andie kept you around indefinitely—which is unlikely—you'd never be able to do that. The parental bond is an amazingly strong thing. You wouldn't understand that, though."

"Not yet." This motherfucker had Mason's buttons lined up in a tidy row. Push, push, push. "Remember when I said I'd give Andie whatever she wanted? Yeah, that."

That brought the little bastard out of his pansy, legs-crossed position. Right into Mason's face, or as close as he could get. They stood inches apart, surrounded by mutual fury.

"You wouldn't."

"Impregnate your ex-wife and start a family with her? In a fucking heartbeat, I would."

"She didn't tell you."

"That she always wanted more kids? Yeah. How impossible that would be since you rarely touched her? I figured that part out for myself while helping her make up for lost time."

Scott backed away, one hand on his temple, rubbing. "Here's some figures for you, doctor…Andie had five miscarriages prior to Dylan. That's five babies, each of which she wanted desperately, all lost. She's youthful and healthy—getting her pregnant shouldn't be a problem. But if you do that to her, you'll be giving her more heartbreak, not a second chance at a family."

The stress and fatigue headache he'd been fighting all day reared up and slammed against his skull. He dropped into his chair. Scott Finch was a miserable asshole, but this information about Andie's history put things in different perspective. She would've told him when the time came. Or would she? They'd had unprotected sex twice and she hadn't said a word about her medical issues. Fuck.

"I've checked you out, Lang. Thoroughly." Scott paused, inspecting his professionally buffed nails several times before getting back to his speech. "You're barely thirty. You're from a close-knit family. Odds are you'll want one of your own in the future. My ex-wife isn't the woman for you."

"You don't know me. You don't know Andie anymore, either. I love her. I'm not going anywhere."

Scott smirked and shook his head. "How sweet. So you love her, but does she love you? She's a very open person, direct and demonstrative with her affection and opinions—but I don't have to tell you that, I'm sure. She's told you that she loves you, I assume?"

"Your interest in my relationship with Andie is out of line, not to mention fucked-up." The chair thudded against the desk, Mason pushed it away so hard when he stood. "I've got work to do. I'll tell her you cleared me to meet Dylan."

The lawyer slid his hands into his pockets, as if he was settling in for a long conversation. "Andie and I didn't have a pornographic sex life, but we had a good marriage. Solid. Dependable."

"Sounds like a Volvo. Guess she's interested in a performance model now." If the prick was going to ignore the obvious dismissal, it was open season.

"You're finally getting it. It's normal for women her age to have a spike in their hormones prior to menopause. When Andie's ends—and it will, that's simple biology—she's going to want her family back, not some young stud who'll still want the sex she's no longer craving. You love her?" A vindictive smile replaced the controlled, straight face. "She lusts for you, junior, it's not love."

By four o'clock, the crazies had set in. Scott had dropped Dylan off hours earlier. After tolerating her mushy hugs for a full three minutes, Dylan had broken free and asked for food, as on any normal day. It was over veggie quesadillas in the kitchen that he'd brought up the boyfriend topic. Damn Scott and his technicalities. She hadn't asked him not to tell Dylan... so, of course he'd told Dylan about the email. And her sweet boy had been okay with it. More than okay. He'd even said it was about time. After a bunch of questions he'd closed the discussion by saying Mason sounded cool.

She had the best kid in the world. That kid had kissed her goodbye half an hour ago. Dylan loved the cottage and spending time with his dad, but he hated missing out on hang time with his friends. She had a couple more hours until he came home for refueling. Enough time to check in with her boyfriend and share the news that had her bouncing off the wall. Oh, and tell him she loved him. Definitely that.

Her legs shook as she walked from her car to the front door of the West End Veterinary Hospital. Anticipation, not nerves like the first time she visited. If a little bird landed on her shoulder and started singing a happy tune, she wouldn't be surprised. Everything was that right in the world.

"Good afternoon, Mrs. Finch," Cara said at the top of her voice when Andie walked through the door.

Andie rolled her eyes. Not even Mason's irritating receptionist could ruin her mood this afternoon. The juvenile antics were getting old, though. One of these days, the ditz would have to accept that Mason wasn't interested in her sexy offers.

"Wait... you can't go back there right now."

Out of respect for Mason's business, she stopped at the desk. "Is he with a client?"

"He's doing a surgery... and it could be awhile. I'll tell him you stopped by."

Her chest tightened. Surgery in the afternoon wasn't good news. Poor Mason, what a horrible day. "Another emergency? Maybe I should wait in his office."

A manicured hand shot over the desk to stop her. "No, you shouldn't. It's not an emergency, just a routine neuter appointment."

Something was definitely up. A little rope and the airhead would probably wrap it around her neck and tie a pretty bow. "Well, that's a relief." She leaned over the reception desk. "Hey, is it a cat or dog?"

"I think it's a," Cara shuffled some papers on the desk and fiddled with her computer, "cat. Yup, there it is, a cat named Princess, scheduled for neutering."

"First of all, Cara, Mason does those procedures first thing in the morning." She leveled a stare at the bimbo. "And not only does neutering a cat only take about fifteen minutes—a female cat gets spayed, not neutered. When lying through your teeth, it's a good idea to know some basic facts."

Cara's lips puckered open and shut. The fishy face matched the fishy story.

"Fine." Cara sighed, as if talking to Andie was an enormous pain in the butt. "He's not here right now and I didn't want you hanging around until he gets back. Sue me for not liking you."

The bitch was still lying about Mason. His truck was around back, its rear end visible from the front lot to anyone who cared to look. Andie issued Cara the middle finger and marched straight to Mason's office. The knob rattled in her hand. Locked door.

"I told you, he's not here," Cara said from beside her.

"His truck is here."

"He went for a walk. Said he needed the fresh air after the day he's had."

Finally, a sensible answer. "You could've said that from the start. Mason's not going to be happy about the hard time you gave me." And yes, she was totally tattling later. For now, though, she just wanted to find him. Do whatever she could to make his day less crappy. She fished her phone from her purse and tapped his number while moving toward the front door.

The ringing stopped her cold.

One of the sweet, romantic things Mason had done was personalize his cell for her calls. Not a generic ringtone that could come from anybody's phone—a snippet of a song he'd said reminded him of her. One he'd played while dancing with her in his living room. One he'd sang in her ear, late at night while lying in bed. For several seconds, those sweet, meaningful lyrics filled the air.

On her end, the call went to voice mail. She looked from his closed office door to Cara. The girl's eyes were wide, her mouth open in the shape of an O. Andie hit redial. This time, silence from Mason's office. Still no answer on the line. Her heart sank as Cara's lips curled upward in a smug smile.

In the parking lot, she slumped over the steering wheel. Questions and scenarios knocked around in her brain. If his phone had rung with the second call, and if Cara hadn't looked so guilty, Andie would've thought he'd simply forgotten his cell before going out. She wanted that to be true. God, she wanted it to be true. For Cara to be a conniving, jealous twit and Mason to be out taking a much-needed break. But it didn't mesh with the evidence, or with the pang of doom in her stomach.

She'd barely settled in to her surveillance spot up the street when Mason drove away from the clinic. She started the car, put it in gear. What the hell was she doing? The problem with falling crazy in love with somebody—it made you crazy. Whatever was going on with him, whatever caused him to lie and avoid her... she wouldn't let it turn her into a psycho girlfriend. Too much. She engaged the parking break and hit send on his cell number again. Yes, that was a little bit psycho, but at least she wasn't tailing him right now. Weaving lane to lane and staying two car lengths behind to avoid detection. She had complete control over her urges. Uh-huh.

Still no answer. His deep voice instructed her to leave a message. This time, she did.

"Hi, it's me. I stopped by your office to check on you, but you were," she bit her tongue, for now, "out for a walk. Call me when you get a chance. I have some things to tell you." There, a crazy-free message. One he'd reply to as soon as he got home, with an explanation and a huge apology. She hoped.

Chapter Sixteen

"You shit-for-brains dickwad coward." A girly slap in the face followed, courtesy of Andie's best friend.

The guys around Mason roared. A couple wolf-whistled, because hell, Lasha was as hot as she was feisty. Black leather covered the essential areas and not much more. Long legs ended in wicked high heels. She had chin-length dark hair that would've been cute on another woman, but combined with her shocking pink lips and heavily made-up eyes, looked the furthest thing from it. Not his type, but he got why his teammates had their tongues on the floor. The fact that she had her arm around another smokin' hot female only added to the appeal.

"I'll take whatever you're dishing…" Mason rose from his seat on the patio. Nodded outside the gated-off area. "But let's do it away from the crowd."

"Why? You don't want your little baseball buddies to hear what a prick you are?"

More hooting from the table. He leaned into her space to answer, rather than raise his voice. "Actually, I had Andie's privacy in mind." Yeah, that took Lasha down a peg or two.

She recovered quickly enough, kissing the redhead full on the lips in front of a table full of guys hopped up on beer and testosterone. "Baby, I need a couple minutes with this douche of an excuse for a man."

"I'll keep his seat warm," Red said, sliding into the vacant spot and smiling demurely at the men. Nobody at that table would give a shit about anything he and Lasha discussed now.

"I hate sadistic players like you." One pointy finger jabbed at his chest, over and over. "Andie wasn't looking for something serious. She wanted to keep things casual. But it was more fun to fuck with her head and her heart, wasn't it? To convince her that you love her, that you wanted to be part of her life, to have a," Lasha's fingers made air quotes, "real relationship. Then, once you had her head over heels for you, willing to do anything, risk everything, you drop her stuff on the doorstep and dump her with a note. You total piece of shit."

Yeah, it'd been a brutal way to end things. If he'd had to see Andie's face, or even hear her voice, he couldn't have done it. Lasha was right, he was a coward. And a piece of shit. But he was not a player. Not with Andie. Lasha had that part all wrong.

"Everything I said to Andie was legit. My half of the relationship was completely honest." His crossed his arms over his chest before Lasha dug a hole clear through to his back. "And while it's nice of you to jump to her defense, I think she'll be fine." Probably already was.

"Why? Because she hasn't come crawling to your door, or cried into your answering machine, begging you to change your mind? Because she hasn't been texting you and emailing you, telling you how much she loves you? It's a good thing you're pretty because you sure are dumb." She snorted in disgust. "You don't know Andie at all."

Andie clapped softly as Dylan crossed home plate. No screaming or jumping up and down. She glanced at the man to her right. Even Scott was outdoing her in the cheering department tonight, and that said a lot.

She'd agreed to come to the game together. Dylan had asked her to, and he never did that. So he and dad could cheer her up, he'd said. Sweet boy. Over a week had passed since she told her son that he wouldn't be meeting her boyfriend because she no longer had one. She'd been careful not to cry or act melancholy around him, but Dylan was a perceptive kid. No, a perceptive young man. He matured a little more every day—intellectually, emotionally and physically. Seeing how wonderfully Dylan was turning out only made the maternal longings worse. Damn Mason for stirring them up. Damn him for a lot of things.

"You're unusually reserved today," Scott said as he resumed his spot beside her on the bleachers.

"That should please you immensely. I know how much my exuberance embarrasses you."

A thin line took the place of Scott's lips. "Not once have I ever said that."

"No, never in those words. But asking me to tone it down, or suggesting I pick something more appropriate to wear—all of those thousands of times—same thing."

"I've always appreciated your whimsy. But when you're the wife of a respected professional, and when your last name is Finch in this town, there are expectations, And."

This wasn't the place for an argument, but he started it, so… "I solved the first issue with a divorce. Changing my last name just jumped to the top of my to-do list." Angry heat bubbled under her skin. That reserve Scott mentioned was slipping fast. "And, for the millionth and last time, I hate being called And. Not that you'd remember this, but I'm a woman. I am not a conjunction." If it weren't for Dylan, she'd harrumph out of there fast as her peep-toe pumps could take her. Trapped on the home-team bleachers, she settled for crossing her leg over her knee and bouncing one heeled foot hard enough to cause a breeze.

Scott knew her well enough to give her a full two minutes to calm. "Don't change your name."

"Dylan won't have a problem with it, if that's what you're thinking."

"I wasn't considering Dylan for the moment. It pleases me that you're still using my name, that we're still connected."

His name. Didn't the fact that she'd been a Finch most of her adult life make it her name too? Ugh. "We're connected by our son and always will be. But that's all."

"After you've had your... free time... you'll want more of a connection than that. What we had before, the comfort and ease of our family life. Nobody knows you better than I do. I might ask you to change your dress or laugh a little quieter, but at least you always know where you stand with me. No surprises, no disappointment."

The speech seemed like a bunch of backhanded digs, not words from Scott's heart. Coming to the game as a family unit was a mistake. Scott took any tiny act of togetherness as a sign they'd get back together.

"I think you should drop me off at home after the game. The three of us going out for dinner isn't a good idea."

"Dylan will be disappointed. And worried about you."

She must have buttons visible only to Scott. Push here for guilt, in doses from gut-churning low to heart-ripper maximum. "Fine."

"We'll get our usual booth. Like always."

Like always? It'd been over two years since they'd gone out for supper together. There was no usual booth for them anymore. She shook her head. Scott just smiled.

But Scott wasn't the only one with insight. The smile on his face didn't fool her—it was victorious, not genuinely happy. She stared as if her eyes were glued to his face. For years she'd loved this man. With all her heart, she'd thought. Now there was…nothing. Only the tiniest shred of warmth remained. Without Dylan tying them, she'd forget about those years with Scott as easily as she forgot her shopping list every Tuesday. The memories of kissing him, touching him, the other things she'd done with him… She shuddered.

"You should've dressed more appropriately," Scott said, putting his arm around her shoulder. The words, his sermonizing tone, his fingers on her bare shoulder…a ball of vomit crawled up the back of her throat. For her son, she forced it back down.

Mason scanned the small bar area. No sign of Logan yet. He grabbed an empty seat and nodded at the bartender. "The darkest you have on tap, large."

"Getting tanked tonight?" Katie snagged his keys from the bar, then hopped onto the neighboring stool. "Thanks for being on time. Punctuality's one of your better qualities." She leaned over the bar and ordered sparkling water before swiveling to face him. "I sent the text from Logan's phone. Sorry to trick you, big brother, but we need to have a little chat. Now that I have you face-to-face and unable to escape," she jingled his keys in front of his face before shoving them into the front pocket of her painted-on jeans, "you're going to say more than four words about your major screw-up with Andie."

Shit. This conversation would require more than a schooner of beer. "Looks like I'll be running a tab," he instructed the bartender when the first twenty-ounce glass arrived. "And as long as she's here, keep 'em coming."

Katie lifted her bottle. "He wants to pay for my drink as well." Then it was guns loaded and aimed at his head. "I had a magazine picture to show Andie, a sleeve detail for my wedding dress, so I dropped by her place earlier. Unannounced."

He gave a so-what shrug and let a wave of lager roll down his throat. Maybe he should order a shot of Jack Daniel's to speed things along.

"It took her forever to answer the door. When she did, well... she'd obviously been crying. For days, judging by the puffy redness."

"I've seen her when she's upset, Katie. She gets that way after five minutes. I'm sure she's fine, whatever it was."

"Moron." Practiced fingers flicked him on the temple—hard. "You broke her heart."

"No, I didn't." Was going out for a couple of beers on a Friday night suddenly cursed? The episode with Lasha last week, and now this week with Katie. Both of them on his case about Andie. He took another swig of beer, savoring the coolness. A few seconds' relief from a heated female tirade. "I realized we weren't going to be compatible long term. Andie already knew that."

Katie made an indignant, squeak-like noise. "After all the times you told her that the age difference didn't matter? Shame on you!"

"No... fuck. Is that what she said?"

"She didn't say anything. You never noticed those big walls she has up?"

Yeah, he'd noticed. Plenty of times. As sexually uninhibited, fun and warm as Andie was, she tended to clam up when it came to the deeply personal stuff. He'd assumed she held back because she wasn't that invested in their relationship.

"I don't have to be her BFF to get how wrecked she is over the breakup."

Damn, why did that make him feel better, instead of shitty? "I miss her, Katie-Kat."

"So why'd you give her the Dear Jane letter, you big dummy?" Katie stopped his hand from lifting the beer to his mouth. "Talk to me, big brother. You know I'm on your side, even if you're royally screwing things up."

The beer went back on the bar. She'd be relentless if he didn't talk. And part of him wanted to unload. Getting it off his chest might help clear it from his mind. "It was a douchey move, but I knew if I tried to end it face-to-face, I wouldn't be able to."

"From the looks of both of you, that would've been a good thing."

"Long term, I did what was best for everybody."

"I don't see how."

"Turns out I want the whole house including the picket fence and she only wants the bedroom."

"Oh." Her hand touched his arm. "That might change."

He opened his throat and downed the remaining half glass of beer. "She doesn't love me, but she loves her son, and I'm sure as hell not going to be the guy who keeps their family apart trying to serve his own purposes." A fresh draught appeared in front of him. Good man. "Thanks. You have any decent tequila behind that bar?"

"Don Julio," the bartender said. "Eight bucks a pop."

"Hit me." This talk required something harder than beer. The tequila shot left a warm trail all the way to his stomach. Much better.

"I think you're way off base about…" Katie's protest died on her lips. "Oh shit."

Mason followed her sightline to the door. Fucking awesome. This night just kept getting better. He rapped his knuckles on the glossy hardwood to get the bartender's attention. "Another tequila."

"What's he doing with them?" The way Katie clucked her tongue in disgust was a perfect copy of their mother. Any other time, he would've teased her about it mercilessly.

But now, Mason sat very still and quiet. As if that would keep Andie or Scott from noticing him as they followed a hostess to a table. "Having dinner, by the looks of it. With his family."

The second shot of tequila—gone.

"She said she was coming here after Dylan's game. I thought it was going to be her and her son. I thought…" Katie focused on the Finch family night out. "I thought it'd be a good opportunity for you to talk to her—casually, at least. Start working things out."

Mason stared too, solely at Andie. Hair in a ponytail, skin almost free of makeup. Soft looking, irresistible, as always. Jeans that molded to her fantastic legs and ass, tits bouncing slightly in a silky sleeveless top, and shoes that had fuck me written all over them. Only the invitation wasn't for him. Wouldn't be, ever again.

Andie chose a seat facing away from him, leaving him with a view of her hair and shoulders. Not much of a fix when he'd been craving her so badly for over a week. The handful of pictures taken with his phone didn't help, though he'd spent enough hours looking at them. Every cell in his body screamed at him to walk over there. Claim her. Punch that undeserving prick, Scott, in the face. Or drop to his knees and beg forgiveness. Anything to have her back. His, for good.

Katie grabbed his hand as he signaled the bartender with his empty tequila glass. "What're you doing?"

"Numbing." He sure as hell wasn't watching this cozy scene while sober. He tipped his head back and demolished another shot of tequila. The third was hotter than the others, making him wince.

"Better now, you big baby?"

A bit more beer to ease the heat in his gut. "Much. And I don't want to talk about babies."

"Hmm." Katie signaled the bartender. "One more dose of truth serum for my brother, please."

Another shot would carve a hole through his liver. "I will if you will," he said with a loose laugh. Katie'd never go for that deal. But holy fuck, she was nodding. Shit.

Two stubby glasses appeared on the bar. Katie picked hers up gingerly, sniffed it and curled her lip. "Ew. You first."

"Nice try, I'm not drunk enough to fall for that one. Together, on three. One, two, three…" Don Julio the fourth hit bottom and set fire to his stomach, launching an inferno that tore up his throat, straight to his brain.

Katie's shot, on the other hand, came up as fast as it went down. Through her nose and mouth. Eyeballs too, in the form of tears.

She sputtered and gulped the rest of her water. "Why would anybody willingly drink that stuff?"

"Pain relief."

After scrubbing all traces of tequila from her lips, she dug through her purse for gum and popped two pieces. "And… is it working?"

Either Katie was rocking back and forth on her stool, or he was well on the way to fucked-up. "Yeah, it's working."

"Good. Now what's the story behind that baby comment?"

"No story. Just thinking of the last time I drank too much tequila." He narrowly avoided his sister's hug. They were not revisiting the Stacey and baby era, not a chance. "I gotta hit the can."

Fuck sympathy or pity. He splashed cold water on his face, braced himself on the edge of the counter. Getting drunk wasn't helping him forget. If anything, it made things worse. Especially with Andie sitting across the room. He could be the one at that table with her and Dylan right now, if he hadn't ended things.

He'd told Katie the breakup was for the best and he'd meant it. Best for Andie because he wouldn't be in her way when she was ready to put her family back together. And she would. Seventeen years and a child together was a hell of a connection. The fact that she hadn't gone on one single date since the separation should've been his first clue. But no, he'd had damn stars in his eyes. While he was busy falling in love with her, mentally picking out wedding bands and building picket fences, she was dancing around any talk of commitment. Then there were the lies by omission when it came to the subject of kids.

Looking back, it made sense. She'd had no reason to tell him her medical issues. Because she didn't love him. She had no intention of staying with him, let alone having a baby. She hadn't reached out once since he cut things off. Not even to bust his balls for being a prick. That told him everything he needed to know, right?

Ending it was best for him too. His damn heart couldn't take another slice down the middle. Better to get out while it was still a slow-bleeding nick.

The restroom door squeaked as it opened. He cranked the taps on and reached for some soap. Dylan's eyes met his in the mirror, then turned away. The boy didn't know him from the next guy. Mason was some random stranger using the john at a restaurant, nothing more. He'd never be more. For the best or not, the fact made him want to puke.

Mason dried his hands on a paper towel. He should leave, but instead pulled out his cell, pretending to read and answer a text. Dylan moved from the urinals to the sinks. The kid looked like his mom. Same eyes, same complexion. Whatever DNA Scott had contributed, it didn't come through in Dylan's appearance. Hopefully the boy didn't inherit his father's tendency to be a controlling asshole. Not that Mason had acted much better.

He ended the fake text conversation and followed Dylan out of the restroom. Mason made his way back to the bar, but kept one eye on Andie's son as Dylan returned to the table. He wasn't the only person watching Dylan. And Dylan wasn't the only person being watched.

"Andie's ex just made me," Mason said as he sat next to Katie. He slid a credit card across the bar. "I'll pay so we can leave."

Now that the lone bartender had custody of Mason's plastic, servers and customers streamed to the bar. So much for settling his tab and getting the hell out of there. Katie's attention was on her cell phone. His shifted between the Finches' table and the bartender holding his MasterCard hostage. The buzz from the tequila shots wasn't holding, leaving him twitchy to make an exit before Andie noticed him. Looking her in the eye might kill him.

"Son of a bitch."

Katie glanced up at his snarled words and followed the line of his glare. Scott had his hand on Andie's and Andie wasn't pulling away. The snake's eyes met Mason's briefly. A smile slithered into place on Scott's face—one obviously directed at Mason, not his beautiful ex.

"Slimy little fucker." Where was the bartender with his tab? He scribbled on the bill when it arrived, snagged his card, stormed toward the door. "She deserves better than a snooty, uptight little jackhole who doesn't appreciate her."

"I agree," Katie said, trotting to keep up with him. "But you chose to let her go, and now you have to, you know, let her go."

He paused for a last look before pushing through the door. Andie was laughing with her son, wearing a smile of pure happiness. Because he was a selfish bastard, Mason stared until she sensed the weight of it and looked his way. He expected her face to change when she saw him—hostility, indifference—maybe both, maybe worse. And it did change. For a few seconds her eyes lit up, the smile changing to one just for him. How the hell was he supposed to let go of that?

Chapter Seventeen

Scott parked his Mercedes rather than let it idle. "I'd like to come in for a few minutes—there's something I need to discuss with you."

She'd had about all she could take of Scott's advances and assumptions tonight. Now he wanted to come in and talk? Dylan hung half in and half out of the backseat, waiting for her answer. She nodded. The best she could do, and only for Dylan's sake. Thank god she had wine.

"I'm really tired, Scott." Particularly, of him. She waited for the click of Dylan's door closing upstairs. "Your three minutes start now."

"Mind if I pour myself a drink?"

"Yes, I mind very much. Go home and drink. Go anywhere, for that matter." She was being cruel, but she couldn't stop. "I don't want you here. Not tonight, not next week, not five years from now. We. Are. Over."

"I'm having a Glenfiddich—join me?"

Unbelievable. She gaped as he helped himself to a tulip glass and the bottle of eighteen-year-old single malt scotch.

249

Marked as to-do—reorganize the cupboards before Scott's next visit.

"I'll take your silence as a no." Three fingers' worth of amber flowed into the glass. He swirled and sniffed, savoring, disregarding her time limit completely. Entirely out of character, he tossed the entire contents back in two swallows. "You look ready to blow a gasket. Good. You won't have to work up to it when I say what I came in to say."

She threw her hands up. Honestly, what more could there be?

"I'm responsible for your breakup with Dr. Lang."

Okay, that. "What?" She waved him off when he started to speak. "No, let me guess. You told Mason how I'm still subconsciously in love with you and he agreed to dump me so you and I could find our way back to each other."

"You're in the ballpark."

"I don't believe you. Mason wouldn't fall for a load of crap like that."

"Because you frequently badmouthed me?"

"No, but maybe I should have." She snatched the bottle off the island before he could pour another. He absolutely was not crashing on her couch, nor was he leaving his car in the driveway overnight. "Go home, Scott."

"I'm not finished."

"Too bad—I am." Bottle in hand, she marched away, only to have Scott spin her around before making it out of the kitchen. The shock of such a spontaneous, physical response from her passionless former husband left her momentarily speechless.

"I provoked him, I admit. Easy to do with a man whose heart is on his sleeve. He was so straightforward about his intentions—I didn't like it. You were my wife for seventeen years. So I goaded him some more, convinced him that you're having a midlife crisis. I kept chipping away until I could see him doubting the depth of your feelings, and then…" He released her, his arms falling to his sides. "I'm so ashamed, Andie."

For Scott to feel ashamed, more so, to admit it… acid churned in her stomach. "Why? What did you do?"

"He wants a future with you, including children—he said as much. So I told him about your miscarriages. I led him to believe you're incapable of fulfilling that desire."

Sweat beaded along her hairline. Her armpits were sticky and damp, yet goose bumps popped out all over her arms.

"You… you…" There weren't words to adequately describe the hatred and disgust roiling inside her right now.

"Tonight at the restaurant, when you saw him standing there… the way you looked at him, it was all over your face… you love him. It's not a hormonal fling."

"I want you to leave," she said between clenched teeth.

"You have my permission to tell him what I did, how I manipulated him. That I lied about your fertility troubles. Tell him… everything." He went to the door, finally, pausing once more before walking through it. "I did it out of love, And. I was trying to do what's best for you."

"I don't want that kind of love." Tears stung her eyes. "I never did."

Half the night had gone to crying, the other half to thinking until her head hurt. The last time she saw on the clock was five-something. Thank god for twelve-year-olds who got their own breakfast. Dylan had shoved a note under her bedroom door around eight, telling her which friend's house he'd gone to and when he'd be home. Awesome kid, that one.

In a way, Scott's manipulations were a good thing. If she'd stayed with Mason, she would've gotten pregnant, either intentionally or accidentally. And she was forty. Healthy and fit enough to have a baby, but way past being chained to a nursing and napping schedule. A newborn wouldn't let her sleep until eight-thirty.

Of course, the newborn's father would. He'd be the type to help with the feedings and fussiness, no doubt about it. Given his occupation, he'd probably change poopie diapers without scrunching his nose. Dammit.

She sprawled on the couch and took a large, fortifying swallow of coffee. Okay, Mason would be a wonderful dad. And truthfully, she'd give up extra sleep for the joys of motherhood any day of the week. But there was the other thing Scott's manipulations had brought to the surface. Mason had major issues working through problems. The first time he'd cut and run had been partially her fault. The night she'd lied to test his feelings. Ugh, what a mistake.

This, though? Breaking up with her via a note on her doorstep because of shit Scott told him... He hadn't even attempted talking to her. Hadn't bothered to ask if any of it were true. Instead, he'd turned tail and headed for the hills. More silent treatment. Different from Scott's, but just as controlling. Last night she'd told Scott she didn't want his kind of love. If running at the first sign of trouble was Mason's M.O., she didn't want his kind of love, either.

She pulled her cell into her lap and sent Lasha a text. *Love sucks. Pancakes required.*

A reply came back immediately. *Told you so. Be there in twenty.*

She was loosely presentable when the doorbell rang. Lasha wouldn't care about the dark circles under bloodshot eyes. Neither would The Pancake House. Andie threw her purse over her shoulder and pulled the door.

"Oh. Scott." She blocked the opening. With her wedge-heeled sandals, his stature and the step, she looked down on him. Bitchy as it was, she enjoyed it.

"Expecting Mason, I assume."

"Stop making assumptions about me and we'll both be happier people. I'm waiting for Lasha. Dylan isn't here, so, goodbye."

"I should have called first."

"And yet you didn't."

"I didn't think you'd take my call."

"Another assumption." Though probably true.

"I took some things I shouldn't have when we separated. It's time I return them, since I've accepted that... we're over."

"Right now?"

"It's just a few things. They're in the car—I could use a hand, if you have a minute."

"Fine." She huffed after him. Anything to expedite his departure.

"I'll get the box in the trunk. You take what's in the backseat."

The dark-tinted window was partially open. A black nose pressed against the narrow crack, sniffing wildly. Andie's heart skipped a beat. She hadn't seen Minx in almost a year, for Minx's sake, and Scott knew that. What kind of game was this?

"Scott..."

He shut the trunk. Came around to the passenger side carrying a box of chew toys, bowls and treats. "What are you waiting for? Open the door and take your dog home."

For this minute, she hated him a little bit less. She pulled the handle, felt a whoosh of cool as it escaped the air-conditioned interior. Seventy pounds of energized muscle sprang out into her waiting arms. God, how she'd missed her pretty puppy. Minx allowed the immobility briefly before becoming a black-and-tan streak as she blitzed around the front lawn, tongue flopping from the side of her long, goofy face. At ten years old, the sweet Dobie still bounced like a puppy. And she was home.

Mason sat in his truck, staring at the blue streamers and balloons. The giant number one stuck into the front lawn. Kid noise drifted into the cab through the open windows—a mixture of giddy voices and crying babies. He didn't want to be here. Not solo. Not this time around.

He grabbed the gift bag and headed up the driveway to the backyard. Party central. At least a dozen kids in various ages and stages. Close to double that in corresponding adults. Mom, dad, kid. Mom, dad, kid, kid. Then—him. The sore, single thumb. He scooped a beer from the cooler, a lawn chair from the circle and found a shady spot near the fence. Inconspicuously present. And right on time for presents.

The process went faster than it had for Josh and Jane's first kid's first birthday. Hallelujah. This time, no reading every verse on every hokey card, no passing the gift around the circle. A simple announcement of the giver, hold up the present, and bam, done. Pretty efficient—until they came to his.

"Ooh, look at this... the gift bag is actually a pillow case. And it's got trucks all over it. Oh my gosh, it even has Will's name stitched on it!" Jane fingered the tiny card Andie had secured to her creation with an oversized diaper pin. "From Mason and Andie." Jane pulled out the items Andie had chosen on their market shopping trip. When Jane finished squealing like a third-grader, she looked up, searching the yard until she spotted him. "Thanks, Mason and...oh, you're alone today? Too bad."

Yeah, he thought so too. Especially now that everyone who wasn't alone was gawking. Jane's husband whispered in her ear. Aw, hell. Nice going, buddy. Had to enlighten her in the middle of a crowd, huh?

"Oh, Mason, I'm sorry. I didn't know you had...uh..." Jane turned redder than red. "Should I send Andie a thank-you card, or..."

"Let's go with or," he said, raising his beer to the yard full of mostly familiar faces.

The next hour and a half crawled by. He successfully blended into the background. Relaxed as he watched. The odd man out today, and much of the time since he hadn't joined the ranks of marriage and parenthood, he still enjoyed this type of gathering. Surrounded by good vibes, even when one, or several, of the kids started wailing.

Such as now. The birthday boy had passed the tipping point and was completely melting down. Jane was unsuccessfully trying to calm him and looking as if she might join him in the freak-out any second. Out of the throng, Josh appeared. Brushed her hair aside to kiss her cheek, then took their adopted son into his arms and disappeared into the house. No words exchanged. But anybody with eyes could see the love. Everywhere he looked in this group, love was in the smallest actions. Between husbands and wives, parents and their kids...

Well, fuck him. He'd been blind as well as dumb.

Friday, finally. Waiting the entire week had almost fucking killed him. So had Lasha, when he'd called to ask for a favor. Convincing Andie's man-eating best friend that he'd come to his senses—permanently—had cost him three cocktails and a chunk of pride. But it was worth it.

He spotted Andie easily. Automatically, as if he were tuned to her frequency, or some cheesy bullshit like that. Tonight, she wore a formfitting green t-shirt, black shorts that showed off her incredible legs and a ponytail peeking out the back of a ball cap. Similar to the first time he'd seen her. One big difference—sneakers in place of her customary sexy heels. Better suited for dog-walking, a part of her life she'd recently regained. She stood at the fence, well away from the bleachers. Her dog sat dutifully at her side while both watched Dylan's game.

After Lasha had decided to trust him, she'd told him about Scott's big move in returning Minx. The closest thing to an apology for the controlling bastard. She'd also told him Scott had accepted Andie's feelings, or lack thereof. Surprisingly, Lasha had sort of defended Scott. "At least he fought for what he wanted, even though he fought dirty," she'd said. Then she'd demanded to know if he was going to fight for Andie. Fucking right, he was.

Starting now. He removed the wrapper from the baseball he'd brought. Rolled it carefully but directly at the dog. Minx took it into her mouth immediately.

Andie looked down at Minx mouthing the ball. "Minxie, drop that." The dog wasn't having any part of that command. "Minx. Drop it." But the only dropping going on was by Andie, now on her knees, alternating between reasoning, scolding and attempting to pry the ball from Minx's determined jaw. "Don't you dare grumble at me, missy."

Preoccupied by her battle with the dog, she didn't notice his approach. Perfect. "Hey, can I get my ball back?"

"I'm so sorry, she won't give it t—" Her voice faded to nothing as her eyes moved from his shoes, up his legs, all the way to his face. "Mason."

He'd thought about that over and over, the way his name sounded in her soft voice, wondering if he'd ever hear it again. The plan in his head disappeared. All he could do was smile at her and hope she didn't walk away.

"You seem to have trouble controlling your balls," she said, a smile tugging at the corner of her mouth as she stood.

"Yeah, I could use some hands-on practice."

"Good thing you've got two. Passing your balls from hand to hand should build up your control. Or try using your non-dominant hand to do most of the work—it'll improve your focus."

"I've tried those." Frequently, the past couple lonely weeks. "What I need is personal, one-on-one training."

She bent to deal with Minx and the captive baseball again. "I'm sure you won't have trouble finding a partner for that."

Her voice had lost its natural playfulness with that last comment. Time to switch tactics. He crouched next to her, close, but not quite touching hips and knees. Offered his hand to Minx for a sniff the dog couldn't be bothered to give.

"Lasha told me you had Minx back home. I'm happy for you."

"You've talked to Lasha?" The pretty blue eyes flashed to his face, wide and worried.

"A couple of times. First one was the Friday after I made the biggest mistake of my life." Her hand stilled on the dog's fur. He wanted to reach for it and hold it so badly his fingers twitched. "She made quite an impression on my baseball team."

"Lasha, out at a bar on a Friday night… I bet she did."

"I should've listened to her then, but I was still in stupid asshat mode."

"W-what'd she say?"

"Among other things, that I'm a shit-for-brains dickwad. Also, that you were head over heels for me. And that I don't know you at all."

"Well, she had parts of it right."

"Parts?"

"Mmhmm. The dickwad part for sure." Her eyelids fluttered as she looked down. "And… I was head over heels."

He didn't like the sound of that. "You said was. Am I too late?"

"I… I won't be a relationship where I'm not an equal partner, where I don't have choices or the voice to state them, not again. No matter how I feel about… the person."

Silence hung between them like a thick curtain. He hadn't controlled her wardrobe or told her how to behave, as Scott had, but he'd still been a domineering jerk. In the worst way.

The packs of spectators on the bleachers erupted into hooting and yelling. Andie sprang to her feet and he followed, just in time to see Dylan in a rundown between second and third. She added her voice to the commotion, cheering for her son while jumping up and down.

The kid was doing a great job of deking out the infielders. Quick feet and good judgment, impressive for a twelve-year-old kid in a rec league. Mason found himself hollering along with the rest. And when her boy made it safely to third, Mason automatically lifted Andie in a celebratory hug. Damn, her arms felt right when they closed around his neck. He held her tight, heat from her pink cheeks transferring to his face.

He closed his eyes. Inhaled deeply, filling his head with the scent of her hair, her skin. The feeling of her tits against his chest, her heart pounding hard against his. He'd missed her so fucking much.

"Wait," he said when she started to pull free. He dipped his head, let his lips hover a breath away from her soft pink lips. "I want to kiss you, but I know I have to earn that back. And I will, if you let me. I fucked up and I know that." Reluctantly, he let her slide down his chest and away.

"This isn't the place…"

It wasn't a resounding yes, but it wasn't a no. He'd take any opening she gave. "Have dinner with me later."

"It's seven o'clock—I've already eaten."

"Dessert. We can get ice cream and walk Minx through Southside Park."

She hesitated, then waved a finger at his uniform. "Looks as though you have a late game to get to."

"I'll skip it."

"I don't know…"

By the way she was worrying her bottom lip between her teeth, this wasn't going to be an easy sell. Not that he deserved one.

"Babe, I'll skip them all. Whatever I have to do, I'm gonna do it, to get another chance with you."

On the infield, Dylan's game was coming to a close. Both teams had formed lines and were exchanging handshakes. Andie shuffled her feet, her attention shifting between the diamond, Minx's continuing destruction of the ball, and him. Now wasn't the time to press her.

"I'll clear out so you can congratulate Dylan and see him off for the weekend." He took her hand. Rubbed his thumb over the silky soft skin. "But I'm not done. I'm fighting for you. For us."

There it was. The smile he'd been waiting for. One that told him she loved him, still, without her saying a word. Why had he been too stupid and stubborn to understand it sooner? However long it took, whatever he had to do, he'd earn her forgiveness. Rebuild her trust. And this time, keep it.

He kissed her hand, then walked backward toward the parking lot. No way was he giving up another minute of looking at that beautiful face.

"Hey," she called. "I'm sorry about your ball. It's not Minx's style to be so possessive." She shook her head at the dog and the pile of leather and rubber at her feet. "Or destructive."

"Yeah, that's my fault. I've had that ball packed in dried liver powder for two days. Kind of irresistible to dogs." He had to grin when her mouth fell open. Damn, she was adorable when surprised. "Like I said, babe…whatever it takes."

Chapter Eighteen

The seatbelt had barely clicked into place when her cell phone chimed. From Mason, the text simply read, Dessert?

Well, he was determined, at least. He had to be nearby. She peeked over her shoulder, starting a visual sweep of the parking lot. His truck hit her radar and her heart skipped a beat or six. Oh god, he was practically right in front of her. After hugging Dylan goodbye at the ball diamond, she'd put her head down and made a beeline for the car with Minx in tow. Her sole focus had been to get home so she could replay every second of the encounter with Mason. Probably with several glasses of merlot accompaniment.

Forget about conjuring up a mental picture of how hot he'd looked with his baseball shirt hanging open. The way his muscles had flexed every time he moved. She had the real deal not more than a dozen feet away.

His left arm rested on the open window, cell in hand. He waved it at her and another message popped onto her screen. Say yes.

Groveling made most men seem weak. Not Mason. His slightly dominant method sent zingers to her heart...and below the belt. She'd barely resisted his verbal pleas for another chance, had wanted to leap into his arms at the first one. Hearing that Lasha had given him her scheduled location lowered her Mason-resistance that much more. He would've had to make a hell of a case to get Lasha's cooperation.

She met his eyes and nodded. He smiled. She didn't stand a chance.

"Sorry, change of plans," she said to Mason as he joined her in her driveway. "Minx threw up in the backseat, several times. No ice cream and walk in the park for us tonight. Maybe another time."

"Yeah, of course another time. Let me take a look at her." He opened the rear door. Being in vet mode, he didn't even wince at the stench. Just leaned in over the mess. He spoke low and softly while he felt Minx's belly, checked her eyes and gums, then helped her out of the car. "It looks as if she's cleared the contents of her stomach, including her supper. That's a good thing."

For the dog, yes. For the upholstery in her Volkswagen, not so much. Ingesting non-food items wasn't typical behavior for Minx, so Andie hadn't paid close attention while Minx happily shredded the baseball. Thank god it had all come back up. From the sheepish expression on Mason's face, he was thinking the same thing. Only he could look guilty and sexy-sweet at the same time.

"You can probably guess what caused the vomiting."

"Your irresistible balls?" She bit the inside of her cheek, but it was useless. She had zero poker-face ability. Trying to squelch the smile made it that much more obvious.

"Yeah." Now he was grinning too. "I expected a lot of licking, maybe even some biting." He winked, making her blush at the memory that comment triggered. "But I didn't think there'd be swallowing."

Minx took this opportunity to barf a puddle of gooey bile at their feet. Nice.

"Take her inside." The vet was back, replacing the sexy-talking guy. "Burn some toast and feed it to her dry, it'll help settle her stomach. Toss some supplies out and I'll clean your car."

She certainly wasn't going to argue that offer.

Half an hour later, he knocked on her front door. "The backseat's not bad, but if you give me the key, I'll drive over to the carwash and give it a shampoo." The empty bucket and a small, tied garbage bag sat off to the side. His gray uniform pants had puke spots in two places she could see. He probably had some on his top too—now fully buttoned—but it was forgivingly black.

"You don't have to do that."

His hands rested on either side of the door, framing the most incredible man to barge into her life. And run back out of it at the first sign of conflict.

"I'm responsible for the mess. I want to make things right," he said, eyes locked with hers.

Damn him, reading her mind again. "Oh, just get in here." She sighed and stepped aside. In her heart, she'd already taken him back. She might as well let him in the house. "Go up to my bathroom and get out of those clothes." He raised his eyebrows and smiled. She did a little eye roll in return. "No, we're not having make-up sex yet. You still have some stuff here, it's in the drawer." Instead of heading for the stairs, he stood in front of her, his grin bigger than seconds before. "What?"

"You said yet."

He'd caught her little slip. Okay, so it wasn't a slip so much as a hint. Still, he didn't have to stand there looking all revved-up with testosterone. Because even sporting random vomit stains, Mason was borderline irresistible.

She jutted one hip to the side and planted a hand on it. "And now you want to know how long you'll have to wait for it?"

"I'm not gonna lie and say I haven't been missing having sex with you." The space between them got smaller. "But this smile on my face, it's purely because you're considering taking my sorry ass back."

"Well, it's a very fine ass... plus, I am in the market for a veterinarian who gives deep discounts and makes house calls." She popped the top buttons of his shirt and pressed her hand to his chest. Instant butterfly assault in her stomach. Instant flip-flop to her heart. Instant heat wave in all her best parts. "At some point this evening, I'm going to want the dessert you promised, so go clean up."

A bag of his stuff was in the bottom drawer of her vanity, like she'd said. A pair of boxers, gym shorts, a t-shirt, mismatched socks in a loose ball, the toothbrush he'd liberated from her stash of extras the first time he'd slept over. And what the fuck? A whack of condoms.

Quietly, he crossed from the en suite bathroom to her bedside table. Opened the drawer where she kept their supply of protection. None there. She hadn't planned to use their condoms with another man. Damn if that didn't make his chest puff out.

Her soft voice filtered in from the bedroom while he was brushing his teeth. "Can I come in and grab your dirty laundry?"

"Sure," he called around the toothbrush and mouthful of minty paste. He spit, adding, "I mean no." Too late, she was already in the bathroom, cheeks on fire, wide eyes blinking twice as fast as normal.

"Um… your clothes are…?"

"Yeah, I'm not letting you wash my stuff."

She cleared her throat. "How about putting the clean ones on."

If he stayed naked, she'd either leave or they'd make up a whole lot quicker. "You're unbelievably cute in this." He tugged at her ball cap. Let his eyes roam over her sporty little outfit. All that nicely toned leg showing… he wanted to drop to his knees and lick her from ankle to ankle—the long and slow way. "And sexy."

The gamble paid off when she didn't walk out the door. Just the opposite, her eyes did some roving of their own. They landed on his cock and she made a noise somewhere between a squeak and a groan. His cock took the sound as a compliment and stood straighter. Not that it needed extra encouragement when she was around. For now, though, he grabbed the boxers, stepped in and snapped the elastic into place above the straining hard-on.

"From the first time you hit on me, I knew I had to get you on a date."

Her eyes shot up to his face. "I didn't hit on you. You hit me with a ball. On purpose!"

"Which you followed up by complimenting my chest. Pretty bold thing to say to a total stranger. Definitely a come on."

"You're calling me bold? The first line out of your mouth was about virgins and lap dancers. That was bold. I almost laid into you for that comment."

He scooped her hands from her hips. Placed them palms down on his chest and started walking her backward out of the bathroom. "But you went with hitting on me instead."

"It's amazing your head fit through that doorway."

He steered them around the bed, smiling when her mouth turned down at the corners. Yeah, he wanted to go there too. Wasn't quite time for it yet. He guided her onto the cushioned bench in the bay window. Held her hands on his body as he lowered to his knees.

"I've thought about meeting you at that ballpark every day since it happened. At first because it was damn hot, and I wondered how I managed to get so fucking lucky that night." Her cheeks turned pretty pink. He smiled and nudged her thighs wider, shuffling forward until all that separated them was a few scraps of clothing and his wavering willpower. "The luck kept on coming, because you agreed to see me again, and then again. Being with you is natural and easy. But it's also this incredible rush. I've never had this with another person."

"For me too." Her hands slid from his shoulders to the back of his neck, where they toyed with his hair. A piece of heaven he'd been missing.

Her face was close. It'd be so easy to kiss her right now. Skip straight to the making up and moving on. The only way to resist was to pull back, which he did with some difficulty.

"I don't know exactly when it happened, but I started thinking about the day we met and imagining telling the story to our family. At our wedding. To our kids, grandkids."

"Mason..."

"I told you how I felt and what I wanted, more than once, but you never told me."

"Mason, I—"

He brushed his thumb over her lips to stop her. "And I turned into an idiot because of it. I stupidly bought into other people's shit. I let it feed my doubts. So I bailed, and I did it prick-style, because I knew I'd never be able to let you go if I had to see your face or hear your voice. I was a coward and a fool."

"Don't forget dickwad."

"Yeah, definitely that."

Scott had offered to come clean with Mason. She'd been this close to saying yes. Part of her had wanted Scott to suffer for the rift he'd caused—and going to Mason, tail between his legs to confess, would've pummeled Scott's high-and-mighty attitude. In the end, she'd made Scott promise not to set things straight. If it'd been that easy to scare Mason off, she didn't want him back. No matter how badly she wanted him back.

Now here he was, on his knees, begging for another chance. Even though nothing had changed. Or had it? "Did Scott talk to you again?" His muscles tensed at the question. "Yes, I know about his visit to your office. He admitted everything last weekend… after we saw you at the restaurant. I need to know if… if you've heard from him since then."

"No." His jaw clenched. "He said enough the first time."

That he had. Enough to make Mason bolt. She almost didn't blame Mason—Scott won big legal cases because he was unbelievably convincing. And she hadn't exactly given Mason reason to think Scott was wrong.

She wanted to grab him. Bury her face in his chest and tell him everything. But she needed to be sure before throwing the doors to her heart wide open. Again.

"Why now? Nothing's changed since the day you hid in your office and stopped answering my calls." The day he shattered her fragile dreams.

"Yeah, it has. I opened my eyes." He cupped her face in his hands. "You love me, or you did. You showed me every day. All the little things, the big things, the trust you gave me... I don't need the words, babe, I just need you."

A lump caught in her throat. He got it. He got her. "What about the other stuff?" She chose her words carefully. "I know what Scott told you about the miscarriages... and I know you want a family someday. What if I'm incapable of that?"

"You could've told me. Those times I wasn't careful... shit." He shook his head. "Truth is, I think part of me wanted you to get pregnant. To give you a big reason to commit to us when I wasn't sure you would otherwise. But I swear, I will never selfishly put you at risk again."

Not telling him was killing her. "It's sweet that you want to protect me, but that doesn't answer the question."

His thumb swept over her cheek to tuck a wayward strand of hair behind her ear. "Yeah, I want a family."

A different door to her heart opened. The trapdoor.

"I'm jumping the gun, or guns, I guess, but I'd be a great stepdad."

Oh god... he wanted that—to be Dylan's stepfather? "You'd be an amazing stepdad, but would that be enough?" Every second that he didn't answer, her stomach twisted tighter.

"Maybe." His hands fell to his sides. "I don't know."

She blinked hard to force the damn tears back again. Sometimes honesty really sucked.

"What about you? Do you still wish you had more children?"

She couldn't blame him for fishing. They should've had this conversation another time, and under better circumstances. Too late for that.

"There was a point when I didn't think motherhood was in the cards for me at all. I'm grateful to have Dylan. After he was born, I accepted that he'd be my only child. I made myself stop wishing for more. Then you came along and kick-started my hormones." She pasted on a halfhearted smile. "Thanks a lot for that. I'm probably going to turn into one of those cat ladies in an attempt to satisfy my maternal urges."

"There's adoption."

"That's what I had in mind."

"You did?"

"Of course. Look at Hugo, he's a great cat—when he's not eating my casseroles, that is."

"You're talking about adopting cats."

"Can't become a cat lady without cats. And the shelters are always full of them, so—"

He cut her off with an unexpected burst of laughter. "I was talking about kids."

"What?"

The smile that'd accompanied his laughter changed into one much deeper, sweeter. "We could adopt. Or foster. Kids, not cats. But I'm good with having a houseful of those too."

"We?"

"Yeah, I know, jumping the gun again. You haven't even agreed to take me back."

"Yet." Heaven help her, she was smiling too. Ear-to-ear.

"Sounds like the odds are in my favor."

"And mine." She placed a hand on his chest and traced his tattoo. The outline, the tiny details on the Franciscan cross.

She had the design memorized, she'd looked at it so many times, but at this moment, it kept her eyes off his face.

"Hey," he tipped her chin up, "tell me."

He read her so easily. Would another man be able to, if things with Mason flopped? In all the years with Scott, he'd never been as tuned in to her as Mason was after only a few weeks.

"I want us to work out...so much...but I'm scared."

"That I'll fuck up again? I probably will."

"Way to give a girl hope." Her view of his grin was brief, because he tilted his head and moved in. Finally. His soft lips took control. Strong hands moved over her back. Lower, to the hem of her t-shirt, which he peeled up in a smooth, sexy motion. She slid one hand into his boxers and circled a deliciously sturdy erection. "Now this is hopeful."

"Nah. That's a sure thing."

"Satisfaction guaranteed or what, my money back?"

"Or I keep doing it until you're fully satisfied." The button on her shorts opened under his dexterous fingers, followed by the zipper. He lifted her ass enough to wiggle them, and her thong, down and away. The lacy black bra followed. "Fuck, you're so beautiful." He palmed her breasts, thumbed his fingers over the nipples, turning them into tingling bullets. Warm breath fanned her skin as he grazed the tips. "I've missed these."

"Not as much as they've missed you. I'm not too shabby in the flexibility department, but I've never been able to get them to my mouth."

He blinked up at her. "You've tried?"

"Of course I've tried."

"Lemme see."

She cupped the left one. Cracked her neck side-to-side, rolled her shoulder back and stretched, tongue straining and extended. And… not even close. "Sexy, right?"

Mason erupted. Huge grin, clutching his abdomen, he full-out laughed his ass off.

And it didn't bother her one bit. In its own bizarre way, it was nice.

"Give me that," he said after collecting himself and resuming his position. He took soft possession of her breast, sucking the deprived nipple into his mouth, flicking it with his tongue. Nipping with exactly the right amount of pressure to send a jolt of need between her legs.

"Mason?"

"Yeah?"

"I hope you don't fuck up again."

He gave her one of his best smiles, the swoon-worthy, sexy-sweet combo. "Yeah, me too."

Her heart tried to lurch from her chest. This was it. Love, with all its perks and difficulties. He wanted it—and so did she.

He dragged her legs over his shoulders. The smile changed again, to one much more predatory. The sight of it sent shivers through her body. He began stroking, featherlight and borderline tickly. Up and down her slit. A little dip here, a quick circle there. Never enough. She wiggled and shifted. He countered, not giving her what she wanted.

"Mason… please."

"Please what?"

"I want my dessert."

"Greedy girl."

"Needy."

"I like that combo," he said, disappearing to the south.

271

Her hips bucked upward at the first press of his tongue to her clit. She'd gone years without oral sex and managed fine. A couple of weeks without Mason's face between her legs and she was in complete withdrawal. Desperate to come under his mouth.

She leaned back to rest on her elbows. Better for watching the movement of his head as it bobbed up and down, side to side. His eyes flickered open and caught hers. Naughty and sweet at the same time. With one hand, she reached down, threaded her fingers into the thick softness of his hair. Urged him tighter against her body. The growl vibrated against her clit, pitching her closer to the edge. Too soon, too soon, but oh—

"Ow, crap, shit..." Stars rattled in her head as she grabbed it.

Mason's head flew up at the racket. "What the hell happened?"

"Not an orgasm." She cringed and stroked the area of her head that'd bounced off the glass. Dammit, there was actually a goose egg. "What are you smirking at?"

"You. How cute you are when your clumsy kicks in." He nodded at the window. "And the neighbors are looking."

"What?" Instinctively, she wrapped an arm across her chest. Not that anyone could see her through the tinted glass. "Nobody's out there."

"Yeah, I know. Bet you're disappointed." He winked while carefully unfolding her from her somewhat jackknifed position. "So you just—fell into the window?"

"It was your fault. I probably have a concussion."

"Guess I'll have to keep you awake and alert the rest of the night."

"I think that's a myth."

"Trust me, I'm a doctor."

A thoroughly unfeminine snort snuck out. "You're an animal doctor, Dr. Lang."

"And you," he said, scooping her up into his arms, "are my favorite animal."

"Because I'm a cougar?"

"I was thinking vixen." Squishy pillows cradled her as he set her on the bed. "Either way, you're mine." A kiss teased her bottom lip. "Mine to take care of." Each nipple got a turn under his mouth. "Mine to worship." His tongue took the direct route back to the land of unfinished business. "Mine...to...keep," he said, each word separated by a long, sensual lick.

Her legs trembled. Every second, every action, pushed her closer to release. Lick, vibrate, suckle...shuffle and repeat. A hot, swirling ache tugged at her clit. She clutched his head, desperately needing—

"That...oh god..." His fingers moved inside her, stroking the magic spot only he knew how to find. His tongue bore hard and fast on her clit. A thousand stars flashed behind her eyelids. Release hit her like a wave, subsided, then surged again. She rocked against his face, panting and moaning, coming until she couldn't breathe. Until she was a quivering pile of satisfied, as he'd guaranteed.

His kiss had the spicy-sweet taste of sex. Half of it, anyway. "Now you're mine to play with however I want."

"Mmm." A quick flip onto her stomach and she rolled up to her knees, wiggling her butt side-to-side. Taunting the bull. "What're you going to do to me?"

The bull's nostrils flared. He slid two fingers inside. Dragged the lubed fingers upward, teased the rim of her ass while whispering in her ear. "I prefer showing to telling. Let me grab the condoms."

"We don't need them."

"Did you go on the Pill?" He crouched beside the bed, facing her, stroking her hair. "Oh, shit. Babe, from before, are you...?"

Nerves jumbled into a ball in her throat. "No." She breathed as deeply as she could, tried to keep her voice from cracking. "I'm fine. Trust me."

The clock on the dresser ticked off the seconds of silence. The comforter crinkled as Mason shifted his weight alongside. His eyes flitted to the bathroom door, then returned to her face. "Are you sure?"

"As sure as I am that I, um, love you." She squeezed her eyes shut and shook her head. Way to botch what should be a memorable, romantic moment. "Which is very sure." She had to be red as a tomato, her cheeks were so hot. "Wow, that really sucked."

"It worked for me." He stood, pushed his boxer briefs off with one hand. Six feet two inches of male perfection stared her in the face.

Up and down, she soaked in the spectacular sight. Top to bottom, outside and in, she loved it all. His eyes and smile, his muscles, his cock. His intelligence, sense of humor and warmth. Even the insecure parts that made him act like a stupid ass. She loved every bit of him.

"I need you. Now," she said, the words raw, half-choked.

He moved alongside her, shifting her position to face-to-face. He blanketed her with his body, tickling her neck with the soft brush of his lips. "You have me. Now and always."

"Even when I'm old and wrinkly?"

"Yeah, even then."

"Hey... you're supposed to say I'll never be old and wrinkly." She wiggled, the action having zero effect other than to land his cock in a better position. The smallest shift and he'd be inside her.

"If I have my way, babe, I'll be old and wrinkly at your side."

"You are smooth."

"Except when I'm rough." His teeth scraped her neck, making her shiver. He rocked forward, teasing her with the head of his cock, sliding it in and out.

A nervous ball formed in her throat. She needed to tell him now, before they committed to this and couldn't put on the brakes. "What about when I'm swollen and fat... with your baby."

Every inch of his body tensed against her. He rolled her to her back in a blink, stared down, boring into her with intense eyes. "Are you pregnant?"

"No, but I want to be."

"Babe, I want that too. Fuck, I've pictured it plenty of times, but it's not worth the physical risk to you, or the heartbreak. There are other ways. We don't need to mix DNA to have a family."

He couldn't have said anything more perfect.

"The problems I had before... weren't mine. They were his." Telling twisted at her gut. Like a betrayal, as though she was blaming Scott for something beyond his control. Wrong or right, it was also a huge relief. "I'm fully capable of carrying a child to term without issue, just not his."

Understanding flashed in Mason's eyes. "Dylan?"

"Isn't Scott's."

"Does he know?"

"We chose the donor together, one with the closest physical attributes. But Dylan doesn't know—he may never. Nobody else knows, either. Not family members, not close friends. Only the medical staff, Scott, me, and now... you."

"Fuck, that's..."

"Too much?"

"No, babe. Not even close." His palms were warm and assuring, cradling her face. "Thank you for trusting me." He kissed her, sweetness laced with spicier intent. A slow roll of his hips brought his cock tight to her body. A knock on the door, waiting for an answer. "Are you sure about this? We have time, I'm not going anywhere, I promise you."

She hooked her legs around his back, her arms around his neck, and pulled him in. He settled there, buried as deeply as possible. Solid against her. Filling her, body and soul.

Soft, teasing sweeps of his lips brushed hers. He moved inside her, the strokes long and slow. A rhythmic dance with a grind at the end of each pass. Every touch tugged at her heart... a little too much.

"Mason," she said, wrangling enough space to look at his whole face. "Fuck me."

He stopped mid-thrust, eyebrows drawing together at her request. "Uh, I am... or was, before the inadequacy set in."

"When I'm eighty years old with brittle bones and a bum hip, this'll be perfect. Right now..." She raked her nails down his back and clamped on to his perfect, firm butt. "I want the totally hot man that I love to fuck me."

A sexy grin slid into place. "I'm never gonna get tired of hearing that."

"Good, because I kind of like saying it."

"Say it again."

"You're totally hot."

The bed shook as he laughed until he collapsed on top of her, lips pressed just below her ear. "I love you too, babe."

Epilogue

Today they parked in the spot that'd been saved in the driveway, instead of on the lawn. Mason had her door open before she'd freed herself from the clutches of the seatbelt.

"Ready to party with the Lang clan?"

"Not really," she said as she took his hand. The gesture had become utilitarian as much as romantic, because lord knew she needed help getting in and out of the truck these days.

"If it gets awful, just think about what I'm going to do to you later."

The grumpiness lifted a bit. She loved this little déjà-vu dance they did whenever they came to his parents' house. "Give me a clue."

"It involves oil."

"Sounds slippery." She smiled, in vain as it was. They'd never get to the action tonight. Poor Mason. The fatigue was killing their sex life. She'd be asleep before he popped the top on the bottle.

"Your sore feet will be having foot-gasms by the time I'm done."

He meant a foot massage, not sex? She hugged him as tight as physically possible. "Now I'm sure I love you."

"Good thing, because that ring is non-refundable."

"Neither is this," she said, rubbing the watermelon-size bump responsible for her growing list of aches and pains. "Oh... somebody's awake."

Mason's hand joined hers on the top of her stomach. Some random baby part rolled under their palms. Together they watched, amazed.

The beautiful, straight-baguette-cut ruby on her left hand glinted in the late-August sunshine. Mason had bought it in secret at the estate auction of a couple married over fifty years. On his knees at the ballpark this spring, he'd proposed they give the ring another half century of happily ever after. She'd cried then, and dammit, the tears were coming again. She'd be blotchy as well as bloated for the party. Great.

A soft sweep of his hand brushed the moisture from her cheek. "Hormones getting you again, babe?"

"No." The most incredible eyes smiled down at her. "Maybe."

"Go wait in the truck. I'll tell everybody you're not feeling well, grab Dylan and we'll all go home."

And deprive Mason of this special occasion... not a chance. "It's okay, I'm good." She dabbed at her eyes and nose with the tissue he produced. Her man—always prepared, from condoms to snot rags. Next it'd be baby wipes. "Let's go get showered."

Mason held the squeaky gate as she waddled through it. The Lang's backyard was as crowded as it had been for their annual Canada Day bash, which had also been Mason's thirty-first birthday party. Pink and blue decorations replaced last month's red and white. Mary and Katie had gone even wilder for this event, tying balloons to every conceivable item. There had to be hundreds of them. Streamers ran from the deck to the trees. A mountain of gifts sat on a large table.

The best present, though... everybody they cared about was here to celebrate with them. Both sets of parents, Katie and Logan, Lasha, Dylan, dozens more of assorted family and friends. And all of them were smiling.

"This is…incredible. The baby is so lucky to have all these people in his life."

"Or her life." Mason firmly believed they were having a girl. His gut feeling since the day she'd skipped her period thirty-seven weeks ago. "I wish she'd hurry up and get here."

"Me too. I have three weeks left, but I don't think I can stand being pregnant one more day."

"Then let's find you a place to sit and be pregnant, beautiful mama."

No point in arguing the beautiful comment, so she rolled her eyes and accepted it in the spirit he'd given it. Katie waved them toward a hard-back chair brought out from the kitchen, bless her. Halfway to the target, Andie froze.

"Oh my god." She yanked on Mason's arm. "I think my water broke."

His eyes dropped to the deck, then back to her face. "Maybe you peed."

"All over your parents' deck, in front of almost everybody we know?" Another gush of fluid escaped involuntarily, adding to the now-obvious puddle around her practical, flat-soled sandals.

"Okay, maybe not."

"Oh…contraction." Thirteen years since her last one, but suddenly she remembered it as if it were yesterday. And that memory scared the crap out of her. "I can't do this—I'm not ready."

"Don't worry. I'll send Lasha to the house for your bag. Katie and Logan are set to take care of the animals. Dylan can come to the hospital with us now, or stay with the family until later. It's under control, babe."

"It's under control? It's under control?" Everyone was looking. At the crazed expression on her face and her hand digging into Mason's arm. At his beaming smile. "Sometime in the next twenty-four hours, I'm going to pass the equivalent of a ten-pin bowling ball through my vagina, and you're telling me not to worry, that it's under control?"

"You're early, she might not be ten pounds…" He ducked as she swung, then caught her when she nearly toppled, pulling her close enough to tickle her lips with his words. "As soon as you've got your center of gravity back, you can deck me. Hard as you want, to give me a share of your pain."

"You know I won't."

"You know I'd take all your pain if I could."

"You already have—I've never been happier." Dammit, the tears were back.

"Get a room!" somebody called, bursting their private bubble while eliciting a laugh from the party-goers.

Pride boomed in Mason's voice as he addressed the group. "We will… a hospital room. Baby is on the way."

Family and close friends scuttled around them. Helping, or trying to help, but mostly adding to Andie's building anxiety. Contraction number three hit as soon as she'd been loaded into the truck on a pile of Mary's old towels. Nothing the breathing exercises couldn't handle. She hugged her parents and blew a kiss to Dylan, who was following with Lasha, then gave the thumbs up to the man of her dreams.

"Ready?"

"I kind of have to be at this point," she said, drumming her fingers on the rock-hard mound of outbound baby. "What about you… are you really ready for all of this?"

"I've been ready for this day for a long time."

True words. Mason had wanted a family six years ago when his then-fiancée got an abortion behind his back. Even with the overactive pregnancy hormones, no pang of insecurity popped up. With his looks, personality, skills in the bedroom… he could've had a handful of kids by now if he'd wanted. By some miracle, fate had saved him for her. Didn't mean she couldn't tease him, though.

She knitted her eyebrows together and tried not to smile. "Are you using me for my womb?"

"Hell yes. Every other part of your body too."

"Some of my parts have been missing you like crazy." Sex had become pretty limited in the past couple months. Especially by their standards.

His hand found hers and dragged it to his lips. "Yeah? Well I'm looking forward to getting reacquainted with those parts."

If she weren't as wide as a side-split and spewing amniotic fluid, the sexy words and matching kiss would have had her libido thumping. "It's going to be a while before we can do… all of our regular stuff."

Mason's sweet smile grew into a full-fledged grin, accompanied by a belly laugh. "I bet you're the only woman to think about sex while in labor."

"That's why you love me—I'm a dirty girl."

"That and a thousand more reasons, babe." In his peripheral vision, he watched her breathe through another contraction, this one much stronger than the last. "Make that one thousand and one." He pulled into a parking spot in the hospital lot. Leaned over and kissed her, white-hot and sweet as honey. "And counting."

Thank You!

Thank you for reading *Game Plan*!

I hope you enjoyed reading Mason and Andie's hot summer love story as much as I loved writing it! If so, I would greatly appreciate you spreading the word, including leaving a review or star-rating at your favorite online retailer, or wherever you enjoy discussing books. Again, thanks for reading!

Sincerely,

Karla Doyle

ABOUT THE AUTHOR

Karla is a small town girl with some big city experience, happiest living somewhere in between. She studied fashion design in college and spent most of her adult life in that industry. These days, she lives a charmed existence with her two amazing kids, an incredible (and smokin' hot) husband, and the best friends in the world. When she's not writing the sexy stories that swirl around in her head, you can find her lifting weights at the gym, playing Scrabble, or cuddled up with a book, surrounded by a pack of pets.

Visit Karla's website

for a complete booklist and other information:

www.karladoyle.com

Connect with Karla Online:

www.facebook.com/KarlaDoyleAuthor

www.instagram.com/KarlaDoyleAuthor

www.pinterest.com/KarlaDoyleStuff

www.twitter.com/Karla_Doyle

Send Karla an email:

karla@karladoyle.com

More Books by Karla Doyle

Gift Wrapped

After catching her boyfriend cheating the week before Christmas, Brinn is seriously lacking in holiday spirit. So when she looks into the eyes of a last-minute shopper after closing on Christmas Eve, she's sarcastic rather than sympathetic. But Brinn is ever the good girl and her conscience wins out. She offers the handsome stranger ten minutes to select a gift and ends up with a present of her own—a date. On Christmas Eve.

Davis hates Christmas. Especially this year, since a neighborhood heist liberated him of his hard-earned belongings and the few gifts he'd purchased. But the robbery led him to a cute store manager with a sense of humor, smokin' body and no plans for the evening. Mistletoe might be in order after all.

Their Christmas Eve date is like gift-wrapped, sexy satisfaction. But the best gifts keep on giving, and one naughty night may not be enough—for either of them.

Cup of Sugar (Close to Home #1)

Nia has one rule—don't date neighbors. Simple, except the guy next door is single, handsome, and not inclined to close his blinds while naked. When her car dies, Conn takes "being neighborly" to a new level by offering a ride to her long-distance destination. Nia has resisted his looks and charm for months. Surely she can handle a few hours in his truck…

For months, Conn has blatantly put himself on display, hoping his pretty blonde neighbor would tire of secretly watching and come knock on his door for a cup of sugar—or more. No such luck—until an unusual opportunity arises. After a six-hour drive turns into a sweet-and-sexy weekend, Conn wants more than neighborly status with Nia. To get it, he must convince her to break the rule protecting her heart—by putting his on the line.

Icing on the Cake (Close to Home #2)

Nia and Conn's wedding will be fairytale perfect…if their siblings can get along.

Free-spirited, anti-establishment Sara has always been on the outside of her family's fairytale mold. Now she's being forced smack into the middle of it at her sister Nia's wedding. Alongside the cocky and annoyingly sexy best man—Conn's cop brother.

Curtis doesn't buy in to organized romance and fairytales. But for his brother, he'll throw on a tux and fake it for a few hours. His flak vest would have been a better choice around the maid of honor. He should have brought his handcuffs too, because somebody needs to restrain the dark-haired spitfire—and he's just the man for the job.

One night to indulge the spark between them, then goodbye—that was the agreement. Curtis isn't looking for a relationship and he sure doesn't want a troublemaker for a girlfriend. The last thing Sara needs in her daily life is a cop looking over her shoulder, no matter how hot he is.

But giving in to their chemistry is much more fun than giving it up…

Crossing the Line

Lifelong best friends Derrick and Jeremy met Hanna at a bar ten years ago. Both wanted her—one married her. Now the other man has been invited to join in for one hot weekend.

Everything would've been fine if they'd had their fun that weekend, then gone back to normal. But they didn't. And when past demons resurface, things will never be the same— for any of them.

Body of Work

Cassie has fantasized about the ginger-haired personal trainer for months. Brian is friendly, but never more—until he appears on her doorstep and shows her how much her flirting has affected him. The more she's with him, the more Cassie wants the fairytale, not just hot sex with the six-two hunk. She can give Brian full access to her body, but after her ex's reaction to her explicit photography business, sharing her secrets, and her heart, isn't an option.

Brian knows better than to break the rules. Don't date gym members. Keep his inner beast on a leash during sex. Cassie tested his resolve on number one her first day in the gym. Shattered the second rule when he touched her. The petite pixie shares his preferences in the bedroom. She makes him laugh and love—but past mistakes haunt him, emotionally and tangibly. Cassie's worth the price he'll pay for breaking the rules. Now he must convince her to give him her heart.

More Than Words

Their online games turn into games of the heart.

A brutal mugging two years ago left Calli terrified to go out after dark, and incapable of real dating. Hanging out with a resentful Chihuahua every night hasn't filled the void, and all the sex toys from the store she owns could never replace a flesh-and-blood man. An online Scrabble-type site promising anonymous, flirty fun sounds right up her alley. A like-minded geek, that's what she needs. Unbeknownst to her, the man on the other end of the game is anything but geeky.

Travis is tired of the party scene and women chasing after his bad-boy musician persona. He wants somebody who is drawn to his mind, not his profession, and he might have found her—on the opposite side of an internet game board. After heating up the tiles with Calli online, he's determined to meet her in person. Touch her in person. And when he does, their chemistry is undeniable. But when he discovers her tragic past he realizes it will take more than words to win her heart... and her trust.

Stealing Home

When Paige's latest attempt at happily-ever-after with a nice guy tanks, she decides to quit fighting her destiny. She craves bad boys. Men who deliver short-term, panty-melting excitement, not reliability and settling down. If she's going to embrace her true nature, who better to start with than the dark-haired, tattooed ballplayer whose cocky attitude gives her more thrills than any steady boyfriend ever has...

Alex had major league plans for his life until it threw him an unexpected and unwelcome curve ball. Switching gears to pursue his other passion was a rough road, but things are good—aside from his MIA muse. When a chance meeting with a blonde firecracker stirs his creative juices—and more— Alex is game to see where their chemistry leads. Trouble is, his potential Miss Right thinks she's only capable of playing the field.

Visit **www.karladoyle.com**

for a complete list of available and upcoming titles.